1

"If you lo... romantic e... ...pick up *Playing W...* ...The scenes between Jessie and Captain Wilson Rye just crackle off the page."
Cozy Mystery Book Reviews: Keep Calm and Read a Cozy Mystery

"Jessie is a fantastic character, I loved the inside look at her writing life, and I found myself laughing out loud at some of her antics . . . Cindy Blackburn is a new author to watch; her debut mystery is one not to miss!"
Melissa's Mochas, Mysteries and More

"Jessie is a new sleuth that you will want to follow again and again."
Tonya Kappes, bestselling author

"Cindy Blackburn knows how to start with a fast break and run the table, leaving readers applauding her skill."
Linda Lovely, author of *The Marley Clark Mystery* series

"Playing With Poison is a fun cozy mystery that will keep you laughing and on your toes all the way to the nail-biting end."
Dorothy St. James, author of *The White House Gardener Mysteries*

"Jessie Hewitt seems prepared to handle anything life throws her way – except a dead body on her sofa. Throw in a good break with a sexy cop, and this story takes off."
Joyce Lavene, author of *The Missing Pieces Mysteries*

Also by Cindy Blackburn

Double Shot
Three Odd Balls

Playing With Poison

by
Cindy Blackburn

A Cue Ball Mystery

ASIN(Kindle): B009D99R0I
ISBN-13: 978-1480092686
ISBN-10: 1480092681

For John,
who bought me a laptop and suggested
I use it to write a book

Acknowledgements

I could not have written Playing with Poison without gobs of help from gobs of people. Thanks to everyone who offered me their support, encouragement, and time. I am bound to forget someone, but here goes: Jean Everett, Anne Saunders, Sharon Politi, Jane Bishop, Joanna Innes, Bob Spearman, Kathy Powell, Megan Beardsley, Betsy Blackburn, Martha Twombly, Karen Phillips, Shari Stauch, Teddy Stockwell, Sean Scapellatto, Carol Peters and my friends at the LRWA. Special super-duper mega thanks to my husband John Blackburn, my technical guru extraordinaire and my hero.

Chapter 1

"Going bra shopping at age fifty-two gives new meaning to the phrase fallen woman," I announced as I gazed at my reflection.

"Oh, Jessie, you always say that." Candy poked her head around the dressing room door and took a peek at the royal blue contraption she was trying to sell me. "Gosh, that looks great. It's very flattering."

I lifted an unconvinced eyebrow. "Oh, Candy, you always say that."

"No really. I hope my figure looks that nice when I'm old."

Okay, so I took that as a compliment and agreed to buy the silly bra. And before she even mentioned them, I also asked for the matching panties. To know my neighbor Candy Poppe is to have a drawer full of completely inappropriate, and often alarming, lace, silk, and satin undergarments.

I got dressed and went out to the floor.

"*Temptation at Twilight* giving you trouble?" she asked as she rang me up. Candy hasn't known me long, but she does know me well. And she's figured out I show up at Tate's whenever writer's block strikes.

I sighed dramatically. "Plot plight."

"But you know you never have issues for very long, Jessie." She wrapped my purchases in pink tissue paper and placed them in a pink Tate's shopping bag. "Even after your divorce, remember? You came in, bought a few nice things, and went on home to finish *Windswept Whispers*." She offered an encouraging nod. "So go home, put on this bra, and start writing."

I did as I was told, but wearing the ridiculous blue bra didn't help after all. The page on my computer screen remained stubbornly blank no matter how hard I stared at it. I was deciding there must be better ways to spend a Saturday night when a knock on the door pulled me out of my funk.

"Maybe it's Prince Charming," I said to my cat. Snowflake seemed skeptical, but I got up to answer anyway.

Funny thing? It really was Prince Charming. I opened my door to find Candy Poppe's handsome to a fault fiancé standing in the hallway. But Stanley wasn't looking all that handsome. Without bothering to say hello, he pushed me aside, stumbled toward the couch, and collapsed. Prince Charming was sick.

I rushed over to where he had invited himself to lie down and knelt beside him. "Stanley?" I asked. "What's wrong?"

"Candy," he whispered, and then he died.

He died?

I blinked twice and told myself I was not seeing what I was seeing. "He's just drunk," I reassured Snowflake. "He passed out."

But then, why were his eyes open like that?

I reached for his wrist. No pulse. I checked for breathing. Nope. I shook him and called his name a few times. Nothing.

Nothing.

The gravity of the situation finally dawned on me, and I jumped up. "CPR!" I shouted at the cat.

But Snowflake doesn't know CPR. And I remembered that I don't either.

I screamed a four-letter word and lunged for the phone.

***

Twenty minutes later a Clarence police officer was standing in my living room, hovering over me, my couch, and Candy's dead fiancé. I stared down at Stanley, willing him to start breathing again, while Captain Wilson Rye kept repeating the same questions about how I knew Candy, how I knew her boyfriend, and—here was the tricky part—what he was doing lying dead on my couch. I imagined Candy would wonder about that, too.

"Ms. Hewitt? Look at me." I glanced up at a pair of blue eyes that might have been pleasant under other circumstances. "You have anywhere else we can talk?"

Hope drained from his face as he scanned my condominium, an expansive loft with an open floor plan and very few doors. At the moment the place was swarming with people wearing plastic sheeting, talking into doohickeys, and either dusting or taking samples of who knows what from every corner and crevice. Unless Officer Rye and I decided to talk in the bathroom, we were doomed to be in the midst of the action.

"I'll make some tea," I said. At least then we could sit at the kitchen counter and stare at the stove. I glanced down. A far better option than staring at poor Stanley.

"Ms. Hewitt?"

"Tea," I repeated and pointed Officer Rye toward a barstool. I turned on the kettle and sat down beside him while the plastic people bustled about behind us, continuing their search for dust bunnies.

"Let's try this again," he said. "What was your relationship with Mr. Sweetzer?"

"We had no relationship."

"Mm-hmm."

"No, really. He was Candy's boyfriend. She lives downstairs in 2B."

The kettle whistled and I got up to pour the tea. Conscious that this cop was watching my every move, I spilled more water on the counter than into the cups. But eventually I succeeded in my task and even managed to hand him a cup.

"How do you take it?" I asked.

"Excuse me?"

"Your tea. Lemon, cream, sugar?"

"Nothing, thank you." He frowned at the tea. "So you knew Sweetzer through Ms. Poppe?"

"Correct." I carried my own cup around the counter and sat down again. "She and I met a few months ago."

"Where? Here?"

I sipped my tea and thought back. I had met Candy in the bra department at Tate's of course. It was the day after my divorce was finalized, and she had sold me a dozen bras spanning every color in the rainbow. Candy had even mentioned it that afternoon.

"Ms. Hewitt?"

"We met in the foundations department at Tate's."

"The what department?"

So much for discretion. "The bra department," I said bluntly. "Candy sold me some bras."

Rye's gaze moved southward for the briefest of seconds, and I remembered the brand new, bright blue specimen lurking beneath my white shirt.

My white shirt.

If there had been a wall handy, I would have banged my head against it. Instead, I mumbled something about not expecting company.

Rye cleared his throat and suggested we move on.

"Candy and I got to talking, and I told her I was in the market for a condo, and she told me about this place." I pointed up. "I took one look at these fifteen-foot ceilings and huge windows and signed a mortgage a week later. We've been good friends ever since."

"And Stanley Sweetzer?"

"Was Candy's boyfriend. He had some hotshot job in finance, and he was madly in love with Candy."

"So what was he doing up here?"

Okay, good question. I was trying to think of a good answer when one of the plastic people interrupted. "Will someone please get this cat out of here?" she called from behind us.

I turned to see Snowflake scurrying across the floor, gleefully unraveling a roll of yellow police tape. I quick hopped down to retrieve her while the plastic people sputtered this and that about contaminating the crime scene.

"She does live here," I said. They stopped scolding and watched as I picked her up and returned to my seat.

Snowflake had other ideas, however. She switched from my lap to Rye's and immediately commenced purring.

Rye resumed the interrogation. "Did you invite Mr. Sweetzer up here?"

"Nooo, I did not. I was working. I was sitting at my desk, minding my own business, when Stanley showed up out of the blue."

"You always work Saturday nights?"

I raised an eyebrow. "Do you?"

Rye took a deep breath. "You were alone then? Before Sweetzer showed up?"

"Snowflake was here."

More deep breathing. "Did he say anything, Ms. Hewitt?"

"He looked up when he hit the couch and whispered 'Candy.'" I shook my head. "It was awful."

"Could he have mistaken you for Candy?"

I shook my head again. "She's at least twenty years younger than me, a lot shorter, and has long dark hair." I pointed to my short blond cut. "No."

"Well then, maybe he had come from Candy's." Rye twirled around and called over to a young black guy—the only person other than himself in a business suit—and introduced me to Lieutenant Russell Densmore.

The Lieutenant shook my hand, but seemed far more interested in the teacups and the cat, who continued to occupy his boss's lap. His gaze landed back on me while he listened to instructions.

"Go downstairs to 2B and get them up here," Captain Rye told him. "Someone named Candy Poppe in particular."

"She's still at work," I said, but Lieutenant Densmore left anyway.

I looked at Rye. "I really don't think Stanley came here from Candy's," I insisted. "She's at work. I saw her there myself."

"Excuse me?"

"I was in Tate's this afternoon."

Rye took another gander at my chest. "That outfit for Sweetzer's benefit?"

"My outfi—What? No!"

Despite the stupid bra, only a madman would find my typical writing attire even remotely seductive. That evening I was wearing a pair of jeans, cut off above the knee, and a discarded men's dress shirt from way back when, courtesy of my ex-husband. As usual when I'm at home, I was barefoot. Stick a corncob pipe in my mouth and point me toward the Mississippi, and I might have borne a vague resemblance to Huck Finn—a tall, thin, menopausal Huck Finn.

I folded my arms and glared. "As I keep telling you, Captain, I was not expecting company."

"Is the door downstairs always unlocked?"

"Umm, yes?"

"You are kidding, right? You live smack in the middle of downtown Clarence and leave your front door unlocked? Anyone and his brother had access to this building tonight. You realize that?"

I gritted my teeth, mustered what was left of my patience, and suggested he talk to my neighbors about it. "For all I know, they've been here for years without a lock on that door."

Rye might have enjoyed lecturing me further, but luckily Lieutenant Densmore came back and distracted him. He reported that, indeed, Candy Poppe was not at home.

"What a shocker," I mumbled.

One of the plastic people also joined us. "You were right, Captain," she said. "This definitely looks unnatural."

"Yet another shocker." My voice had gained some volume, and all three of them frowned at me. I frowned back. "This whole evening has been extremely unnatural."

Rye turned and gave directions to the plastic person— something about getting the body to the medical examiner. He told Lieutenant Densmore to go downstairs and wait for Candy. Then he scooted Snowflake onto the floor and stood up to issue orders to the rest of the crowd.

I stood up also. Everyone appeared to have finished with their dusting, and I was happy to see that Stanley had been taken away. But it was a bit disconcerting to watch my couch being hauled off.

"You wouldn't want it here anyway, would you?" the Captain asked me. We stood together and waited while everyone else gathered their equipment and departed.

Rye was the last go. "I'll be downstairs if you think of anything else, Ms. Hewitt. Or call me." He handed me his card and headed toward the door. "I can't wait to hear what Ms. Poppe has to say for herself."

"She'll have nothing to say for herself," I called after him. "She's been at work all day."

He turned at the doorway. "Stay put," he said. "That's an order."

"Shut the door behind you, Captain. That's an order."

***

I headed for the fridge, desperately in search of champagne. Given the situation, this may seem odd. But champagne became my drink of choice after my divorce, when I decided every day without my ex is a day worth celebrating. Even days with dead bodies in them. I popped the cork. Make that, especially days with dead bodies.

I opened my door to better hear what was happening below and sank down in an easy chair. Candy got home at 9:30, but Rye and Densmore quickly shuffled her into her condo, and someone closed the door.

"Most unhandy," I told Snowflake. She jumped onto my lap, and together we stared at the empty spot where my couch had been.

The Korbel bottle was nearly half empty by the time Candy's door opened again. I hopped up to eavesdrop at my own doorway and heard Rye say something about calling him if she thought of anything else. Lieutenant Densmore asked if she had any family close by.

"My parents," she answered. "But I think I'll go see Jessie now, okay?"

I didn't catch Rye's reply, but the cops finally left, and within seconds Candy was at my doorstep.

"Oh, Jessie," she cried as I pulled her inside. She stopped short. "Umm, what happened to your sofa?"

"We need to talk," I told her. I guided her toward my bed and had her lie down.

The poor woman cried for a solid ten minutes. I held her hand and waited, and eventually she asked for some champagne. Like I told Rye—Candy and I are good friends.

I went to fetch a tray, and she was sitting up when I returned to the bedroom.

"Do you feel like talking, Sweetie?" I asked as I handed her a glass.

She took a sip, and then pulled a tissue from the box on my nightstand and made a sloppy attempt to wipe the mascara from under her eyes. "Those policemen told me what happened, but I could barely listen."

"They wanted to know why Stanley was here tonight. Do you know?"

She shook her head. "They kept asking me where I was. I was at work, right?"

"At least you have a solid alibi." I frowned. "Which makes one of us."

"Captain Rye was real interested in you, Jessie. I think he likes you."

I rolled my eyes. "Would you get a grip, Candy? Rye's real interested because he thinks I killed your boyfriend."

Her face dropped and she blinked her big brown eyes. "Did someone kill Stanley?"

Okay, so Candy Poppe isn't exactly the fizziest champagne in the fridge. Even on days without dead bodies.

"It looks like Stanley was murdered," I said quietly and handed her another tissue. "Did he have any enemies?"

"That's what Captain Rye kept asking me," she whined. "But everyone loved Stanley, didn't they?"

I had my doubts but thought it best to agree. I asked about his family, and over the remains of the Korbel, we discussed his parents. Apparently Margaret and Roger Sweetzer did not approve of Candy.

"They think I was after his money," she said. She put down her empty glass. "They don't like my job either. I swear to God, his mother comes into the store twice a week to embarrass me in front of the customers. And every time Mr. Sweetzer sees me, he asks how business is and stares at my chest."

While Candy blew her nose, I stared at her chest. The woman is my friend and all, but I could see how people might get the wrong impression. On this particular occasion she was wearing her red mini dress—and I do mean mini—and had accessorized with a truckload of red baubles and beads that would have fit better on a Christmas tree than on Candy's petite frame. An unlikely pair of red patent leather stilettos completed the ensemble.

I stifled a frown. Hopefully, Captain Rye understood she had not known her fiancé was about to die when she wiggled her curvaceous little body into that outfit.

I mumbled something about trying to get some rest. If I still had my couch, I would have slept on it and let Candy drift off on the bed. I lamented such as she got up to leave, but she assured me she would be fine and teetered out the door in those ridiculous red shoes.

Chapter 2

Alexis Wynsome was having a bad day. Trapped in the turret of the vile Lord Maynard Snipe's castle, the heroine of my current literary venture, *Temptation at Twilight*, could not imagine what was taking Rolfe so very long to rescue her. After all, Lord Snipe had kidnapped her the previous evening. And the ruggedly handsome and altogether oversexed Rolfe Vanderhorn usually moved faster than this.

The lovely Alexis paced. Occasionally she ventured over to the narrow window of her cell and scanned the surrounding hills, searching in vain for any sign of her hero. But without the help of yours truly, dear Rolfe did not possess the mental acuity needed to save his lady. And considering my mood that morning, Alexis appeared doomed. She sat down on the one hard wooden chair Maynard Snipe had seen fit to provide and sighed dramatically, her bosom trembling even more than her delicate hands.

***

I, too, sighed dramatically. My bosom, however, remained pretty much inert. Despite spending a restless night worrying about Stanley's murder, I had stuck to my normal routine. I was up at five, showered, and at my desk by six. But here it was close to eleven, and I had written next to nothing. I closed my laptop and stared out the window. From her perch on the windowsill, Snowflake stared with me.

Well, no wonder we were distracted. Two vans from the local TV station were parked in front of The Stone Fountain and were disgorging people and equipment at an alarming rate. The news crew spent some time filming who knows what on Sullivan Street, but everyone appeared even more agitated when Gina Stone arrived to open the bar for Sunday brunch.

She tried to keep Channel 15 from following her inside, but she didn't have much luck. Everyone and everything, other than the vans themselves, disappeared into The Stone Fountain.

"What was that all about?" I asked Snowflake.

The cat didn't answer, but why was I sure it had something to do with Stanley?

A knock on my door pulled me out of my reverie. "Maybe it's Prince Char—"

I blinked at the cat. "Never mind."

Captain Rye was leaning on the doorframe when I got there. He presented quite a commanding figure, but I stood my ground and blocked his entry.

"It's Sunday morning," I offered as a greeting.

"I'm aware of that, Ms. Hewitt, and I'm sorry to disturb you. May I come in?"

"When can I have my couch back?"

"We have a problem. May I come in?"

"Do I have a choice?" I waved him inside and toward an easy chair, but my desk caught his attention, and he wandered over in that direction instead.

It was irritating, but I really couldn't blame the guy. My desk occupies the best spot in the condo, where the row of south-facing windows intersects with the row of west-facing windows. From there I can watch all the activity at the corner of Sullivan and Vine Streets, and also have a view of the Blue Ridge Mountains in the distance.

Rye put his hands on his hips and stared down at Sullivan Street, affording me ample opportunity to notice the holster and gun under his suit jacket. I whimpered only slightly and joined him at the window.

Two women pushing baby carriages were crossing Vine Street. And Fiona Greeley, the woman who manages the artists' co-op next to The Stone Fountain, was on a ladder installing a banner over her doorway. An old man shod in dark socks and sandals stopped to watch her progress, and she enlisted him to hold one end of the banner while she tacked up the other.

"You like it here?" Rye asked.

"I do. Clarence is just the right size city—not too big, not too small." I watched the kindly old man help Fiona off the ladder. "And I love living downtown."

I pointed to Fiona. "I bought all the paintings of sunflowers and daisies you see in here at that gallery." I moved my hand toward The Stone Fountain. "And I love that bar. It's in such a great building, don't you think?"

The Stone Fountain occupied the ground floor of an old brick warehouse similar to the building I lived in. Instead of condos, that one had been converted into retail and office space.

"Sweetzer was spotted there last night," Rye told me.

"I thought so." I pointed out the Channel 15 vans, and Captain Rye groaned. "Are they a problem?" I asked.

"You do know about Jimmy Beak and his crew?"

I shook my head. "I don't watch much TV."

"Well then, you're smart. Beak's a menace. He and his supposed news team don't think they're doing their job unless they're getting in my way and screwing up whatever investigation I have going."

He cocked an eyebrow in my direction. "Be careful, Ms. Hewitt. They're bound to be up here harassing you before long."

"What? You didn't tell them about me?"

"Absolutely not. But someone down there is bound to mention Ms. Poppe. I guarantee Jimmy Beak will be figuring out where Sweetzer died soon enough.

"Which reminds me." His tone changed. "When do you plan on putting a lock on that door downstairs? Anyone and his brother has access to this building. You realize that?"

Yes, I did. It was kind of hard to forget, what with Rye's constant reminders.

"You should get a lock," he continued lecturing. "You'll see what I mean when Beak comes knocking at your door."

As if on cue, the news crew emerged from the bar. A very tall guy in a plaid suit ran into the street and started waving both arms at our building. Rye and I jumped away from the window as the man carrying the camera lifted it in our direction.

"Is that him?" I asked. "The guy in plaid?"

"Steer clear."

I folded my arms and thought about it. "Stanley must have been over there waiting for Candy last night."

Rye glanced down at me. "Before he came up here?"

"Well, clearly it wasn't after he came up here."

We stepped even further from the window, and Rye again noticed my desk. He touched nothing, but seemed to be taking a mental inventory of what was there—my laptop and a clutter of papers, pens, and sticky notes.

Eventually his gaze landed on the nearby bookshelf, and again the mental inventory. The poor guy. To the uninitiated, my masterpieces must all look the same—inch thick paperbacks with lots of pastels and flowers decorating their spines.

He pulled out one of the tomes and studied it. "What exactly do you do for a living?"

I reached over and tapped the cover. "That's me."

He lowered the book to look at me. "Say what?"

I took a closer glance and understood why the man was so incredulous. I had pointed to a buxom—no, let's be accurate—very buxom, youthful redhead wearing a pink petticoat and looking more than sufficiently ravished by the muscular hunk gently caressing her swooning and lithe body.

I jabbed my finger at the name below the woman's bodice. "I'm Adelé Nightingale."

"You mean, you actually read this stuff?" Rye was still perplexed.

Again, I pointed to my name, clearly printed in metallic pink script. "No," I said, "I write this stuff. Adelé Nightingale's my pen name."

"Adelé Nightingale." He took another look at the book and read out loud, "*A Deluge of Desire.*" He turned it over and read the back cover. "You mean, you actually write this stuff?"

I crossed my arms and glared. "Yes, I actually do. Believe it or not, my steamy sex scenes are the stuff of legend in romance circles. I'm damn good."

A slow grin made its way across his face. "Oh, Ms. Hewitt, I'm sure you are."

I grabbed the book and jammed it back on the shelf. "What is it you want, Captain?"

He lost the grin and pulled a tape player out of his suit pocket. "We need to talk," he said and placed the machine on the two inches of clear space on my desk.

Snowflake moved from her perch on the windowsill to the top of my computer, where she had better access to the new gadget. She tapped it with her paw while I stared at it, aghast.

"Are you recording this?" I forced myself to ask.

"No, but your conversation with the dispatcher last night got recorded. It's standard procedure."

"Oh?"

"And I'd like you to hear it."

Rye hit the play button, and we listened as the dispatcher answered my call of distress. She asked what type of emergency I had, and I said a murder. Then she asked me where, and I told her my couch.

"The address, ma'am," she said. "I need the address."

I gave her that, and after getting a few more details about Stanley, she told me to stay with the body until help arrived.

"Great idea," I had said sarcastically before hanging up.

Rye stopped the tape and stared at me.

"What?" I asked. "Isn't that exactly how I explained it last night? As I recall, it took us hours to go over what that dispatcher got out of me in a mere minute or two."

"How did you know he was murdered?"

I blinked twice. "Excuse me?"

He slipped the tape player back in his pocket. "You agree that you point blank told the dispatcher Stanley Sweetzer was murdered?"

"Yes?" My heart had started beating way too fast.

"But there was no blood, no gunshot wounds, no stab wounds, the guy wasn't beaten up. Nothing." He paused. "So how did you know it was murder?"

I turned and walked away before the cop could notice that my hands were shaking. How had I known it was murder?

* * *

"You don't have to be nervous, Ms. Hewitt."

Rye had followed me into the living room, and we were now sitting across from each other. We may have been in easy chairs, but trust me, we were not relaxed. How could anyone relax with his pesky, pesky, question hanging over us?

"I have no idea how I knew." I forced myself to meet his gaze. "I'm a writer, okay? I have more intuition than the average person. I know things about people. Really, I do. I'm not lying."

"There's no reason to be nervous."

Why did he keep saying that?

I hesitated and then just blurted it out, "Do you think I killed Stanley?"

"Probably not."

"Probably?" I squeaked.

"But what I think doesn't matter if that's where the evidence leads us. You understand that?"

I failed to answer, since I was too busy remembering how to breath.

"Since you're so sure it was murder," he continued relentlessly, "what killed him? Your intuition tell you that?"

I stared at my bare feet and lamented my unprofessional appearance. Maybe if I were wearing a business suit, this cop would be less inclined to accuse me of murder. But there I was, impersonating Huck Finn yet again.

"Ms. Hewitt?"

I looked up. "Stanley Sweetzer was poisoned."

Rye stared at me as if I had suddenly turned green and sprouted antennae from my forehead.

"Well?" I said. "He was, wasn't he?"

"Yes, he was." He kept staring. Apparently my antennae had started growing. "Now do you see the problem? How do you know all this?"

"What? You think I know because I'm the one who did it? Get a grip, Captain. What possible reason could I have for killing Stanley?"

Rye didn't answer, so I insisted again, "I had no motive. You can't arrest me without a motive."

"I'm not here to arrest you."

Thank you, God.

"However, someone who had a mind to might be able to argue a motive."

I sat up and braced myself for who knows what. "Okay, enlighten me," I said. "What is this supposed motive?"

"Jealousy."

"Jealousy! Jealousy of what?"

"Of Ms. Poppe."

I offered Rye the glare he so richly deserved. "That, sir, is absurd. Absolutely absurd."

He held my eye. "It's conceivable—conceivable mind you—that you were jealous of your friend's love life." I glared harder, but still failed to discourage him. "It's happened before. A lonely woman—let's say, a woman of a certain age—"

"I'm fifty two," I interrupted. "And I am not lonely."

Rye hesitated a moment before continuing, "—sees a younger woman with a rich and handsome boyfriend, and she gets jealous."

I crossed my arms so as not to slap him. "Are you always this charming?" I asked.

The captain winced, which was satisfying indeed. That is, until Snowflake jumped onto his lap. He stroked the cat from head to tail, and she purred accordingly.

"I'm sorry," he said to me, "but it looks bad. Especially considering your choice of career."

"Excuse me? What are you talking about now?"

"Any prosecutor worth his salt would have a heyday with the kind of stuff you write. They would argue you have an overactive imagination when it comes to these things."

"I'm a hack, Captain. A hack! I write stories just for fun. No one in their right mind takes them seriously."

No response.

"Oh, for Lord's sake." I threw my hands in the air. "Now you're wondering if I'm in my right mind, aren't you?"

After enduring a few more uncomfortable seconds of silence, I decided to ask a few questions myself. "Okay, so how exactly was Stanley poisoned?" I held up my hand. "No, no, let me re-phrase that. How exactly did I go about poisoning the guy?"

Rye focused on the cat. "I'm not at liberty to tell you that," he mumbled. "I will say, though," he spoke up, "that homicide by poisoning is pretty uncommon nowadays. But for a nonviolent woman of a certain age—"

"Use that phrase one more time, Captain, and I will demonstrate homicide for you."

Rye took a deep breath. "Can we have some tea?" he asked.

Tea! Was the man insane?

"Are you insane?" I didn't wait for a reply. "You come in here and call me an ugly, old, bitch murderer, and then expect me to serve you tea?"

"I never said you were ugly."

***

I closed my eyes and prayed for strength.

When I opened them again, I ascertained that Rye had not miraculously disappeared. I sighed dramatically and got up to make the damn tea as he took his barstool from the night before.

"Tell me about the other people who live here," he asked as I put the kettle on.

"Karen Sembler and Peter Harrison live on the first floor." I banged around getting our cups, et cetera. "This whole building used to belong to Mr. Harrison. When he retired he had it converted into condos to make some money. At least that's my understanding."

"You bought this place from him?"

"I did. I never dealt with him personally—the realtors handled it—but he was the seller."

I poured the tea and shoved a cup in front of Rye. He offered an extremely polite thank you, but I continued to bang things around anyway. "That's all I can tell you about Mr. Harrison. He's very old and very reclusive."

"He gives piano lessons down there?"

It dawned on me that Rye had already talked to my neighbors. I ceased all the unnecessary activity and tried to calm down. "The only time I ever even see Mr. Harrison is if I happen to be in the lobby when he opens his door and a piano student pops in or out."

"And Karen Sembler?"

"Karen's become a good friend." I somehow sensed the need to defend her. "She works at home, too. She's more or less converted her condo into a workshop. And she has a nice-sized private yard. She needs it to do all her welding and such."

"She told me she's a carpenter."

"Karen's an everything. She can build or fix anything. But mostly she builds fancy furniture for all the interior decorators down in Charlotte."

"What about her personal life?"

"What about it?" I asked defiantly. "Do you think she was jealous of Candy, too? Maybe we were in on Stanley's murder together? Is that it?"

"Answer the question, please."

I petted Snowflake, who had jumped onto the counter and was pacing back and forth between us. "Okay, so I really don't know that much about Karen's personal life. She values her privacy." I caught Rye's eye. "As do I."

"Is she involved with anyone?"

"You're very nosey. Do you know that?"

"Yep. And what about you?"

"What about me?"

"Are you involved with anyone, Ms. Hewitt?"

"That, sir, is none of your business."

"I'm investigating a murder. Everything's my business." He pointed to my chest. "Where'd you get that?"

"Excuse me?"

"Your shirt," he said. "It belongs to a man. So did the one last night."

I rolled my eyes. "Would you give me a break? This stupid shirt is at least ten years old."

"You remember where you got it?"

"Once upon a time, it belonged to my ex-husband, if you must know."

"Oh, really?" Rye seemed far too intrigued.

"Read whatever you want into that, Captain. But I assure you—it's just a shirt."

"Mm-hmm."

I drank my tea and wondered if the ordeal would ever end. Apparently not, since Rye insisted on hearing about my neighbors on the second floor. Oh well. At least we were moving away from the altogether depressing topic of my love life.

I explained that Candy Poppe and Bryce Dixon both rented from Mr. Harrison. "Bryce is in 2A above Karen, and Candy has 2B. You've already questioned Candy, correct?"

"I've talked to everyone here, but right now I'm interested in your perspective."

"Well then, you know how much I care about Candy. I like Bryce, too." I confirmed what Rye had already learned for himself—that Bryce Dixon is about Candy's age, and a perpetual student.

"He just switched majors again," I said. "Something to do with business this time. And he tends bar at The Stone Fountain. Candy, Karen, and I are over there a lot."

"He ever involved with Ms. Poppe?"

I shook my head. "They're just friends, as far as I know. As far as I know, Candy's never dated Mr. Harrison, either."

"Or Dixon?"

"No, Bryce hasn't dated Mr. Harrison, either."

"Ms. Hewitt," he scolded. "Can't you try to help me out here? Please?"

I rolled my eyes for the umpteenth time. "Okay, here's the rundown on everyone's love life." I counted my neighbors off on my fingers, starting with my thumb. "I do believe Peter Harrison lives like a celibate monk. As does Karen." I held up my index finger and kept thinking. "And you know what? So does Bryce." Middle finger. I looked at the cat and raised my ring finger and pinky. "I suppose I better put myself in that category, too. And Snowflake."

I slapped the counter. "There, so you see? Every single one of us must have been living vicariously through Candy Poppe's love life."

Rye ignored the sarcasm. "Bryce Dixon's the only neighbor not from around here? Is that right?"

"Other than me," I said. "Karen and Candy even went to the same high school. At different times, though. Karen graduated about ten years before Candy. And I assume Mr. Harrison's family has been here since before dirt. Bryce is from some small town in Missouri. He was just home for vacation."

"What about you?" Rye asked.

"I'm from South Carolina. But I've been a resident of North Carolina since college, and a law-abiding citizen of Clarence for over twenty years."

"And you're the only one up here on the third floor?" Rye scanned my condo yet again. "This is a big space for just one person."

I waved a hand. "Alas, the lonely old bitch of a certain age."

***

With heroic effort and even more patience, I finally got rid of Rye and got back to work. But I accomplished next to nothing. Alexis Wynsome got so bored she actually took a nap.

However, while Alexis tossed and turned on the narrow and lumpy cot chained into the mustiest corner of the turret, Rolfe Vanderhorn arrived on the Snipe estate. He emerged at the clearing at the edge of the forest and stood frowning at the formidable castle of the evil Maynard Snipe.

Something waving in the winds at the top of the north turret caught his eye, and he looked up. Could it be?

Yes! Yes, it was one of the lace hankies that the lovely Alexis was fond of dabbing her dewy brown eyes with. What a smart girl! To tie it outside her window like that, so he would know where to find her!

Suddenly, Rolfe resumed frowning. For our dear, dim, hero had nary a plan for scaling the walls of Lord Snipe's fortress and rescuing his lady love. His horse had no clue either.

And if they were expecting any coaching from me, they were destined for disappointment. I was far too distracted by my own problems to offer any assistance. How irritating would it be if Captain Rye decided to drop by every day until this whole Stanley Sweetzer thing was resolved?

Speaking of irritating—while Rolfe was busy watering his horse, I glanced over at my bookshelf and noticed a gap where *A Deluge of Desire* should have been. That damn cop had stolen my book.

Chapter 3

I barely had time to enjoy my righteous indignation before someone else was pounding on my door. I muttered something about Grand Central Station and went to answer.

But thank God, Jimmy Beak is the impatient type. He announced himself just as I reached for the doorknob, and I froze. Captain Rye was right—that didn't take long.

"Go away," I said cordially.

"You need to answer a few questions about Stanley Sweetzer." Jimmy Beak banged on the door with renewed vigor. "Open up!"

I double checked the deadbolt.

"The public has a right to know what happened here last night," Beak argued. "One of Clarence's finest young men has been murdered. Don't you even care about that, Miss Hewitt?" He jiggled the doorknob. "Miss Hewitt?"

What to do? I gestured to the cat, and we tiptoed back to my desk. But even from behind the door and across the room, I could still hear Jimmy Beak, apparently reporting to the public, who apparently had the right to know.

"Channel 15 News has just learned that Stanley Sweetzer died right here!" Beak was getting excited. "Behind this very door! In the home of Miss Jessica Hewitt, a recent divorcée!"

He knocked yet again, and I was certain the cameras were rolling.

"We also know that Captain Wilson Rye, Clarence's highest ranking homicide detective, has just left the premises. What do you have to say about that, Jessica Hewitt?" Jimmy directed his voice inside. "I know, and more importantly our viewers know, that if Captain Rye's involved, it means trouble." His tone grew even more menacing. "And this time it means trouble for you. You can bet on it.

"Whether or not Jessica Hewitt agrees to cooperate, our viewers can rest easy." Jimmy must have turned back to the camera. "The entire Channel 15 News team will be following up on her involvement with Stanley Sweetzer. The public has a right to know what happened behind this very door."

He rattled my doorknob one last time, and I whined at Snowflake. She hopped into my lap and squeaked back.

"Maybe Alexis Wynsome is on to something," I told her. Being trapped in a nice, solid turret in a castle far, far, away suddenly seemed ideal.

***

"But what about Jimmy Beak?" Karen asked when I called her later.

"What about him?" I asked. "I've been hiding at home for the past twenty-four hours, and all I've gotten for it is a corpse on my couch, a cop in my kitchen, and a creep in the corridor. It's time to go out."

"And risk seeing Jimmy? He put that little scene outside your door on the news tonight, you know?"

I reminded her that I didn't know, since I don't watch TV.

"He's out to get us, Jess. He showed a similar scene outside my own door. I refused to talk to him, too."

"Then we deserve a night out."

When I had decided on an evening at The Stone Fountain to commiserate with my friends, I expected Candy to be the reluctant one. But she had jumped at the chance. She said something about going stir crazy sitting around home and promised to be ready at eight.

Karen, however, was proving harder to convince.

"Come on, Karen," I said. "Even Candy says she's up to it."

"Kiddo's coming with us?"

***

We agreed to call it off at the first sign of Jimmy Beak, but at eight o'clock the coast was clear, and the three of us ventured across Sullivan Street. Despite the disconcerting circumstances, we had risen to the occasion and at least looked our normal selves. Candy may have been a little wobblier than usual, but she was still in stilettos. Karen wore jeans and a T-shirt, and I was also in my evening uniform—slacks, sweater, and pointy-toed flats.

Jim Morrison was singing "Light My Fire" over the sound system as we entered the bar. I took note of the happy fact that it was The Doors night at The Stone Fountain as Gina Stone scurried past us with a tray of drinks.

"Nachos coming up," she called over her shoulder.

"I'm starving," Candy said, but Gina was already long gone.

We waved at Matthew Stone, presiding over his half of the bar, and he offered his standard frown. Matthew pretends to be grumpy, but everyone knows it's just an act. We smiled anyway and maneuvered our way through the crowd. Bryce was pointing to our three favorite barstools, but I took a moment to greet my pals at the pool table before sitting down.

Bless his heart, Bryce had already poured Karen's Corona, and had the Korbel at the ready when I finally turned around. He did a little Bryce-bounce and glanced at Candy. "It's on the house," he told her. "Or whatever you want."

She pointed a hot pink fingernail at the champagne bottle, and we were offering a toast to Stanley when Gina popped over with a plate of nachos.

"I'm starving," Candy reminded us and dug in with gusto.

I shrugged at Karen. "You see?" I said. "Business as usual."

"Usual?" Bryce disagreed. "Haven't the cops been bugging you guys about Stanley?"

"Oh, yeah," Karen said and squeezed some lime into her beer. "Captain Rye wasted half my day, snooping around my workshop and asking why I was home alone last night." She took a sip. "I guess I have no alibi."

"He wasted the other half with me," I said. "Asking why Stanley chose to visit me of all people."

"You guys had it easy," Bryce insisted. "Rye and that lieutenant bugged me over there and over here. They claim Stan had to be poisoned in one place or the other." He held onto the edge of the bar and rocked back and forth. "So guess who looks guilty?"

"But you work over here," Karen said.

"And you live over there," I added.

Bryce kept swaying. "Lucky me."

I sighed dramatically. "Apparently Rye's interested in all of us—our jobs, our love-lives—you name it. We simply fascinate the guy."

"He wanted a list of everyone I've built anything for in the last ten years," Karen said.

"He took a copy of my class schedules for the last ten semesters," Bryce agreed. "He kept asking why I switch majors all the time."

"Why do you switch majors all the time?" Candy asked.

Bryce thought for a moment. "I guess because I always wanted to be a vet like my mom."

I cringed and thought of poor Bryce's allergy to my cat. "Not an option?" I asked.

He pointed to his nose. "First it was cats, then dogs, then horses, then—you guys get the picture. If this business major doesn't work out, I'm thinking of journalism next."

"You could write books like Jessie," Candy suggested.

"Speaking of which, Rye stole one of mine."

"Girlfriend!" Karen stared at me aghast. "He did not."

"Oh, yes he did. There's a big gaping hole on my bookshelf where *A Deluge of Desire* should be."

"That one's my favorites," Candy said. She stopped wrestling with the guacamole and glanced at each of us. "Y'all have to promise me something, okay? Be nice to Captain Rye?"

We groaned in unison.

"No, really," she insisted. "He's just doing his job."

"Yeah, but so is Jimmy Beak," Karen said. "Sorry, Kiddo, but no way I'm being polite to that jerk."

"Jimmy's been bothering everyone?" I asked.

Karen shuddered, Candy whimpered, and Bryce complained that, like Rye, Jimmy Beak had bothered him both at home and at work.

"Matthew and Gina are totally fed up. But I'm the one he bugged the most." Bryce frowned. "Lucky me—I mixed Stan's drinks last night."

"But you're the bartender," I reminded him.

"Everyone's still real interested. Matthew and Gina both claim they didn't serve him anything. Just me."

"Stanley always loved your Long Island Iced Teas." Candy said quietly. "Everyone does."

"Everyone but you."

"Bryce isn't the only one who looks bad," Karen said with an ominous glance at me.

"Jimmy knows you're Adelé Nightingale," Bryce explained. "He talked about it on TV tonight, Jessie. He acted like your books are illegal or something."

"Oh, but he showed a real nice picture of you!" Candy said, and I almost choked on my champagne. "The one from the back of *Windswept Whispers*?"

I drank some more.

The fact that Jimmy Beak had shown any picture of me was horrifying in and of itself. But using the photograph from *Windswept Whispers*? Proof positive that the man is evil. I was having a bad hair month when that picture was taken, and for a few misguided and unattractive weeks, I had gone grey.

"Help me," I begged no one in particular.

"At least Kiddo did okay." Karen patted Candy's knee. "You did great handling Jimmy's questions."

Candy finally gave up on the nachos. "He seemed real nice when we were talking. But then when I saw myself on TV, it was like he tricked me or something." She turned to me. "I probably shouldn't have told him where Stanley died, huh?"

I told her not to worry about it and tried to believe Karen and Bryce, who claimed that Jimmy has a very short attention span. According to them, he would soon find another supposed story to worry himself and everyone else about.

"Maybe the cops will get busy somewhere else, too," Bryce suggested.

"No way," I said. "Rye's having far too much fun accusing me. He insists bitchy old women like me are prone to poisoning people."

"You are not a bitch," Candy said.

"I'm not a murderer, either."

"I bet Old Man Harrison did it," Bryce said, and the three of us jumped. "Think about it, guys." He tapped his index fingers on the bar, playing imaginary drums. "If the cops keep blaming someone in our building, it had to be Harrison."

"But why would Mr. Harrison hurt Stanley?" Candy asked. "Everyone loved Stanley."

"Old Man Harrison hates everyone," Bryce argued.

"He refused to talk to Jimmy Beak," Karen added.

I raised an eyebrow. "So did we, Karen."

The two of us blinked at each other until Candy broke the silence. "Umm, Bryce?" she said. "Did Stanley say anything last night? You know, when he was over here?"

"About what?"

She shifted in her seat. "Gosh, I don't know. Anything?"

"You think he might have mentioned something important?" I asked. "Like a clue?"

"Maybe?" She looked at Bryce, but he told her to keep dreaming.

"I barely talked to Stan. He hung out with the Dibbles, mostly."

"The Dibbles?" I asked. "You are jok—"

"Shhhit," Karen hissed. "Ten o'clock! Ten o'clock!"

We jerked our heads toward ten o'clock, where Jimmy Beak stood in the doorway, armed with his cameraman.

"Shhhit," we hissed in unison.

But Gina Stone was on it. She walked right up to Jimmy and spilled a drink on his bow tie. That gave Matthew time to get over there. He stepped in front of the cameraman and blocked our view of whatever followed next.

"Turn around!" Bryce demanded.

We twirled around on our barstools and faced the pool table.

"Jimmy's blocking the door, Jessie!" That was Candy.

"And no way we can get past the camera guy," Karen said.

"The public has a right to know." I heard Jimmy's voice over Jim Morrison's baritone and knew he had made it past Matthew.

I blinked at the pool table. More to the point, I glanced under the table and then at my pool-playing pal Kirby Cox.

Bless his heart, he read my mind and cleared a path.

"Dive!" I ordered.

Karen went down first. Candy followed, and I took up the rear.

I sure did hope Jimmy's cameraman was still preoccupied, because the sight of Candy Poppe's miniskirt-clad bottom wiggling its way under that pool table was more than the public had a right to know. Trust me.

We crouched out of sight while Kirby rearranged the pool table crowd. "About face!" he whispered loudly. "Secure the perimeter!"

Have I mentioned Kirby is an ex-Marine?

***

"Gross," Karen muttered and pointed to the bare toes surrounding us.

What is it with this town and sandals, I asked myself, not for the first time. Okay, so I have a thing about bare toes. I do not like them, and I do not like looking at anyone's feet. And just then, I was looking at a lot of feet.

I recognized Kirby's toes, and assumed the others belonged to Gus, and to Bernie and Camille Allen. "TMI," I mumbled.

Jimmy was causing a commotion, but other than those ugly feet, we couldn't see a darn thing. We got ourselves as comfortable as possible, which wasn't very, and waited.

"I'll never forget the day Audrey found out I'm a Libra, just like her," Karen whispered at some point. "She's wanted to commiserate with me ever since."

I shifted slowly, since quickly was not an option, and glared at my friend. "Excuse me?"

"Audrey Dibble," Candy reminded me. "Bryce said Stanley talked to her last night."

I may have groaned, but perhaps it did make sense to discuss Audrey Dibble in the present circumstances. The situation was surrealistically weird. As was Audrey.

From what I could tell, she and her husband Jackson lived in their booth at The Stone Fountain. The one time I had spoken to them, Audrey asked for my birthday. I had given her the date, only to be subjected to a twenty-minute dissertation about the perils of being a Pisces.

"Was Stanley friends with the Dibbles?" I had to ask.

"Sometimes the four of us would talk," Candy said. "Audrey's always so interesting."

Karen caught my eye. "Who can argue?"

"All clear!" Matthew Stone announced, and an uproar of applause exploded around the bar.

The sandals parted, and we were just about to crawl out from our lair, when I spotted a pair of Oxfords at my fingertips. They might as well have had "COP" emblazoned across the toes.

I closed my eyes and prayed for strength.

Chapter 4

Rye squatted down and stuck his head under the table.

"Ladies," he greeted us. He glanced at the three of us until his gaze halted at me. "Pleasure to see you again, Ms. Hewitt."

I attempted a most unladylike gesture, bumped my head, and muttered an unladylike word.

Rye offered his hand, but I slapped it away.

"I am perfectly capable of standing up on my own," I informed him with as much dignity as a fifty-two-year-old woman could muster while crawling out from under a barroom pool table.

I stood upright, more or less, brushed the debris from my hands and knees, and gratefully accepted a bar towel from Bryce.

"And people wonder why I spend so much time home alone with my cat," I mumbled to Karen. Lieutenant Densmore had helped her out and was in the process of getting Candy to her feet.

Rye continued staring at me.

"Unless you're here to arrest me, Captain, I'll excuse myself." I tossed Bryce the towel and led my friends to the ladies room.

"Let's get out of here," I said as the three of us lined up at the sinks and pumped gobs of disinfectant soap into our hands.

Candy caught my eye in the mirror. "But what if Jimmy Beak's waiting for us?"

"What? Like lurking outside, ready to ambush us?"

She shrugged and grabbed a handful of paper towels.

"Let's wait a while," Karen suggested. "I could use another Corona anyway."

Testimony to my whimsical and flexible nature, I agreed to one more glass of champagne. "I'll need it if Rye's still out there."

Which of course, he was. He was talking to Gina Stone, but immediately stopped harassing her when he saw us return to our barstools.

I turned my back as he approached.

"Champagne?" he asked over my shoulder.

"It's what she always drinks," Bryce answered. He pointed back and forth between Candy and me. "We keep a stock of the stuff just for the two of them."

"We're not being disrespectful to Stanley, sir." Candy had turned to face Rye, and seemed to think he deserved even further explanation. "It's just what Jessie and me drink is all."

Karen also jumped on the be-nice-to-Rye bandwagon. She patted the empty seat beside her and actually asked him to join us.

I was contemplating a return to my cozy spot under the pool table, but Rye stepped away. He claimed he didn't want to bother anyone, joined Densmore, and the two of them got lost in the crowd.

I was really, really, ready to go, but Karen reminded me of the Jimmy Beak hazard, and Candy seemed content watching the pool game going on behind us. This seemed a pleasant enough diversion. I turned to watch the game, but also kept a wary eye on the cops.

Densmore sat down with the Dibbles, but much to my chagrin, Rye had also gotten interested in the pool game. He stood in the back corner, and I noticed he had taken off his suit jacket and tie. Apparently, he had lost the gun also.

Eventually, Kirby invited him to play. Kirby Cox is, by far, the worst pool player I have ever met. But what he lacks in skill, he more than makes up for in enthusiasm.

No big surprise, Captain Rye won the game against Kirby. Then he played Gus and beat him also. He was looking around for another victim when Candy jumped up and pointed to me. I could have killed her.

"Jessie's real good, sir. Ask her to play!"

I refused, as did Rye, but then Densmore appeared and whispered something to his boss. Rye stared at me while listening to the lieutenant and apparently changed his mind. In fact, he grinned from ear to ear and asked me to reconsider.

The two of them probably had some plan to force a confession out of me in the middle of the game, but I decided to take my chances. After all, someone had to wipe that stupid grin off his face.

I hopped off my barstool as Bryce produced my cue from behind the bar.

That got Rye's attention. "You mean you have your own cue stick?"

We locked eyes as I screwed my cue together.

"When she dies we're gonna dip it in gold and hang it over the table," Bryce told him.

I chalked up and asked Kirby to rack the balls. Then I turned to my opponent. "Do you plan on arresting me when I win?"

"When, Ms. Hewitt?" He kept grinning. "Don't you mean if?"

I repeated my question, verbatim, and gestured for him to break.

"Oh, no," he said, offering a false bow. "Ladies first, I insist."

"You'll be sorry," Karen sang from behind me.

I approached the table.

***

While Kirby stood at attention saluting, I broke, knocking the three ball into the left corner pocket while I was it. I scanned the table and enjoyed a bit of Jim Morrison singing "LA Woman" before continuing. The five and the two balls also fell easily, but the seven ball was going to be a challenge. I looked at where the cue ball had rolled and decided to bank it off the far bumper, clip the four and then pocket the seven.

I walked over to where Rye was standing, stupefied and dumbfounded. He didn't seem to notice he was in my way, so I tapped his chest with my index finger and asked him to please step back. He still looked perplexed, so I explained my plan for the seven ball.

He glanced at the table. "No way," he said. "No one can make that shot."

"Way." I applied a bit more pressure with my index finger, and he finally moved.

When the seven ball cooperated, Karen and Bryce high-fived each other across the bar, and Kirby saluted again, bless his heart. Candy bounced on her barstool and applauded, and even Densmore emitted a low whistle of appreciation. I smiled at the captain, who, I noticed, had suddenly ceased grinning.

I smiled some more and returned to the table. But the cue ball hadn't landed exactly where I had hoped, and I didn't see much else to work with. I knocked a couple of balls into inconvenient spots and gave Rye his turn.

While he studied the table, I chatted with Lieutenant Densmore. "I thought you guys weren't supposed to drink?" I asked.

"We're off duty, ma'am."

Rye sunk the ten ball, and then the thirteen.

"So you're here just for the fun of it?"

"Stanley Sweetzer was here last night."

"With the murderer?" I glanced away from the game and up at Densmore. "Maybe?"

He shrugged noncommittally and watched Rye miss the fourteen ball.

"What do you know about the Dibbles?" Densmore asked me.

"They drink Long Island Iced Teas by the bucketful and Audrey's a Libra." I excused myself from the lieutenant and returned to the table. But Rye stopped me just as I was about to call the one ball.

"I've been thinking about our discussions," he said quietly.

"Oh?" I tried walking around him, but he blocked me from the table and actually turned us around to face the wall.

"And you still haven't told me why Sweetzer showed up at your place last night."

"Maybe because I don't know why."

"Another thing you haven't told me." Rye lowered his voice even further. "Is if he made a regular habit of calling on you. Alone, that is—without your friend Ms. Poppe in tow."

I held onto my cue with both hands and blinked at the brick wall in front of me. "Aren't you off duty?" I asked.

"Answer the question, please."

I continued studying the stupid wall. "There was nothing unseemly going on between Stanley Sweetzer and me." My tone was firm.

"So he had never visited you before?"

"There was nothing sordid going on." I dismissed the wall and glared at Rye. "Sorry to disappoint you."

I turned and somehow forced my way around him and back to the table. "One ball," I announced a bit too loudly. I knocked at the pocket near my right hip and made the shot. And before Rye could think of any more pesky questions, I took care of the rest of the solids and pointed to where the eight ball would fall.

Candy hopped off her barstool and walked over to Rye as I made the shot and finished the game. The small group of onlookers clapped accordingly, and I offered a modest curtsy.

"You see?" Candy said. "I told you Jessie's good."

"Yes, Ms. Poppe." Rye frowned. "It appears your friend has many talents."

I handed my cue back to Bryce and joined them. "Yeah, you know? Shooting pool, poisoning people, whatever." I held out my hand and the captain shook it.

"Where'd you learn to play pool like that?" he asked without letting go of my hand.

I pulled back. "Once upon a time my father taught me."

I failed to share my family history with Captain Rye, but my father put the working half of a cue in my hand the day I could stand upright on my own. Our pool table presided over the dining room, and Daddy would drag a chair around for me to stand on until I was tall enough to reach over the rail. I was beating my older brother by the time I was seven and had even won a few games against my father since then. Rarely, but sometimes.

Candy was still bragging to Rye. "I've never seen Jessie lose. Ever!"

I looked at the captain. "She's right," I told him. "I seldom lose."

"Neither do I, Ms. Hewitt."

***

"Oh my gosh, Jessie," Candy squealed as we arrived back home. "Captain Rye really likes you. I mean, he could not take his eyes off you while you were downing those balls right and left." She pranced around the lobby, pretending to play pool with an imaginary stick. Apparently Stanley's demise had slipped her mind.

"Help me," I asked Karen.

She shrugged and unlocked her door. "The guy did keep his eyes firmly planted on your backside every time you bent over to take a shot."

"Charming, no?"

"Actually, for some weird reason it was." She walked inside and turned to Candy. "Call me if you need anything, Kiddo," she said and closed the door.

"He's not married," Candy said as we walked up the stairs to our own places.

"Candy," I spoke sternly, "I do not care about that stupid cop's marital status." We reached her door. "Okay, so how do you know this?"

"Like, duh!" She tapped her ring finger. "There's no ring, okay? And I asked Lieutenant Densmore just to make extra-double sure." She was quite proud of herself. "Captain Rye is single. And perfect for you." She poked my shoulder with a hot pink fingernail.

I folded my arms and glared. "You seem to forget the guy thinks I killed Stanley."

Mention of Stanley distracted Candy for a bit, and I was sorry I had spoken so gruffly.

I patted her hand. "Okay, Sweetie. Tell me why Captain Rye and I are so darn perfect for each other."

She found a tissue in the tiny sequined purse she was carrying, blew her nose, and enlightened me. "Well, you're both single," she said, and I nodded. "And you have the same haircut."

I thought about that. Rye's was dark with some graying at the temples, and mine was blond, with some help from my hairdresser. But I couldn't argue there either.

Encouraged, Candy continued, "And you're both tall, and you both play pool, and you're both old—" She caught herself. "Older, I mean. Captain Rye's forty-seven."

"And how exactly do you know this?"

"I asked him!"

I did the math. "That would put me in cougar territory."

"So?"

I closed my eyes and prayed for strength.

When I opened them again, Candy was smiling broadly. She turned around to unlock her door. "Gosh he's a hunk, even if he is old. I mean, how could you not notice those eyes, Jessie?"

I admitted that I had noticed the Captain's lovely blue eyes. Lord knows I had glared into them often enough.

Candy stepped inside her apartment. "And don't you think the graying at his temples is to die for?"

I told her she was giving me a headache and walked upstairs.

Chapter 5

The following morning Rolfe Vanderhorn got busy being heroic. He forded Lord Snipe's moat and fought his way into the castle, fending off several guards and Maynard Snipe himself along the way. Alexis couldn't see the struggle from behind the heavy door of her turret, but she heard the commotion in the winding stone stairwell, and prepared herself for the impending moment, when Rolfe would barge through the door, sweep her off her feet, and carry her to freedom, at last. To say the woman's bosom trembled in anticipation would be an understatement.

Rolfe did not disappoint. Indeed, he swash buckled his way into the turret, rescued a most grateful Alexis Wynsome, and delivered her forthwith to his charming cottage on the outskirts of the village.

And now our hero was in the process of unbuckling a few things when a commotion arose outside my own door.

"Go away," I heard Captain Rye tell Jimmy Beak.

"Grand Central Station," I mumbled to Snowflake. I closed my computer and the two of us walked over to hear more.

Rye's arrival was adding a new mix to the mayhem, but Channel 15's finest had been camped out in the hall all morning. Apparently Jimmy Beak was under the impression that if he waited long enough, I would break down, open my door, and confess all, preferably while the camera was rolling.

"Get lost, Beak," Rye demanded. Jimmy offered some lame argument, but the captain was unfazed. "You can leave, or you can get yourself arrested for trespassing. Take your pick."

I heard retreating footsteps, but Rye had to assure me Jimmy and his cameraman had left the building before I opened the door.

"We've got a problem," he said when I peeked out.

"Why am I not surprised?" I crossed my arms and blocked his entry.

"May I come in?"

"Could you really have arrested Jimmy?"

"As long as this hallway is private property, he has no right to be here. Not without your permission."

"Thank you," I said sincerely. "I'll remember that."

"Like when you remember to put a lock on that door downstairs?"

So much for gratitude. I ushered Rye inside, but something about how he hesitated made my heart beat in a disturbing way.

"What's wrong now?" I had to ask.

Rye took a deep breath. "I'm here to search your house."

"What!?" I screamed, and he held up his arms in self-defense. "Over my dead body!" I continued screaming. "Don't tell me you're looking for the poison?"

"That, and we need to check your financial records."

"My financial records!?"

He mumbled something about Stanley's job as a financial advisor and pulled a truly sinister-looking document from his pocket.

"Is this a warrant?" I stared aghast at the paper he handed me, and Rye confirmed that it was indeed a warrant.

I let this startling information sink in for a few seconds before looking up. "Where's my book?"

"Excuse me?"

"My book, Captain. The one you stole from me yesterday." I shoved the warrant back into his hands. "You plan on taking anything else while you're at it?"

I kid you not, the man actually grinned as he again reached into his suit pocket. This time he pulled out *A Deluge of Desire*. "You can't blame a guy for being curious, can you? I read it when I got home last night."

I grabbed the book. "Even my most loyal fans need more than one night to finish one of these."

"Well," he sang. "I only read the parts you were bragging about yesterday."

I folded my arms and glared. "Learn anything?"

Lieutenant Densmore cleared his throat from the doorway, and we both jumped.

I tossed *Deluge* on the coffee table. "I suppose you're here to help sack the place?"

Poor Densmore glanced at his boss, and Rye explained that while he searched for the poison, Densmore would be checking my financial records.

My financial records. I blinked twice as it finally struck me what these cops were looking for. "You won't find anything," I said.

"Why didn't you tell me you were one of Sweetzer's clients, Ms. Hewitt?"

"Because I'm not. I haven't invested a dime with Stanley." I folded my arms and resumed glaring. "I'm not lying."

"You're not exactly telling the truth either. All those times I asked about your relationship with the guy? And you failed to mention this?"

"I've been checking Stanley Sweetzer's records at his job, ma'am." That was Lieutenant Densmore. "He had a file on you. On your finances."

"That's impossible," I argued. "Stanley knew nothing about my finances."

"It's a pretty detailed file," Densmore added.

"Detailed? But how—" I stopped short when I noticed the latex gloves emerging from the lieutenant's pocket.

Rye waited until he caught my eye. "You have any questions before we start?"

Where to begin? I mumbled a no, and resigned myself to the inevitable as Densmore continued delivering the bad news. "After I finish here," he told me, "I'll also be talking with your bank, and with your accountant."

I plopped into an easy chair and groaned.

The cops stared. "You do have an accountant, ma'am?" Densmore asked.

"I'm, umm, between accountants right now."

"Between accountants?" Rye said. "What does that mean?"

"It means my ex-husband is a CPA. Ian Crawcheck." I groaned again. "I haven't replaced him yet."

I focused on Snowflake, who was sitting at my feet nonchalantly cleaning her paws, and thought about the ominous implications of Densmore talking to Ian.

Rye hovered until I looked up. "You have a right to stay and watch," he informed me and headed to the kitchen.

"Well then," I said quietly, "I will."

***

Rye began an altogether futile attempt to discover poison in my refrigerator, but I was far more interested in Lieutenant Densmore's task. I directed him to the large cardboard box under my bed. He pulled it out and set it between us on the coffee table. Then he delved on in with an enthusiasm my bank statements and tax returns truly did not merit. Even more remarkable—Densmore studied each document as if he actually understood the mumbo jumbo.

Eventually, he came to some mumbo jumbo even he didn't comprehend. "Tell me about these, ma'am?" He held up a stack of the statements my publisher sends me every quarter.

"They're my royalty statements from Perpetual Pleasures Press."

"Ma'am?"

"My publisher, Lieutenant. I never understand the stupid things."

Densmore furrowed his brow and did his best to understand the stupid things. He even took out a pocket calculator and started crunching the numbers while I watched in awe.

"Maybe I should hire you as my new accountant," I suggested.

Densmore said no thank you, and we were sharing a bit of nervous laughter when Rye passed by.

"Bathroom's next," he said and headed in that direction.

I stayed in the living room since I saw no need to watch Rye search my medicine cabinet. My calcium supplements and an outdated bottle of Advil couldn't be all that incriminating.

"Feel free to scoop out Snowflake's litter box while you're in there," I called out, and Densmore chuckled again.

Oh yes, I was thinking this search thing wasn't so intimidating after all when Rye moved into my bedroom and started rummaging through my dresser drawers.

I remembered my underwear drawer, filled to the brim with highly unsuitable lacy things purchased at Tate's Department Store, and decided I was getting a headache. I picked up Snowflake and headed toward the door.

"We'll be on the roof," I announced. My civil rights be damned, I needed some fresh air.

***

I lost track of time sitting in my garden, staring off at the Blue Ridge, but eventually Rye emerged onto the roof. I folded my arms and refused to look up.

"Where's Densmore?" I asked.

"You couldn't pay the lieutenant to come out here. He hates heights."

With that, Rye invited himself to sit beside me. He leaned back and looked quite comfortable indeed.

"Man, this is incredible." He waved an arm at the various flower pots surrounding us. "Did you do all this?"

I stood up and made a show of moving to the opposite bench. "Are you flirting with me or arresting me, Captain Rye?" I folded my arms and glared. "Make up your mind."

While Rye made up his mind, Snowflake hopped onto the spot I had just vacated. I glared at her, too.

"I'm not arresting you," he said eventually.

"Oh, so you didn't find the poison then?" I do believe he caught the sarcasm.

"I'm ninety-nine percent—" He stopped and corrected himself. "I'm ninety percent sure you're not the murderer."

"Gee thanks."

He tossed the plastic bag he was holding onto my lap. I glanced down and recognized the five or six brochures of bogus companies Stanley had given me over the past few weeks.

"I thought I recycled those," I mumbled.

"Getting rid of evidence doesn't help your cause, Ms. Hewitt. We check recycling. And garbage."

"Lovely."

"You need to tell me the exact nature of your relationship with Sweetzer. The whole story this time."

I reminded him I had no relationship with Sweetzer, and we had ourselves a little stare down.

Rye leaned forward and offered his sternest cop-like look. "I might think you're innocent," he said quietly. "But the chief of police—my boss—does not. So this is where we're stuck, and where Jimmy Beak is stuck, until you level with me." He sat back. "You get it, lady?"

Okay, so maybe I did. I took a deep breath and blurted it out. "Stanley was trying to sell me some stocks. He used to visit me when Candy was at work."

Rye turned to Snowflake. "Now she tells me."

"But nothing happened," I insisted. "Stanley came by three or four times. I listened to his stupid sales pitch and accepted his stupid brochures. I never gave him any money." I tossed the bag of brochures back to Rye. "I was just trying to be polite," I continued. "He was Candy's boyfriend after all. But his act got old pretty quickly."

"What act?"

"Stanley tried to charm me out of my money, Captain. Apparently he thought a lonely old bitch like me would be flattered by the attention." I raised an eyebrow. "Sound familiar?"

"I never actually called you a lonely old bitch."

"Gee thanks."

Rye frowned. "Why all the secrecy? Why not tell me this sooner?"

"Because I am sick of discussing my private affairs—" I stopped and tried again. "Of discussing my finances with men. First of all, I've just gone through an extremely contentious divorce. Other than Snowflake, I had to fight for everything I took away from my twenty years of marriage."

Rye glanced at Snowflake, as if verifying I had custody.

I continued, "I survived that ordeal, only to get Stanley Sweetzer harassing me about money. And then you come along asking all kinds of personal questions, implying I'm guilty of who knows what."

My voice had been rising steadily throughout my diatribe, and I practically shouted as I thought of one more issue. "Oh, and let's not forget Densmore! Who is probably, right this very moment, talking to my ex-husband. My ex, for Lord's sake!" I waved my arms in exasperation. "So much for the right to privacy."

Rye, of course, was watching me. After calmly witnessing my minor breakdown, he calmly thanked me for my honesty.

I closed my eyes and prayed for strength.

"Speaking of my privacy." I opened my eyes. "What exactly is in this file Stanley had on me?"

"He knew where you do your banking, and where you hold your mutual funds."

"I suppose he also knew my bank balance?"

Rye named a figure, and I almost fell off the bench.

"Accurate?" he asked.

It was the exact amount of my divorce settlement. Ian had gotten the house, and I had gotten a lump sum of cash. I reluctantly explained the details to Rye.

"But how did Stanley know all this?" I asked.

"You ever confide in Candy Poppe?"

"No way. I haven't discussed my divorce settlement with anyone. Until now."

"Well then, that's another mystery to solve."

I wracked my brains for some explanation of Stanley's sixth sense.

"How much money—cash—do you have in your house right now?" Rye asked me.

"Didn't you guys just search my wallet?"

"Humor me."

"I don't know," I said. "Maybe fifty dollars?"

"You have forty-six and some change."

"And this is significant how?"

"Stanley Sweetzer had a little over twenty-seven thousand dollars cash in his apartment the night he died." I sat up straight and Rye nodded. "Intriguing, huh?"

"Maybe he gambled," I said without thinking.

Rye looked at me with even more interest than usual. "You know something from Ms. Poppe about this?"

I shook my head. "Candy's pretty innocent and naive. She'd never imagine anyone gambling like that."

"How come you imagine it?"

Oops.

I decided to use the same excuse I had given the day before. "Intuition." I tapped my temple. "I'm a writer, remember?"

Rye chuckled. "Oh, Ms. Hewitt, I'm not apt to forget that. I have read *A Deluge of Desire*, after all."

The numerous scenes of unbridled passion between Devon Larkin and Chase Gable, the energetic and enthusiastic stars of *Deluge,* came floating back to me.

"Take your mind off it, Captain."

"You're one to talk. From what I can tell, you make a living putting people's minds on it."

"There's more to my books than the sex, you know?" I actually said this with a straight face. "But then again, how would you know? Since, as you say, you only read the good parts."

"Twice."

Chapter 6

"So!" I sprang up and decided it was time for a stroll. "How do you like my garden?"

"I love your garden." Rye stood also, and we began pacing the roof. It was a perfect day to be up there—late August, a bit breezy, sunny, but not too hot.

"Did you do all this?" he asked, and I explained that the garden was my idea, but that my neighbors had pitched in also.

I pointed out the wrought iron railing around the perimeter of the roof. "That was the first step—making it safe to be up here. Karen said she'd install it if I paid for it. She also made our fountain." I waved at the old fashioned bathtub on claw feet Karen had converted into a water feature.

"What about all the plants?"

I looked around with a fresh eye and had to agree the garden looked fantastic. "I like yellow flowers," I said. "So I started with a few daisies and marigolds. But Candy's so sweet. She keeps bringing home more and more." I pointed to a yellow hibiscus. "That's my current favorite."

I pointed again. "I hunted the antique shops for those big urns and the benches. And Bryce is our muscle. He got everything up here. No easy feat, considering the elevator doesn't make it to the roof, even when it is working."

Rye had wandered toward the skylight above my kitchen. "You're not worried your neighbors can spy on you from up here?"

"Not really." I walked over, and we gazed down at my stove. "I don't make a habit of sunbathing naked down there." We moved to the skylight over my desk. "And I doubt anyone's all that interested in watching me sit at my computer."

"You guys really need to start locking the front door. Anyone and his brother could get up here."

"Now, where have I heard that before?" I promised I would look into it and headed toward the stairwell. "What's next?" I asked.

Rye hesitated. "You're not gonna like it."

"I hate it when you say that."

"Stanley Sweetzer made out a will the week before he died."

I stopped and turned at the top of the stairs. "And?"

"And your friend Ms. Poppe is the sole beneficiary."

He was watching me for a reaction, so I decided it was best not to have one. I called to Snowflake and kept my eyes on her as she hopped down from Karen's railing and took her sweet time to come to me. Still conscious of Rye's gaze, I led the two of them down the stairs.

"Good for Candy," I said over my shoulder. "I'm sure she deserves it."

"Do you think she knew about that twenty-seven thousand dollars?"

"I don't like what you're implying, Captain." We had reached my door. "Besides, Candy has an alibi for Saturday night. She was at work."

"No, she wasn't."

"What?"

"Densmore's checked into it. She took close to a two-hour dinner break that night."

What? My mind raced back to Saturday. I had actually seen Candy at Tate's that afternoon. And then, that night, after Stanley had died? Candy had told me she was at work the whole evening. I furrowed my brow. Hadn't she?

"Ms. Hewitt?"

I glanced up. "Candy must have an explanation," I said with conviction.

"If she does, she's refusing to talk about it. She told Densmore it's too embarrassing."

"So let me get this straight." I spoke slowly. "If I'm not the murderer, my friend Candy must be? You have a lot of nerve, you know that?"

Rye didn't respond, and we stood there glaring at each other until we both got tired. I finally gave up and walked inside, but then something else occurred to me.

"What exactly killed Stanley, anyway?" I faced Rye again. "What was this poison you were looking for?"

"You didn't read that warrant very carefully, Ms. Hewitt. Phenobarbital. Sweetzer died from a combination of Phenobarbital poisoning and alcohol. Those Long Island Iced Teas he was so fond of didn't help him any."

"They're the house specialty over there." I tilted my head in the direction of The Stone Fountain. "They're pretty potent."

"Especially when they're mixed with Phenobarbital."

I asked about Phenobarbital, and Rye explained the basics of barbiturates. Apparently, someone as young and healthy as Stanley would have to consume massive amounts of the stuff to be killed by it.

"Which leads to another question," he said. "Where'd the killer get the drugs? Forensics informs me Phenobarbital's not that easy to come by these days. It's seldom prescribed anymore."

I leaned on my doorframe and thought about Stanley. "So, we think someone slipped this barbiturate stuff into his drink that night?"

"Yes, Ms. Hewitt. That's what we think." He emphasized the we.

"And then he walked all the way across Sullivan Street and up three flights of stairs to die on my couch?"

"That, or else he was poisoned over here." Rye peeked around me and into my living room.

I told him he was giving me a headache and shut the door.

***

Desperate for an Advil, I headed to the bathroom, where further trauma awaited. Not only had Rye failed to scoop out Snowflake's litter box, but the bottle of Advil in my medicine cabinet wasn't expired—it was empty. I went downstairs to beg some pain reliever from Candy. No one was home, so I tried Karen instead.

Bless her heart, she answered her door in typical Karen fashion—wearing goggles and work gloves, and holding a few scraps of sandpaper. She stepped aside to let me in and I noticed the smell of raw wood. Karen's perfume.

"What's up, Jess?" She took off her gloves and slipped the goggles onto the top of her head.

I explained my purpose, and she went to fetch some Advil, leaving me standing in the midst of what should have been her living room. But in reality the room is part of Karen's workshop. On that particular day an enormous four-poster bed that would have seemed cramped even in my bedroom stood in the middle of the room.

The bed and matching six-foot tall dresser were surrounded by an even scarier assortment of power tools. I recognized a drill, but would need a lesson on whatever else was lying around.

"It's hideous, isn't it?" Karen had emerged from the bathroom and handed me a bottle of generic Ibuprofen.

I continued staring at the bed. "It would be beautiful if it were ten sizes smaller. Why do people want furniture anywhere near that big?"

She shrugged and a few tools on her tool belt clanged together. "Heck, I don't know. But I'm making a small fortune on that eyesore.

"Let's get you some water," she said and led me into the kitchen. Other than the sink, which looked like it belonged in a garage, this room was almost normal. I sat down at the table while she washed her hands and came over with two glasses of ice water.

"You're looking a little frazzled there, girlfriend. What's up?"

"Captain Rye is up."

She raised an eyebrow and I took a pill.

"He searched my place this morning," I grumbled. "Believe it or not, he actually had a warrant."

"Did he find anything?"

"Karen!"

"Relax, will you? At least he didn't arrest you."

"Thank God for small favors." I reached for a second pill and spoke to my water glass. "He searched my underwear drawer."

"Oh boy."

"The poor man has probably never seen so much lace in his life."

Karen let out a hoot. "Candy Poppe strikes again. If it makes you feel any better, he'd find about the same in my dresser." She tilted her head. "Maybe I should invite him over sometime?"

"Yeah, right. Don't take this wrong, Karen, but you don't strike me as a woman who's hiding anything more than a few pairs of cotton waist highs in her underwear drawer."

"But you're forgetting I've been neighbors with Candy for three years." She tapped her tool belt. "You simply can't imagine how much lace is lurking under here."

I mumbled that I had a vague idea.

Karen rested her elbows on the table and looked at me. "So, like, you didn't happen to watch the news this morning?"

"I will not give Jimmy Beak the satisfaction."

"That's probably for the best."

Something in her tone revived my headache. "What?" I had to ask. "What did he do this time?"

"He read an excerpt from one of your books." Karen waited to see if I would explode before continuing, "The one with that picture of you on the back cover. You know, with the grey hair?"

I closed my eyes and prayed for strength.

"They put a picture of Stanley on the screen, too, and Jimmy read your description of some character named Lance Votive."

I groaned and dropped my head onto the table. "Votaw," I said to the Formica.

"Huh?"

"Lance Votaw," I repeated. "He's the hero of *Windswept Whispers*."

"Yeah, well, anyway. Jimmy implied that you based this Lance Votaw guy on Stanley." I started banging my head as she continued, "Because you were obsessed with Stanley."

She reached over and lifted my chin. "Can I get you some more drugs, Jess?"

I sat up. "You know what's really absurd? Jimmy Beak and Wilson Rye both stayed up last night, reading my books."

Karen shrugged. "Hey, maybe they learned something."

I glanced out the window and watched the lunch crowd file into The Stone Fountain.

"Umm, Karen?" I ventured. "Did Stanley ever approach you?"

Her shoulders stiffened. "What about?"

"About making some investments?"

She groaned and reached for the Advil.

"I'll take that as a yes. Did you give him any money?"

"What do you think?" She swallowed a pill. "How about you?"

"My father taught me never to gamble on anyone's talent but my own."

"That rules out Stanley then."

"Did he visit you?" I asked. "When Candy wasn't around?"

She got up to refill our water glasses, and I apologized for being so nosey. "I've gotten so used to Rye's rude questions, I've forgotten my manners."

"Stanley came over once or twice." She handed me my glass. "But I always kicked him out. The guy was way too slick for my taste."

"Can't you just see it?" I asked. "He'd bug you, get nowhere, and then come upstairs to bother me. Lord help me, I actually served him tea!"

Karen shook her head at me. "You need to get over that southern manners thing, Jess. You're way too hospitable."

"And you're not?" I pointed to the plate of Oreos she had set before me, and she told me to eat a damn cookie.

"At least I didn't offer Rye any tea today," I said in my own defense. "You know, when he was serving me the warrant?"

"Way to be tough, girlfriend." She pointed me toward another Oreo and took two for herself.

We spent a few moments eating cookies and gazing out her window. Bryce was crossing Sullivan Street on his way to work.

"I wonder if Stanley bothered him, too," I said.

"What for? Bryce can barely pay his rent most months. Stanley had bigger fish to fry." Karen turned back to me. "Does Rye really still suspect you, Jess?"

"He says he's ninety percent sure I'm innocent. Reassuring, no?"

"But that's great. He's looking into other possibilities, then?"

"Candy Poppe," I said.

"Oh boy."

I thought about Candy. Okay, so she wasn't exactly the epitome of the grieving girlfriend. And then there was Stanley's will to consider. And the twenty-seven thousand in cash, and Candy's extra-long dinner break on Saturday night.

I caught Karen's eye. "You don't think she could have done it?"

"No way." Karen seemed confident. "But she did have a motive."

"What!?"

"Think about it, Jess. If Stanley had lived, and Candy had married him, our little Kiddo would have gone through life as Candy Poppe-Sweetzer." She took the last Oreo and twisted it open. "It's enough to drive any woman to murder."

Chapter 7

And where was Candy anyway? I called her several times that afternoon to no avail, and tried her door one more time on my way down to get the mail. Still no answer.

I was sorting through my junk mail in the lobby when Mr. Harrison's door opened and out popped a piano student. The pretty teenage girl thanked him and he reminded her to continue practicing her Chopin piece.

"It needs work, Miss Taylor," he said. "Work."

Miss Taylor shrugged and waved a handful of fingers at me as she skittered across the lobby and out the front door.

I glanced up just in time to see Peter Harrison's door slam shut.

Once upon a time—like a week ago—that kind of thing would have discouraged me. But a week ago I wasn't looking for a murderer. I tossed my trash in the waste basket and knocked on the door. When it opened again, I was ready with my friendliest smile.

"I'm sorry to bother you, Mr. Harrison," I lied.

Mr. Harrison glared with about as much encouragement as I gave Captain Rye every time he appeared unannounced at my own doorstep. "Is there a problem?" he asked.

There were all sorts of problems, the most immediate being I had no idea what I was going to say next. But then I spotted the huge piano inside.

"I'm, umm, I've been thinking of taking piano lessons," I said. I turned my gaze from the piano back to Peter Harrison. "And I was wondering if you offer lessons to adults?" I opened my eyes wide and feigned great interest in his response.

"Have you ever played?"

I confessed that I had never touched a keyboard in my life. "But I'm quite curious to try." I smiled broadly and tried looking eager.

Much to my dismay, Mr. Harrison did not instantly invite me inside to give it a whirl. Indeed, his glare was now joined by a most discouraging frown.

"I have had enough strange people knocking on my door over the past few days," he scolded. "And I am not in the mood for charades. What is it you want, Miss Hewitt?"

I gave up the charade. "I want to figure out who killed Stanley Sweetzer," I said. "As I'm sure you know, Candy Poppe's boyfriend died on my couch the other night."

"And created quite a ruckus in the process."

Mr. Harrison seemed to expect an apology about that. I gave him one, but this only encouraged his self-righteous indignation.

"Boyfriends traipsing the hallways at all hours of the day and night, policemen coming and going, Jimmy Beak and his news crew." He pursed his lips and continued frowning at the same time. "When I sold the third floor unit to a middle-aged woman who writes books for a living, I did not expect this sort of thing. I trust this will not become a habit?"

"Umm, noooo," I said, perplexed. Did Old Man Harrison really expect a steady contingent of men to be dropping dead on my couch? On a regular basis?

He offered yet more frowning, glaring, and pursing of lips. If I had needed to practice my Chopin piece, I am sure his disapproval would have inspired more earnest effort.

"Mr. Harrison," I pleaded. "I just want to find out what really happened on Saturday. Did you see anything?"

"I most certainly did not. I was asleep until the police arrived. Sleep, Miss Hewitt. I'm 78 years old, take 9 prescription medications every day, and teach 18 unruly piano students every week. I need my rest." He made a show of looking at his watch. "And now, it is well past my nap-time. If you'll excuse me."

He tried to shut his door, but I put my foot out and stopped it from closing.

"There's a good chance either Candy or I are going to get blamed for the murder." I, too, spoke firmly. "But whatever you might think of us, sir, we are not killers."

I removed my foot and stepped back. The door remained open.

"So then," I continued in a softer voice. "Even if you were home in bed, maybe you heard something unusual? Anything?"

Mr. Harrison tore his gaze away from my foot and looked up. "I hear rather a lot of unusual things around here, don't I? Considering the number of boyfriends Miss Poppe has, this kind of thing was bound to happen." He tut-tutted for effect. "I only wish I had evicted her long before now."

"Have you tried to evict Candy?" I am sure I sounded shocked and dismayed.

"I know the law," he snapped. "The girl pays her rent on time and she's quiet. I wouldn't have a leg to stand on." He smiled for the first time. "Mr. Dixon, on the other hand."

My head was reeling. "Have you tried to evict Bryce?"

"He plays loud music and his rent's always late. Since you're so concerned, why don't you tell him I'm considering it? You are bound to run into him, aren't you? At that bar you spend half your life in?"

He looked down, ascertained that my foot was not in the way, and shut the door.

* * *

I stood riveted to the spot and blinked at Old Man Harrison's door. Eventually, I recovered enough to climb the stairs to my own place. I dropped the mail on the coffee table and went out for a walk. I needed the exercise, I needed to shake off the sheer hostility of my encounter with Mr. Harrison, and most of all, I needed to think.

But the weather had turned since my rooftop rendezvous with Rye, and a storm was brewing. Despite the growing cloud cover and rising winds, I hastened down Sullivan Street toward Hamilton. I almost hoped to get caught in a downpour. The shock might jolt my imagination—and my imagination could use a jolt.

First of all, I had no idea what further perils awaited Rolfe Vanderhorn and Alexis Wynsome now that Alexis was safe from the clutches of Maynard Snipe.

And even more pressing than the plot of *Temptation at Twilight*, was the plight of Candy Poppe. Were Peter Harrison's insinuations about her many boyfriends valid? And where had she been the night of Stanley's murder? Where was she at the moment, for that matter? And if Candy didn't kill Stanley, and I was ninety percent certain she hadn't, who did?

I trudged up the steep incline of Hamilton Avenue and pondered the possibilities. Where did that random twenty-seven thousand dollars in Stanley's apartment fit into all this? Was it connected to his murder? Or maybe his job?

Stanley's job. I turned right onto Summit Street and headed into the wind. Had Stanley been cheating some of his clients? Even though Karen and I hadn't squandered our hard-earned cash with him, someone likely had. Captain Rye must have thought the disgruntled client theory had credence, too. Why else would he have Densmore checking into my finances and talking to Ian?

Ian. I groaned out loud, and a street musician playing a really, really, bad rendition of "Mr. Tambourine Man" stopped singing to ask if I was all right. I put a dollar in his cap, he grabbed it before it blew away, and I kept walking. How the heck had Stanley known about my divorce settlement?

Back to Stanley's job, I reminded myself. A list of his clients would be mighty handy. But how in the world would I ever get hold of something like that? Rye might be flirting with me, but I doubted I could charm him out of that kind of information.

I stopped suddenly. But maybe I didn't need Rye. I turned around and headed for home armed with one clear fact—Stanley had either been poisoned in my building or at The Stone Fountain. Whoever killed him had been at the bar on Saturday night. I was sure of it.

I climbed the stairs to my condo with a plan in mind and a smile on my face. I lost the smile when I almost tripped over Jimmy Beak.

***

He and his cameraman were sitting cross-legged on the floor at my doorway looking quite comfortable indeed. Jimmy glanced up and snickered, and I was reminded of the evil Lord Snipe.

"Go away," I ordered.

He turned his head right and left, pretending to search for something. "Oh dear," he said with another snicker. "Where is that pool table when you need it most?"

"Now, Beak," I said, veritably channeling Captain Rye. "You can leave now, or I'll have you arrested for trespassing. Take your pick."

Jimmy made a show of standing up and brushing off his suit, which was a weird, almost metallic, shade of blue. He straightened his bow tie and combed his greasy hair while I tried not to be physically ill. The cameraman had also stood up. Instead of attending to his personal grooming needs, he worked on getting the camera up and running.

"Here she is," Jimmy began as soon as his microphone was in place. "Jessica Hewitt, in the flesh."

I wish I could report he was speaking into the camera, but I was well aware that the lens was directed at me.

"Jessica Hewitt," he continued. "A.k.a. Adelé Nightingale, the prime suspect in the ongoing Stanley Sweetzer murder investigation. Let me remind our viewers that Mr. Sweetzer expired right here, behind this very door."

You guessed it—he banged on my door.

"We're here at the scene of the crime, where Miss Hewitt has finally agreed to answer a few questions."

"Go away," I repeated.

"So tell us, Jessica, why was Captain Wilson Rye here again today? Along with the entire team of investigators from the Clarence police force? Did he have a warrant? Did he find the drugs you used to kill your young lover?" Jimmy wiggled the microphone under my nose. "The public has a right to know."

I contemplated my options and considered throwing him down the stairs. He was taller than I, but I was confident I could take him. The cameraman was another issue, however. He was a lot more bulky than his boss, and

I doubted I could toss him anywhere. He was also apt to capture the whole episode on film.

"You're thinking too hard," Jimmy scolded me. "Just tell our viewers what happened here, behind this very door, last Saturday night." He again banged his fist on my door, and the camera took an all-too-brief hiatus from filming me. "After all, Jessica." Jimmy shoved the microphone back in my face. "If you're as innocent as you claim, you have nothing to hide."

"Go away," I repeated, still refusing to look at the camera.

He tried again. "Exactly how long have you been obsessed with Stanley Sweetzer, Jessica? Have you based the heroes of all your novels on him? Just tell the truth. Can you do that, Jessica? Tell the truth?"

I grabbed the microphone and started talking. "Okay, here's the truth, Jimmy." I made sure to say his name with at least as much derision as he had used saying mine.

The cameraman was beside himself. He lunged toward me and must have gotten quite a nice close up of my nose. I put my index finger smack in the middle of the lens and pushed. The cameraman took a slight step backwards.

I removed my finger and calmly continued, "Basing all my characters on Stanley Sweetzer would be quite a feat, Jimmy, since I've been writing my books for over twenty years, and I only knew Stanley for the last three months."

"Three months!" Jimmy shouted and wrestled me for the microphone.

I kept a firm grip, and testimony to my maturity and self-restraint, refrained from bopping him over the head with it. Eventually I did hand him the stupid contraption, but only after I made him say pretty please.

He clutched the mic with both hands while he caught his breath. "So then," he said. "You admit that you and poor Stanley Sweetzer were having an affair for the last three months? I will remind our viewers that poor Mr. Sweetzer was a good twenty years younger than Miss Hewitt." Beak feigned shock, but the camera was pointed at me, likely getting a close up of the evil old hag's wrinkles.

"Well, I am shocked you admit it, Jessica," Jimmy was sneering again. "But at last the truth emerges. Does Captain Rye know about this? And what about young Candy Poppe? Does she know about this sordid little tryst of yours? Did Stanley Sweetzer threaten to tell her about it? Is that why you killed him?"

"Go away," I said weakly.

Proof that there is a God in heaven, they did. Just as I was about to wring his scrawny little neck, Jimmy's cell phone rang. He mumbled something to his cameraman about the school board meeting at the other end of town and off they ran.

I took a few deep breaths, listened for the front door to close behind them, and unlocked my own door. Snowflake scolded me the second I entered, and I admitted that I never should have argued with Jimmy Beak.

"It won't happen again," I promised.

And if it did, I wouldn't hesitate to toss him down the stairs, with or without the stupid cameraman.

***

I had made it back to my desk, and gotten Alexis and Rolfe sufficiently disrobed for things to get interesting when the phone rang. Talk about frustration.

"Jessica!" Louise Urko shouted when I answered. "What in the world is going on down there?"

"Going on?" I asked. Surely my literary agent, fondly referred to as Geez Louise throughout the publishing world, hadn't heard about the Stanley Sweetzer fiasco all the way up in Manhattan?

"Babe! I'm looking at your latest numbers. In the past twenty-four hours your local sales have skyrocketed. I mean, through the roof!"

Louise was excited, even by Geez Louise standards.

"So fill me in," she insisted. "What kind of publicity have you found for yourself? Who's been interviewing you? What about book signings? What's your secret,

Jessica? I mean, because whatever you're doing, I want all my clients to take a lesson!"

"How much coffee have you had today, Louise?"

"I've never seen numbers like this from you. Ever! Not even after you got that two minute segment on public radio last year." Louise came up for breath. "So?" she asked. "What's up? Tell me, tell me, tell me!"

"I'm under investigation for murder," I told her.

"Murder! But that's fantastical! How on earth did you come up with such a brilliant idea?"

I rolled my eyes at Snowflake. "My neighbor's boyfriend died on my couch the other night," I said. "He was murdered."

"By you?"

"Oh for Lord's sake, Louise! What do you think?"

With my warped agent interjecting a few 'fantasticals' whenever the urge struck, I summarized the basics. I emphasized I did not kill Stanley Sweetzer, and even mentioned that Captain Rye was ninety percent convinced of my innocence. Louise ignored that trivial detail, and insisted on hearing more about my ill-gotten publicity.

"The local news has been all over it," I explained. "We have this reporter, Jimmy Beak. He's having a field day implying I had some sort of sordid affair with Stanley, and then killed him in a fit of jealous rage."

"Oh, but wouldn't that be fantastical? Just think of the publicity!"

Patience, I reminded myself. "Jimmy's claiming that my books somehow reflect my real life. He actually compared Stanley to Lance Votaw. Remember him?"

"From *Windswept Whispers*? But of course I remember Lance! What red-blooded woman under the age of ninety could forget Lance Votaw?"

Geez Louise didn't wait for an answer. "So what about *Temptation at Twilight*, Jessica? How's that one coming along? Because the sooner we get it in the stores and on the shelves, the more we benefit from all your newfound fame!"

"I hate to burst your bubble, Louise," I said in an attempt to burst her bubble. "But all my newfound fame has done nothing to stimulate Rolfe Vanderhorn's libido."

Chapter 8

"Where is everyone?" Bryce asked as he popped the Korbel cork.

Good question. As far as I knew, Rolfe and Alexis were home in bed, but not necessarily asleep. Candy, on the other hand, still wasn't home. Frankly, I hadn't a clue where she was. At least I was sure about Karen. She was sanding that ugly bedroom suite and supposedly far too busy to spend another evening at The Stone Fountain.

"Just me tonight," I said and pointed to the bubbly. "But I'll gladly share that with anyone willing to talk to me about Stanley."

Bryce stopped pouring and stared. "Say what?"

"I am going to find out who killed him." I offered my most determined look. "And I'll start by learning what happened in here on Saturday."

Bryce continued staring, the champagne bottle poised aloft. "Captain Rye still giving you a hard time?"

"He's after Candy now."

"Candy?" The poor guy almost dropped the bottle. "But she didn't do it!" He thought a second. "Did she?"

"You've known her for a while, Bryce?"

"Two years."

"And she's been with Stanley that whole time?"

"You're kidding, right?" Bryce again looked up from pouring and I began to wonder if I would ever get my drink. "Candy's been with lots of guys, Jessie."

"With you?"

He chuckled and shook his head.

"Why not?"

Bryce looked at the ceiling, searching for an answer. "Let's just say she doesn't like my Long Island Iced Teas," he said eventually.

"What about the other men in here? Any former boyfriends?"

"Lots of them." He handed me my drink and scanned the room. "Joseph, Marty, Arthur, Ted—"

"Okay, okay," I interrupted.

"—Kirby, Gus—"

"Bryce!" I waved a hand in front of his face to break the momentum. "Let's simplify things, okay? Which of these guys was here Saturday?"

Bryce blinked at me as it dawned on him what I was asking. "You're thinking someone killed Stan over Candy?" he whispered. "Someone in here?"

"I'm not thinking anything very clearly," I admitted. "But it's worth considering, no?"

Bless his heart, he again glanced around at the various and sundry ex-boyfriends of Candy Poppe littering the room.

"Sorry, Jessie, but I bet all the guys were here. Everyone's here on Saturdays." He turned back to me. "I'm kind of surprised you weren't."

"I was working," I reminded him. "But stay with me, Bryce. Who in particular talked to Stanley that night?"

Bryce scanned the room yet again. "Stan hung with Evan for a while." He tilted his head to Matthew's end of the bar, and I spotted Evan McCloy, a Stone Fountain semi-regular who had worked with Stanley. "I think they were talking about their jobs."

"Perfect!" I said with a big, happy smile. I had never spent much time chatting with Evan, but that was about to change. "Did Evan ever date Candy?"

Bryce shook his head. "I bet Evan and I are the only guys in here who haven't."

"Who else did Stanley talk to?" I asked.

"The Dibbles."

Oh, Lord, the Dibbles. I stopped smiling and hazarded a glance toward their booth. Audrey was leaning across the table jiggling an earring at her husband. She seemed pleased with what must have been some new jewelry, but Jackson Dibble looked less than thrilled. He gulped his drink, and when that was empty, picked up his wife's.

"Do you know if they invested with Stanley?" I asked.

"They must have. How else could they afford all those Long Island Iced Teas?" Bryce looked back at me. "Why?"

I shrugged. "If it wasn't one of Candy's old boyfriends, then maybe a disgruntled client killed him."

"But Stanley made all kinds of money for people, Jessie. He was really good at it."

"You're sure of that?"

"Well, no." Bryce started tapping his index fingers on the bar, playing imaginary drums. "But that's what he told everyone."

"Did you invest with him?"

"Me?" He stopping drumming and pointed to himself. "No way. I can't afford anything like that."

"Who could? Anyone in here?"

Bryce hesitated. "If I name someone are they automatic suspects?"

"Do I look like a cop?" I reminded him I had no idea what I was doing as Gina Stone scurried past.

"Gina and Matthew?" I whispered, and he cringed.

"Please don't go bugging them about it, Jessie. Matthew's mad enough as it is."

Poor Bryce. Matthew Stone's grouchiness might seem endearing to the regulars, but Bryce had to work for the guy. I promised not to bother the Stones, at least not right away, and asked if there were anyone else I should talk to.

"How about Kirby and Gus? And maybe the Allens? They were all here Saturday. Shooting pool."

And apparently a couple of them had dated Candy. I turned to watch the game. As usual, Kirby Cox was being clobbered, but not by one of the regulars.

"Who's that with Kirby?" I asked over my shoulder.

"John something."

"Was he here Saturday?" I twirled back to face the bar, and Bryce shook his head.

"John's new. He just moved here."

I assessed the situation. Talking with my buddies at the pool table would be easiest, so I would tackle that last. And it might be better to approach Audrey Dibble after I had consumed a bit more alcohol. I decided to interrogate Evan McCloy first.

He was at the opposite end of the bar, deep in conversation with a young woman, whom he seemed to be impressing with who knows what. I kept my eye on him and waved when he looked up. His frown reminded me I was old enough to be his mother, but this was no time to take offense.

"Get Evan over here, will you, Bryce?"

He tapped the bar until I looked up. "Be careful," he said. He stood still while I let that sink in, then went to retrieve Evan.

***

As Karen would say, Evan was slick. Just like his friend Stanley, he was a little too handsome and a little too well dressed. Evan McCloy was definitely not your sandal-wearing kind of guy.

Bryce wasn't nearly as well heeled or sophisticated, but bless his heart, he was persistent. He talked, he bounced, he drummed, and he tapped, while Evan and his lady friend scowled and frowned. Eventually, Evan got tired of watching all the fidgeting. He gave up and stood up.

Yeah, Bryce! I got a whiff of heavy cologne as Evan came closer, but I smiled anyway and reintroduced myself.

"I know who you are," he said and shook my hand. "Where's Candy?" He looked over my shoulder as if I might be hiding her somewhere.

"She's not here," I said firmly. I asked Bryce to refill whatever Evan was drinking, and then watched Evan look everywhere but at me.

"What is it you want, ma'am?" His eyes finally found mine as I handed him a Long Island Iced Tea.

"I want to know who killed Stanley Sweetzer," I said, and Evan almost choked on an ice cube.

Okay, so maybe that was a bit abrupt. I waited until he stopped coughing and tried a more subtle approach. "I understand you talked to Stanley on Saturday night?" I said in my most soothing voice.

"I've already spoken to the cops about it. Three times."

"Oh?" I raised an encouraging eyebrow, but Evan only frowned.

"Like I told the police, I don't know anything," he said and started to walk away.

"I invested with Stanley," I blurted out.

Evan stopped and turned.

I blinked twice but decided it was too late to take it back. I dug my grave a little deeper. "And now, of course, I'm looking for a new financial advisor." I tried looking woefully inept about finances—a task which was not all that difficult.

Evan smiled, and as I gulped champagne, offered what sounded like an infomercial on his place of employment. He droned on and on about how many decades Boykin and Dent Investment Management had been protecting the financial interests of the fine residents of Clarence. The report was altogether riveting, but I interrupted anyway.

"I'm wondering about Stanley's other clients?" I said. "I would just love to talk to them. You know, to find what they're doing now that Stanley's gone?"

Evan backed away, and I remembered too late about the value of subtlety.

"You really think I'm that stupid?" he asked.

Well, I was rather hoping.

"I just can't go spouting off about our clients." He took another step back. "It's unethical. And it's against the law, even if I did know what Stan was up to."

He finished his drink in one gulp and shoved the empty at me. "I'm out of here," he said and practically ran for the front door.

Bryce walked over and refilled my glass. "That went well."

"Gee, thanks."

Bryce wandered off to replenish Gina's tray, and I gave myself a pep talk. Surely this sleuthing stuff would get easier the more I practiced? With that in mind, I turned my attention to the Dibble's booth, where Audrey was now showing her husband one of the many trinkets adorning her neck.

"What are all those things Audrey wears?" I asked when Bryce came back.

"Crystals," he said without even a peek in her direction. "But don't go asking her about them. Make that mistake and you'll end up with a big old bag of rocks."

"Excuse me?"

"Really, Jessie. I've seen it happen." Bryce held out his arms and stumbled around, pretending to hold a very large imaginary bag of rocks.

"I won't mention the jewelry," I promised. "But I should buy them a drink, no?"

Bryce produced two more Long Island Iced Teas. "These will get them talking," he said. "Talking nonsense, but talking."

I mumbled something about how Captain Rye probably didn't have to ruin his monthly booze budget getting information out of people and picked up the drinks.

***

Subtlety, I reminded myself as I approached the Dibbles. They looked puzzled, but I refused to be discouraged and asked ever so politely if I could talk to them about Stanley. Indeed, I practically curtsied as I set the Long Island Iced Teas before them.

"May I join you?" I asked.

Jackson grunted and reached for the drink, which I interpreted as a yes. Audrey also was welcoming. She moved over, her jewelry clinking and clanking, and patted the seat next to her.

"We were just talking about you," she said as I sat down. "We saw you on TV, and I reminded Jackson you're the only Pisces I know. It's uncanny, isn't it?" She appealed to me with her bulbous eyes, and I agreed that it did seem uncanny.

"And it's uncanny you're the one who found Stan." Audrey leaned a bit too close. "Pisces have to watch out for things like that, you know?"

"Oh?"

"Well, yes! Stan did die in your house, didn't he?"

I nodded. "On my couch to be exact."

"But how awful for you!" Audrey stared at me with a fascination I don't believe I merited, even considering I was the only Pisces she knew.

"Where are you living now?" she asked. "And what about your couch?"

"Excuse me?"

"My wife believes in ghosts." Jackson grunted. "I'd bet good money she thinks your place is haunted."

"You can't possibly sleep in a house where someone just died! Murdered, no less!" Audrey shuddered at the prospect, and as if on cue, the weather outside broke.

As the first thunderclap boomed, I confessed that I was still living in the same place. Audrey looked horrified, so I tried to ease her distress. "My couch is gone, though. It was confiscated by the police." I shrugged. "I do hope to get it back someday."

"Oh no, Jessie!" Audrey shuddered again. "You really must get rid of that couch. Do not allow it back into your home!"

"Huh?"

Jackson looked up from his drink. "She's serious, you know? Listen to her long enough, and you'll start thinking everything's haunted."

With that, the Dibbles started arguing over the validity or absurdity of Audrey's claims, and Audrey was spouting off some rather complicated statistics of ghost sightings before we could stop her. I interrupted a detailed explanation of the hazards of unhappy poltergeists and insisted I hadn't seen any trace of Stanley or his apparition since he had died.

"I don't see why he would haunt me, anyway," I said. "I didn't kill him."

The Dibbles stopped bickering to stare at me.

"I'm innocent," I told them.

They continued staring.

"That's probably true," Audrey said eventually, although she didn't sound all that convinced.

I cleared my throat and moved on. "If Stanley were going to haunt someone, who would it be?"

She sat up straight and set some crystals a-clanking. "I see what you're getting at, Jessie. You think Stan would haunt the person who killed him, right?"

"Maybe." Personally, I didn't think Stanley's ghost would be bothering anyone, but if that was the way to approach the question, why not?

I watched Audrey think and Jackson drink until my patience ran out. "Do either of you have any ideas about the murder?" I asked point blank. "For instance, could anyone in here be responsible?"

I scanned the crowd, and invited the Dibbles to do the same. Audrey looked around with me, and we waved at Bryce, who was watching us from behind the bar.

"Oh, I just don't know." She sounded quite forlorn, but then perked right up and yanked on her earrings. "These will help though!"

I stared at the black rocks Audrey held aloft from her ear, and instinctively touched the small diamond studs that adorn my own earlobes.

"They're lovely," I lied.

"I bought them today! Aren't they wonderful?"

Jackson grunted. "You're supposed to ask her why her stupid earrings are wonderful."

I asked.

"Well now, all crystals are beneficial to one's chakras." Audrey waved a hand in the air. "Erasing negative energy, improving one's intellect and intuition, and so forth. But these are obsidian. I bought them especially to improve my insightfulness."

"Ask her how much improving her insightfulness chakra set us back," Jackson ordered.

Audrey pursed her lips. "I think Jessie here understands that we need some insight if we're ever going to help Stan."

"I think Jessie here understands Stan don't need no more help."

Audrey ignored her husband's obtuseness. "The dead will not rest until justice is served," she announced.

"Oh?" I said, feeling a bit obtuse myself. I had no idea how the dead might rest, for instance, and I was clueless as to what a chakra was, or was not. Most of all I was puzzled about how our conversation had gone off on this odd tangent.

"So!" I said brightly. "What did you and Stanley talk about Saturday night?" I looked back and forth between the Dibbles. "Anything important?"

"Nope." So much for Jackson's contribution.

I appealed to Audrey, but she was in some sort of trance. She had her eyes closed and was rubbing both of her earrings between her thumbs and index fingers, garnering up all her insightfulness chakras as it were.

I sighed dramatically and caught Gina's eye. "Bryce is keeping my tab," I told her and pointed to the Dibbles. "And perhaps you would bring my champagne over?"

"That's it!" Audrey hit the table with both palms, and Gina scurried away.

"I need to consult Ezekiel." She opened her eyes and blinked at me. "I'll go tomorrow."

"Ezekiel?"

"Ezekiel Titus. He's my astrologer. I'll ask him who could have done this terrible thing to poor Stan. Let's just hope he can fit me in on such short notice."

She started rummaging through her purse as Gina came back with our drinks.

"Scorpio!" Audrey proclaimed triumphantly, and Gina ran away again.

I glanced at the handful of frayed notes Audrey was brandishing before me and recognized what she was so proud of—her infamous list of the birth dates and sun signs of everyone she knew, however remotely.

"Here's my list for The Stone Fountain." She ran a ring-clad index finger down the page and tapped my name. "You see, Jessie? You really are the only Pisces."

I took a wild guess. "And Stanley was a Scorpio?"

"Mm-hmm." Audrey pointed to his birthday. "November 13, 1983. I can't wait to hear what Ezekiel makes of that!"

"I can't wait to hear what Ezekiel charges you," Jackson said.

Audrey rolled her eyes at me. "I really must consult Ezekiel before I say anything further." She put away her notes. "You understand, Jessie?"

Not really.

I turned to Jackson. "Do you have any ideas about Stanley?"

He said he'd get back to me after his next session with his psychic advisor and commenced humming the tune from *The Twilight Zone*.

"Laugh all you want, Jackson Dibble. But if you had just listened to Ezekiel when you had the chance, we wouldn't be in this mess, would we?"

Audrey spoke to me. "My husband simply does not know how to handle money. Ezekiel offered us such good advice on these things, but would he listen?"

She waved a dismissive hand at Jackson, and I actually smiled. Maybe we were finally getting somewhere.

"Stanley was a financial advisor," I ventured. "I understand he was quite good at it." I tilted my head and waited for a response.

Nothing.

"I invested a little with him," I lied with a huge smile on my face. "How about you?"

I looked expectantly at the Dibbles. But just my luck, Audrey had returned to a trance-like state, and Jackson got busy devouring his drink.

I took my leave before he could order another round on me.

Chapter 9

"Cue please?" I asked as I swept past the bar, Gina Stone style.

Bryce handed me my cue, I handed him my glass, and I kept on going. Next stop, the pool table—the blessed place where I understood the rules of the game.

"Jessie!" Kirby called out as I approached. "Play me a game?"

"Oh, if you insist." I smiled and reached for the triangle, but Gus took it and racked the balls while I announced my purpose to the small group of regulars. Thanks to Jimmy Beak, everyone knew more than enough about Stanley and where he had died.

"I'll play left-handed with anyone who can tell me anything useful about what happened that night," I said as I chalked up.

"Can you do that?" Kirby asked.

"Ask about Stanley? I don't see why not."

"No, no, no. Can you actually play left-handed?"

"Not very well," I answered honestly and motioned for him to break.

The left-handed approach worked, at least to some extent, and at least playing against Kirby Cox. But our game took a lot longer than usual, giving the pool table gang plenty of time to reminisce about Stanley. Or argue about Stanley, as the case may be.

As I coached Kirby on how best to make a fairly straightforward bank shot for the seven ball, Bernie and Camille Allen got into it. I would have felt guilty about introducing what was clearly a touchy subject, but I had seen the Allens bicker before. I do believe they were better at it than the Dibbles.

Bernie kept insisting Stanley wasn't nearly as rich as he pretended to be, but Camille was convinced otherwise.

"You can't fake a thing like that, Bernard." The irritation in her voice made me glance up from the table. "Bernie's just jealous, is all," Camille told me. "Stan Sweetzer was a class act. Period."

"Did you invest with him?" I asked, and her mouth dropped open. "I did," I chirped. This ridiculous lie was getting easier by the minute.

But it still wasn't getting the results I was hoping for. Camille bent down to tighten a strap on her sandals. I turned and appealed to Bernie.

"Ain't hardly likely," he mumbled with his eyes on his wife.

"Why's that?" I asked.

He rubbed his thumb and fingers together. "Cash-o-la, Jessie. We didn't have enough for Stan to bother."

And that seemed to be the general consensus. Stanley ignored the little people, as Kirby put it. He frowned and pointed at the two ball, nestled against the left rail and blocked by my fifteen. The poor man was never going to pocket that one.

I turned to the new guy. "Do you even know who we're talking about, John?"

"Not really, but I've seen the news. And Sweetzer's girlfriend." He let out a slow whistle.

"Candy's cute, isn't she?"

"Oh, yeah."

I looked around at the various male heads nodding in agreement and wondered how a person might approach the next delicate topic. I had no idea.

"So, Gus?" I gave up on subtlety altogether. "I understand you used to date Candy?"

The loud clanking of balls from behind startled me, but not nearly as much as the cue ball, which landed at my feet.

I spun around, and Kirby saluted. "Your turn," he said.

Gus bent down and handed me the cue ball. "It was a long time ago, Jessie. Besides, practically everyone's been with Candy."

"Until Stanley," Bryce called over from the bar.

Kirby agreed with Bryce. "None of us had a chance after that."

"What are you getting at, anyway?" Camille Allen scowled at me.

I shrugged and told her, quite honestly, that I had no idea.

"Well, I do," she said. "You're trying to pin this on one of us."

She took a step toward me, and I backed away and onto Kirby's foot. Instead of yelping, he held onto my shoulders and steadied me.

"Jimmy Beak's practically court-martialed Jessie," he said. "You'd be trying to prove your innocence, too."

Gus threw his hands up. "Oh, for God's sake, people." He continued waving his arms. "Jessie's innocent, I'm innocent, you're innocent, we're all innocent." He waved at me. "Would you finish the game, already?"

That did seem like a good idea. I cleared the table. Then I played Gus.

He's a little more skilled than Kirby, but then again, Snowflake's a little more skilled than Kirby. Gus is one of those guys who swings way too hard, apparently believing that if the balls make enough noise banging into each other, something—anything—is bound to go in. His is not the most successful strategy, but playing with Gus does add some drama to the game. He's also trainable. If I can catch him before he blows it, I can usually calm him down enough to make a decent shot.

That evening I did some quick coaching, and Gus was pleased to make a couple of tricky shots. In fact, he only had one ball on the table when I sunk the eight ball in the side pocket.

"Nice shot, Ms. Hewitt." I froze with my back to him, but Captain Rye walked around me until I had to look up. "But I think you'll need your right hand for the next round."

***

"What the hell are you doing here?" I asked cordially.

"Getting even." Rye refused the cue Gus offered him, and walked over to the rack to find something better. He turned to me while he chalked up. "The best of three?"

I raised an eyebrow. "Do you planning on arresting me when I win?"

Gus racked, and I motioned for Rye to break, unnecessarily reminding him he had lost when he had given me the break. He mumbled something about my fine manners, downed the six and the four balls while he was at it, and left me with very little to play with.

I rose to the occasion, however, and pocketed three stripes before giving the table back. But Rye must have gotten distracted when Kirby asked me how Candy was holding up, and he missed an easy shot at the one ball. That clinched it. I ran the rest of the stripes and finished the game.

Rye racked as I continued talking with Kirby. "What exactly did you think of Candy and Stanley?" I asked him. "Were they a good couple?"

Bryce caught my eye and jerked his head toward the captain, who seemed impatient that I break.

"They were okay, I guess." Kirby answered me at the exact moment I took the shot. "But Candy could do better for herself. We all thought so."

Not one ball went anywhere useful. Not one. I stepped back in dismay and asked Kirby to explain, hardly noticing the clinking and clanging of the balls Rye was hitting behind me.

"Candy's gorgeous," Kirby reminded me.

"She's way too good for Stan," Bryce said.

"Even if he was rich," Bernie added.

"Oh, spare me." That was Camille.

I braced myself and took a chance on further irritating her. "What do you think?" I asked.

"I think Candy Poppe dresses like a hooker." She pointed to the pool table. "And I think you're about to get your butt kicked."

Yeah, right. I turned around to pay attention. Rye made two impressive shots while I watched. When given my turn, I stepped up to the table and sunk three solids.

"Where is Candy, anyway?" John the New Guy asked, and I completely flubbed on the two ball. "Isn't she usually here with you?"

John's questions got Rye's attention. But he must have believed me when I said I did not know where Candy was. He studied the table again, shot in the fourteen and called the eight ball.

The eight ball? How the heck did that happen? I started concentrating on the game, only to watch as the eight ball rolled into the far right corner pocket, just as the Captain had predicted.

A veritable hush fell over the crowd as I stared at the spot on the felt where the eight ball had been. Gus picked up Kirby from where he had pretended to faint, and Bernie examined my cue stick for signs of tampering.

"What's the matter, Ms. Hewitt?" Rye broke the silence. "Haven't you ever lost before?"

I shifted my gaze from the middle of the table, to the pocket where the eight ball had dropped. "Not since my father died last year," I said honestly.

"I'm sorry."

I shook my head and snapped out of it. "No need to apologize." I glanced up at him. "I like playing with someone who gives me a challenge."

He bent over and whispered in my ear, "I was talking about your father."

Oh.

I offered Rye the slightest smile and racked the balls for game three, which I won. I must confess, I do not know how I would have reacted had I lost that game, too. I haven't lost two games in a row since I was ten, except to my father, of course.

I held out my hand to Rye. "Good game, Captain. You're very good." I ignored the grin. "But I really must be going now."

I bowed to Kirby and Gus, handed Bryce my cue, and headed for the door. I tried not to notice Rye was following me.

***

He caught up as I waited for the light to change on Sullivan Street. I turned around and spoke over the rain, which was drenching us both. "What, may I ask, are you doing now?"

"I'm walking you home."

"No, you are not." I pointed across the street. "I am quite capable of making it all the way over there on my own. Even in the rain."

"But I'm still walking you home." He took my elbow and escorted me across the street as the light changed.

I waited until we had gotten underneath the awning at my building before pulling away.

"I do not like being bullied, Captain." I folded my arms. "And you are not getting invited upstairs, if that's what you're thinking."

Rye chuckled. "Don't flatter yourself, lady."

I continued glaring.

"What exactly did you think you were doing in there?" He jerked his head in the direction of The Stone Fountain.

"What?" I asked. "I was playing some pool."

"Yeah, right. What were you doing?"

I sighed dramatically. "Okay, so I was trying to learn what happened on Saturday. Wasn't it obvious?"

"Dammit!" Rye lost any trace of a grin and seemed to expect further explanation.

"You have to know I'm a little interested in the outcome here?" I raised my voice again as the rain came down even harder. "Believe it or not, going to jail isn't all that appealing. For me or Candy."

I tried to storm away but he reached out and pulled me back.

"Let's try this another way," he said when I was standing still again. "What do you think I was doing in there tonight? And last night, for that matter?"

I watched a few cars drive by the bar before answering. "Maybe trying to learn what happened the night Stanley was killed?"

"Very good. Now do you see why I'm walking you home?"

"In case I learned something useful?"

"Did you?"

Chapter 10

"Not much," I admitted. "Stanley wasn't nearly as well loved as Candy likes to think. But Candy couldn't be more loved." I thought about Camille Allen. "At least by all the guys."

"What else?" Rye asked.

"She didn't kill him."

"Someone tell you that?"

"Bryce." I thought a second. "And Karen, earlier. And myself, of course. People who know Candy know she didn't do it."

I listened to the rain patter on the awning overhead while Rye waited for who knows what.

"Audrey Dibble may have a theory," I offered. "But she won't say what it is until she consults her astrologer. Stanley Sweetzer was a Scorpio."

"Excuse me?"

"The Dibbles may have invested with him," I said. "As did the Stones. And I'm pretty sure Camille Allen's in that group, too." I looked up and batted my eyelashes.

"You got something in your eye?"

I smiled sweetly despite Rye's most discouraging frown. "You know, Captain," I said. "Having a list of Stanley's clients would be very useful."

"Mm-hmm. What made you talk to Jimmy Beak?"

I lost the smile. "You watched the news?"

"It's part of my job, unfortunately."

"Okay, so he caught me off guard. And before you say it, I already know fighting back like I did was really, really, stupid. But he just made me so furious."

Rye told me not to kick myself too hard. "Beak's had a lot of practice harassing people until they break." He actually chuckled. "But you should have hit him with that microphone when you had the chance. I, for one, was rooting for you."

"How bad did it look?"

"You mean you didn't watch it yourself?"

I shook my head. "The only thing I'm apt to catch on TV is a Duke basketball game."

"Well then, you'll be happy to know the segment with you was blessedly short. The disturbance down at the Board of Ed took up the greater part of Beak's report this evening."

I asked what had happened, and Rye explained that two members of the school board had gotten into a fist fight over which elementary school should receive new desks.

"Hopefully no one was hurt?"

"The superintendant. She made the mistake of stepping between the fists. Beak ended up interviewing her from the emergency room."

I cringed, but Rye told me to look on the bright side. "She'll be fine—a black eye and one bruised rib. But this news certainly trumps your sordid little tryst with Sweetzer. Beak should be leaving you alone, at least for a day or two."

I decided to ignore the sordid little tryst comment. "What about you?" I asked. "Do you plan on leaving me alone? At least for a day or two?"

"Heck, no, Ms. Hewitt. You'd miss me too much."

He turned to open the door, and we walked inside, where I endured a stern lecture up the two flights of stairs about how we needed to get a lock on the front door, and how I needed to be more careful, and not put myself in danger. Yadda, yadda, yadda.

"Don't you believe in taking the elevator?" he asked as we made it to my condo.

"People our age need the exercise," I said. "Besides, that one seldom works, as I'm sure you've noticed."

I unlocked my door and stepped inside. "Well, thank you for your concern, Captain." I turned around to face him. "But as you can see, I'm home now. All safe and sound."

"What was your father's name?"

"Excuse me?"

"You mentioned him earlier. What was his name?"

I blinked twice. "My father's name was Daddy," I said and shut the door.

***

I had made it into my pajamas when someone else knocked. But I was sick of panicking every time Jimmy Beak came calling, no matter what the time of day or night.

"The man has no mercy," I told Snowflake and climbed into bed. "That, or he's a vampire."

"Jessie?" Candy called out, and I sprang up. "Are you still awake?"

I called back that I was coming and stumbled through the condo.

"Oh, Jessie!" She rushed in as I opened the door. "Where have you been?"

"Where have I been?" I wandered around, turning on the lights. "How about, where have you been?"

She hesitated. "I asked you first."

"Over at the bar," I said. I put the tea kettle on while Candy tottered into an easy chair. "Now you."

"I guess I took a long walk."

"All day?"

"I met an old friend for lunch," she said as I rummaged around for cups. "I thought it would make me feel better. You know, to be with old friends? Then after lunch, I kept walking."

Her stiletto heels caught my eye.

"I called you before I went out tonight." I spoke more or less to the shoes. "And you still weren't home."

"Gosh, I must have just missed you." Candy leaned forward, all wide eyed and smiley. "You met Captain Rye at The Stone Fountain, huh? I heard you guys in the stairway just now?"

I folded my arms and glared. "He saw fit to search my condo this morning."

"So he was here twice today?"

"He had a warrant, Candy. He was looking for the poison."

At least she frowned at that.

"And Lieutenant Densmore checked my financial records." I took a deep breath and told her I had a confession to make.

She bounced onto the edge of her seat. "About Captain Rye?"

"No. About Stanley." I handed her a cup and sat down with a thud. "He was trying to sell me some stocks. I'm sorry, Sweetie, but he used to come up here."

I waited for a reaction, but she seemed not at all concerned.

"Without you," I added.

Candy nodded, and it dawned on me that this was not the earth-shaking news I thought it would be.

"You knew about this?" I asked.

"Stanley wanted to help you with your finances, Jessie. He said divorced women need help."

I swallowed a groan. "Did he happen to mention any particulars to you? About my finances?"

"Gosh, no! That's none of my business, right?"

I double checked that last point, but Candy insisted Stanley had never told her any details about my net worth, or how he had obtained such information.

"How about our neighbors?" I asked. "Did any of them invest with him?"

She considered the question. "Definitely not Mr. Harrison."

"How about Bryce?" Lord forgive me, I had to ask.

She shook her head.

"Karen?" Lord forgive me again.

"No. Don't tell her I said so, but Stanley didn't like Karen very much."

I thought a second. "What about the folks at The Stone Fountain? Were any of them clients?"

Candy scowled at me. "Is Captain Rye interested in Stanley's job?"

"Maybe," I said. "I really have no idea what he's interested in."

"In you!" The woman was positively gleeful. "What happened tonight, Jessie? Did you guys play pool? Did you beat him?"

I rolled my eyes and assured her it was anything but a romantic encounter.

"But he walked you home." She clapped her hands. "That is so sweet!"

"Will you get a grip?" I hissed. "The only reason that stupid cop walked me home was on the pretense that maybe, just maybe, one of us is not the culprit."

The smile faded. "One of us?"

"Yes, Candy. You do realize you're a suspect?"

She started chewing her knuckle, and I felt a little guilty about my impatience. But I still asked the next question. "Umm, Sweetie," I said quietly. "Did you have anything to do with Stanley's death?"

"Of course not! Oh, Jessie, how could you think such a thing? I loved Stanley, right?"

Why the heck was she asking me? I sipped my tea and thought about how to proceed. "Rye told me some things," I said eventually. "For instance, did you know Stanley had a will?"

She bit her lip and a tear or two landed in her teacup. "He left everything to me," she whispered.

I went over and knelt in front of her. "Do you know the details? What exactly he left you?"

Candy swallowed hard. "You mean about the twenty-seven thousand dollars?"

I toppled backwards.

"So!" I said as I scooted back into my chair. "You knew about the money, then?"

"I didn't know anything until Lieutenant Densmore told me," she wailed. "Really, Jessie. You've just gotta believe me."

I insisted that I did believe her. Snowflake hopped into my lap and we stared at each other.

I did believe Candy, didn't I?

"It would help if we knew where all that money came from." I glanced at Candy. "Was it related to his job somehow?"

"Gosh, I don't think so. Stanley didn't take cash, did he?"

Why the heck did she keep asking me these questions? I sighed dramatically and pondered the money.

"Okay, what about gambling?" I asked.

"Huh?"

"If Stanley gambled, that could explain things."

"He used to play poker on Thursday nights," she offered.

"For high stakes?"

"Huh?"

I slowed down. "Did they gamble for a lot of money at these poker games?"

"Gosh, I don't think so."

"Who did he play with?"

"His father and a couple other guys. I never paid that much attention." She started crying again. "I needed to be a lot smarter, didn't I?"

"You needed to be exactly who you are," I insisted and sent Snowflake over to cheer her up. "But I do have another hard question."

Her shoulders tightened.

"Where were you Saturday night?"

She hiccupped. "You know about that, too?"

"I know you were AWOL from work, yes."

"I swear to God and hope to die, I didn't do it, Jessie!" She hiccupped again.

"But where were you?"

She petted Snowflake and refused to look up. "With Stanley," she mumbled.

"What!?"

Candy jumped and poor Snowflake scurried into the bedroom. "Now do you see why I didn't tell anyone?" she asked.

I stood up and started pacing.

"It gets worse," she said.

"I can't imagine how that's possible, Candy!" I stopped and turned. "How?"

"We had a fight."

"Oh, for Lord's sake!" I plopped back into my chair and calmed myself. "Okay," I said eventually. "Where were you, who saw you, and what on earth were you fighting about?"

"We were sitting in Stanley's car in the parking lot at Tate's. But I promise no one saw us."

I closed my eyes and prayed for strength.

"I broke up with him that night, Jessie."

***

That revelation certainly opened my eyes. I stared aghast at my friend, who was slumped back in her chair staring at the ceiling.

"What am I gonna do?" she whined. "I'm so scared Captain Rye will find out, and it will look like I killed Stanley, huh?"

"But why did you break up with him?" I may have whined a bit myself. "I thought you were madly in love?"

"If I tell you, you have to promise not to hate me, okay? No matter what?"

I rolled my eyes, but Candy refused to answer until I had promised—and crossed my heart and hoped to die—that I would never hate her.

"I kind of ran into Carter O'Connell last week," she said.

I asked who Carter was, and Candy explained they had gone to high school together.

"He went away to college. But now he's back."

"And let me guess, Carter's an old boyfriend. The old friend you just happened to spend all of today with?"

"There, you see!" Candy threw her hands up. "I knew you'd hate me."

"I do not hate you," I insisted. But I did frown as I pondered the complex and perilous topic of my young friend's love life. "Are there any other old boyfriends?" I asked. "Maybe from the bar?"

Her shoulders tensed.

"Someone who was jealous of you and Stanley?"

Candy gave it some thought, and I could almost see the extensive list scroll through her brain. "Definitely not Kirby or Gus," she said. "Or Teddy, or Joey." She squinted at the ceiling. "Or Marty, or Arty, or—"

I lost track after some guy named Burt and interrupted, "What about Bernie Allen?"

She jumped. "Gosh, no! Bernie's married, Jessie."

"So then, that rules out Matthew Stone and Jackson Dibble?"

Candy wrinkled her nose.

"What about Bryce?"

She shook her head vigorously.

"Evan McCloy?"

"I never dated Evan, either." She blinked a few times. "Evan was there, though."

"There, where?"

"When I met Stanley. We met at The Stone Fountain. Did you know that?"

I did not, so Candy filled me in on the first time she ever saw Stanley. Apparently, it had been love—or at least lust—at first sight.

"Who else was there that night?" I asked.

"Lots of people, I guess. Bryce, of course. And Karen." She scowled at me. "Is this important?"

I told her I had no idea and apologized for being so nosey.

"Does it look bad, Jessie? That I was with all those guys?"

"You're young," I said with a shrug. "It's probably good to play the field. And you were smart to break it off with Stanley."

"Really?"

"Trust me, Sweetie. You don't want to get married unless you're absolutely, one hundred percent sure."

"But breaking up like that still looks bad, huh? Since Stanley got killed and all?"

Well, let's see. Candy knew about Stanley's will, knew about the twenty-seven thousand dollars, had found herself a new boyfriend, and had broken up with Stanley on the night he was murdered. Yes, I had to agree, it did look bad.

"But it looks worse that you're not telling the cops what happened," I said. "Promise me you'll call Rye?"

"Would you do it for me, Jessie? He really likes you."

I shook my head. "Sorry, Sweetie, but you need to do this yourself. You know that."

She took a deep breath. "I guess I'll call him tomorrow," she said. "I'll have all day, since I guess I'm not going to the funeral."

"Why's that?"

"Stanley's mother says I'm not invited."

"Excuse me?"

Candy actually hung her head. "I called to see if I could do anything to help, and that's what she said."

"Candy! No one gets invited to a funeral. More importantly, no one gets turned away."

"Really?"

"You're going," I insisted. "Better yet, we're going."

"But Mrs. Sweetzer will be furious."

"That's just tough." I saw the horror stricken look on my friend's face. "Come on, Sweetie. Stanley loved you, correct?" She agreed. "And you loved Stanley? At least at one time?"

She agreed with that also.

"Well then, you need to be there. Stanley would want you there."

"You're right, Jessie." Candy offered a determined nod. "Stanley would want me there."

About then, I remembered Jimmy Beak. But this was no time for cowardice, especially since Candy Poppe was looking downright courageous.

Chapter 11

Stanley may have wanted Candy at his funeral, but I doubt even her former fiancé would have been thrilled with her outfit for the occasion. She had called after lunch the next day to say she was running late and would meet me at my car. But little did I suspect what she would meet me in.

The best I could say for her outfit is that it was indeed black, right down to her fingernails. Maybe I should start with her hair. Already a deep brunette, Candy had decided that a rinse of Goth black was in order for the occasion. The result would have been alarming even without the black lace mini dress, and I do mean mini, the black fishnets, and the stilettos—black patent leather, but of course. Alarming about sums it up.

"Is this okay, Jessie?" she asked as she approached the car. "Black is the color you're supposed to wear to funerals, right?"

I nodded meekly and climbed into the driver's seat of my Porsche.

Candy scooted into the passenger seat. "But you're not in black at all," she said as she assessed my outfit.

It was true that I had chosen a blue pinstripe pant suit for the occasion, and had even ventured away from dark colors enough to tie a baby blue chiffon scarf around my hair. I explained that all black was no longer required, as long as one remembered the solemnity of the occasion and dressed accordingly.

"Gosh, Jessie." She looked relieved. "I'm glad you noticed."

***

I entered the church with much trepidation. First of all, there was Candy's show-stopping outfit to consider. And even if that didn't produce pandemonium, Jimmy Beak might. Somehow I doubted that the solemnity of the occasion would mean much to the Channel 15 News team.

But luckily the church was crowded, and Jimmy was nowhere in sight. I scanned the sanctuary a second time to make sure of that happy fact and said a little prayer for the speedy recovery of our school superintendant. Rather contradictory, I said another prayer of thanks for the elementary school desk debacle, hoping it would continue to distract Jimmy for a long, long, time.

We sat near the back and were singing the first hymn when Rye and Densmore arrived. They approached our pew, but I gave Rye a look that would ward off a pack of wolves and the two of them backed away.

I leaned toward Candy. "Did you call him this morning?"

She whispered that she had. "But let's not talk about it right now, okay? I'm kind of nervous as it is."

Candy made it through the church service with only a few tears, and no one even noticed as I eased my car into the procession to the nearby cemetery. Indeed, things were going so smoothly that I imagined we might survive the day without incident. But as we left the car and were walking toward the gravesite someone shouted Candy's name.

She whimpered and reached for my hand. "It's Stanley's father, Jessie. Brace yourself."

"Candy!" he called again from across the expanse of lawn and gravestones. If only he had managed to keep his big mouth shut. But after observing Roger Sweetzer for about ten seconds, I concluded he likely had never managed to keep his big mouth shut.

"It is Candy, isn't it?" he bellowed as he got nearer. "Margaret! Come see Candy!" He gave Candy more than a future father-in-law type hug. "I'm glad you decided to come. I didn't see you at the church." More bellowing as he waved a finger at her. "Where were you hiding?"

For the father of the deceased, Mr. Sweetzer certainly seemed cheerful. I got the feeling his wife Margaret was less so. And she was less than inclined to come see Candy. She did, however, want to shut up her stupid husband, and as she tiptoed her way over, Candy whimpered again.

"Oh, yes, Rog." Margaret drew closer. "It is Candy, isn't it?" She smiled and I wondered if the woman made a habit of sharpening her teeth. "And what an exceptional outfit, Candy." She bared her teeth in my direction. "Did your mother help you coordinate it?"

Perhaps that was meant as an insult, but I smiled pleasantly. Maybe I wasn't the only person in Clarence who had yet to see Jimmy Beak's reports.

"I'm Jessica Hewitt, Mrs. Sweetzer." I held out my hand. "Candy's neighbor. I'm so sorry about your son."

Margaret ignored my hand to take off her glasses and get in my face. "Candy's neighbor?"

I maintained my most neutral expression as I watched her mind race. And then it dawned on her.

"Oh my God!" Margaret Sweetzer shrieked just as well as Roger Sweetzer bellowed. "Get this woman out of here, Roger. She's the one who killed our Stanley!"

Candy wobbled noticeably, and I must admit, I was also feeling a bit shaky when Captain Rye appeared at my side. He spoke in a quiet but firm voice and asked the Sweetzers not to get too upset. "Ms. Hewitt's been very cooperative during our investigation," he told them.

Excuse me?

I was mouthing a 'Gee, thanks' to Rye when I spotted my ex, and even worse, my ex's new wife, making their way over to our little gathering. I blinked twice, hoping to dispel the hideous specter.

No such luck. Clarence is a small city, and running into Ian on occasion was a hazard I resigned myself to after our divorce. But I had never bargained on seeing him—or God forbid—Amanda, at quite such an awkward moment.

"Could this day get any worse?" I mumbled under my breath.

"Gosh, I hope not," Candy whispered back.

"My ex-husband is here," I explained and turned to Rye. "I assume you've met Ian?"

He nodded, and I concluded that, yes, the day could get worse.

Ian was calling out in a voice loud enough to raise the dead at our feet. "Don't worry about it, Rog. Amanda and I will take care of it." He waved a hand in my direction so that everyone would know I was the 'it' to which he was referring.

Margaret and Roger Sweetzer wandered off toward the gravesite, and while I searched desperately for a large tombstone behind which I might seek refuge, Ian and Amanda exchanged pleasantries with Rye.

My ex-husband turned to me and there the pleasantries ended. "What the hell did you do to your hair?"

I smiled slowly. "You like it, Ian." That wasn't a question, it was a statement. And trust me, he did. I hadn't been married to this fool for close to twenty years for nothing.

Amanda spoke next, coming up close to me, just as Margaret had, and straining her neck to inspect my roots. "Oh my, it is rather extreme, isn't it?"

She smiled, and I decided Amanda must use the same tooth-sharpening tools as Margaret.

"I've been telling Ian all week that picture of you Jimmy Beak keeps showing can't possibly be recent," she said. "You look much younger in that picture. Did you know that, Jessica?"

Rye cleared his throat and took three giant steps backward while Candy quietly reminded me about the grey haired photo of yours truly that Jimmy Beak had been using.

I spoke to my ex over the top of Amanda's head. "What are you doing here?"

Amanda answered, trying to look me in the eye. "Oh my," she said. "The Sweetzers and my family go way back, don't you know? Margaret and I practically grew up together. She used to babysit me every Saturday night." Amanda tapped her husband's chest. "And Ian here has taken up playing cards with Roger and his cronies. Can you imagine such a thing, Jessica?"

I assured her I no longer wasted my time imagining what Ian does and turned to Candy.

"Ian and Amanda Crawcheck, this is my good friend, Candice Poppe." I used my gentlest voice. Anyone listening might even think I was mature and polite. "Candy was Stanley's girlfriend," I explained helpfully.

Amanda stared at the fishnets, and I must admit, I really couldn't blame her. "Girlfriend?" she said. "I wasn't aware Stanley had a serious girlfriend?"

She looked Candy up and down before bursting out. "Oh, I know, Ian! This is the bra girl." She faced Candy again. "Am I right? You're the bra girl from Tate's?"

I already had my arm around Candy's back, so I was able to tug on her hair without anyone noticing. With a little help from my puppeteering, Candy held her head up.

"Oh, yes, Amanda." I mocked her tone but not her volume. "Everyone in town knows Candy. At least all the women. She is so good at her job, isn't she though?"

I looked straight at Ian, who, I am here to tell you, had not taken his eyes off me. "Why, even today I'm wearing some nice things Candy found for me." His mouth dropped open. "Royal blue," I added with a flutter of eyelashes.

Bless her heart, Candy caught on to the game. "Jessie has such an amazing figure, don't you think?" She glanced back and forth between Ian and Amanda. "She looks wonderful in everything I offer her."

A lie if ever there was one, but I was not inclined to stay and argue. I grabbed Candy's hand and headed toward the gravesite.

As we stepped away from Ian, I caught a glimpse of Rye lurking behind a large tree. I kept moving and called back over my shoulder, "That's right, Captain—royal blue, yet again."

"Again?" Ian squeaked.

***

Lucky me. After the committal service, Candy insisted on attending the reception. I would have skipped it altogether, but I had promised her my support. I braced myself and drove to the Clarence Country Club.

At least the place was crowded, and I entered the ballroom with high hopes of avoiding another embarrassing encounter with my ex. Or the Sweetzers. Or Jimmy Beak, for that matter. Oh well. If all else failed, I noticed a nice roomy buffet table. I could hide under there if all hell broke loose.

Evan McCloy saw us, or perhaps I should say he saw Candy, and rushed over. With barely a frown in my direction, he whisked her off to join a group of stressed out looking financial types, who I assumed were Stanley's co-workers.

The spot beneath the buffet table did seem inviting, but I decided to risk it, and instead found an inconspicuous corner from which to people watch. I was assessing each individual who passed by for murderer possibilities when Rye joined me.

"Don't you have anything better to do?" I asked.

He handed me a glass of red wine. "You looked like you could use this. Sorry, but there's no champagne."

I mumbled a 'thank you' and noticed he himself was drinking nothing. I also noticed he was staring at me in that disconcerting, cop-like way.

"What is it this time?" I had to ask. "What lies has Ian been telling you?"

"It wasn't Ian."

"Amanda, then."

Rye shook his head. "I'm thinking it's you who's still lying."

"Oh?"

"You've been telling everyone and his brother you invested with Sweetzer."

"Oh, shit!"

"Yep, Ms. Hewitt. That about sums it up."

I grimaced. "Someone at The Stone Fountain tattled on me?"

"Mm-hmm."

I asked who, but of course he wouldn't divulge his source. And as I thought about it, it could have been anyone. I had indeed announced that stupid lie to everyone and his brother.

"I was just trying to get people to open up to me," I said in my defense. "It would be very helpful to know who Stanley's clients were."

"Mm-hmm."

I took a deep breath and then repeated the question I had asked Rye who knows how many times before. "You still believe me, don't you? That I didn't invest with Stanley?"

He waited a solid minute before answering. "I still believe you," he finally mumbled. "But I doubt Jimmy Beak will."

"Oh, shit!"

"That about sums it up."

I whimpered. "You're thinking someone at the bar actually believed my lies? And they'll tell Jimmy?"

"Yep."

"And Jimmy will tell the world." I whimpered some more, but Rye offered no sympathy whatsoever. Instead, he muttered something about how simple and serene his job as a homicide detective used to be—back in the good old days before he met me.

I interrupted his trip down memory lane and tilted my head toward the crowded room. "Aren't you worried about being seen with me?" I asked. "You know, consorting with the enemy and all that?"

Rye grinned. "They probably think I'm making an arrest."

"Gee, thanks."

"That's some fancy car you drive, lady. A silver Porsche?"

My car? I asked if he were referring to my ten-year-old Carrera with 140,000 miles on it. "Do you mean that fancy car?"

"It looks nice." He grinned again. "Adelé, huh?"

I shrugged. "Okay, so I have vanity plates. Is that a crime?"

"At least it's accurate."

"Ah, so you get it?"

"I caught on when I saw the license plate." He said my pen name again, emphasizing each of the three syllables. "Add-a-lay. That's certainly what *A Deluge of Desire* was all about."

I decided not to argue, informed Rye that I planned on spotting the murderer at this shindig, and turned away to people watch.

He lingered, apparently under the impression I was enjoying his company.

After a few moments of silence, he bent down and whispered in my right ear. "I figured out who your father was."

"Oh?" I continued to study the crowd.

"Leon Hewitt," he said. "Your daddy was Leon Cue-It Hewitt."

"Oh?"

"He was a shark, Miss Hewitt." Rye was speaking a bit too loudly and I told him so. He lowered his voice. "Cue-It Hewitt was one of the best pool players south of the Mason Dixon Line. In his heyday he took on Minnesota Fats a few times. And usually won."

The Captain seemed so proud of his earthshaking report that I failed to mention quite a few hustlers had taken on the Fatman and won. Heck, even I had played him once or twice. I didn't win, mind you, but I adored Mr. Wanderone. He was the guest of honor at my ninth birthday party.

"Congratulations," I said. "You've discovered my deep dark family secret. And what, pray tell, does what my father did for a living have to do with Stanley Sweetzer's murder?"

"Oh." Rye sang the word. "Probably nothing."

We watched as Candy and the financial gurus maneuvered their way over to the buffet table. I was marveling at how much food she could pile onto her miniature plate when Rye bent down and whispered again.

"I know your deep dark secret, too," he said.

My shoulders tensed. "Oh?"

"You were arrested for hustling back in 1980."

Chapter 12

I spun around and almost spilled my wine. "You do know what kind of hustling?"

"At pool, of course." The damn cop was grinning. "You got busted at some dive outside Winston-Salem after hustling a little over five hundred dollars out of the sheriff's nephew in a little under an hour."

"I won that money fair and square."

"Oh, Ms. Hewitt, I'm sure you did. But gambling on a pool game is a misdemeanor, isn't it?"

I glared with all my might. "If Jimmy Beak ever gets wind of this, I will never speak to you again. That, sir, is a promise."

Rye assured me my secret was safe with him. "My job is to protect the public, remember?"

"Gee, I feel so much better now."

"What I can't figure out is how you got off so easy. You never even paid a fine from what I can tell."

"I wore a low cut dress and smiled real pretty at the judge." I continued glaring. "Believe it or not, that kind of thing worked for me once upon a time. The old coot didn't even slap my delicate little wrist."

"And?" Rye asked. "Can we assume you quit your night job after that?"

"Hell, no. I still had another year's tuition at Duke to pay for."

He laughed out loud. "You're a little scary. You know that?"

I didn't argue.

Rye cleared his throat. "So, when did you quit hustling? Or have you?"

"I just told you." I finished my wine and placed the empty on a tray that was passing by. "When I got my degree. Believe it or not, I hated gambling. And a girl hustling at a pool table could get herself into some fairly tight situations." I raised an eyebrow. "You can imagine that?"

Rye's face dropped.

"Oh, don't look so alarmed, Captain." I patted his forearm. "I haven't played for anything more than the occasional bottle of champagne for decades. I'm what Daddy used to call a lamb. I could play for money, but I choose not to."

Whether or not he believed me, we stopped talking and went back to people watching. I still hadn't mastered the skill, but I continued scanning the crowd for murderers.

Eventually I gave up and asked Rye how he did it. "How do you recognize a murderer?" I said. "For instance, when did you decide I'm not the killer?"

He continued perusing the crowd. "Who says I've decided?"

"When?" I asked again.

"The night Sweetzer died," he said. "When you served me tea."

"Oh, really?"

"I've been a cop for twenty five years, Ms. Hewitt. And never once has a killer offered me a cup of tea at a murder scene. Much less wondered if I take cream or sugar."

"So all this harassment you've been giving me since then has been for the fun of it?"

"Remember my boss. The chief wasn't as convinced as me." Rye shrugged. "Heck, I might still be wrong about you."

"Yeah, right."

I turned my attention back to the crowd and spotted Candy. She had finally finished eating and was back to talking with Evan and his colleagues. She said something that had everyone laughing.

"Candy called you this morning?" I asked over my shoulder.

"Yep."

"She didn't do it, you know?"

"Yeah, right."

I turned around. "Come on, Captain. Surely even you can see why she didn't tell you everything? Her argument with Stanley doesn't mean anything at all," I insisted. "Except that she's fickle about men, correct?"

Rye stared straight ahead. Straight at Candy.

"Listen," I said as a wave of panic swept over me. "If you're so willing to let me off the hook based on some sort of intuition, why not give Candy the benefit of the doubt, too?"

Rye finally caught my eye. "She's never served me tea."

***

Bless his heart, Lieutenant Densmore relieved me of the captain, and they wandered off to harass someone else for a nice change of pace. I took a few deep breaths and walked over to join Candy.

"Serve champagne at my funeral," I told her. "Promise me?"

She looked up from Evan, who was kneeling in front of her, doing who knows what with her shoe. "I'm sorry, Jessie. What's that?"

"I said, be sure to serve champagne, preferably Korbel, at my funeral."

"Okay." She startled me by starting to cry. "Oh, Jessie, don't you die, too!"

I reached across Evan and gave her a little hug. "Introduce me to your friends, Sweetie."

Evan stood up and frowned. "We've already met," he said and mumbled an almost inaudible 'unfortunately.'

Vikki Fitkin and Blaine Notari also seemed less than thrilled at my intrusion. They were about the same age as Evan, and I wondered how these people, who were so very young, managed the investments of people my own age. Thomas Fell was a couple of decades older than his co-workers and much more eager to please. He shook my hand, and insisted that he hadn't believed a word of what Jimmy Beak was saying about me.

"We all work at Boykin and Dent." Thomas continued pumping my hand. "With Stan. What a great guy! And sharp. Did you invest with Boykin and Dent, Jessica?"

I yanked my hand away. Why the heck did that subject have to come up?

But before I had a chance to think of a response, Evan jumped in. "Jessie was working with Stan," he announced in a loud and clear voice.

"But that's great!" Thomas, too, was almost shouting. "I'd be happy to take over for you, Jessica! Now that Stan's gone!"

He looked at me, his eyes wide, and I tried not to curl my lip.

"We've been talking about Stanley," Candy explained unnecessarily.

"Candy here's been telling us about a side of Stan we never saw at the office." Blaine Notari chuckled at his colleagues. "The lighter side of Sweetzer—who would have guessed it?"

"Certainly, not I." Vikki pursed her lips and scowled at Candy. "Stan probably liked you because then he didn't have to be serious with you."

Candy may not have caught the bitchy tone of that, but I did. I studied Vikki, and Rye's old theory that jealousy might have prompted Stanley's demise popped into my head.

But Vikki certainly had no reason to be jealous of Candy's looks. The woman was adorable. She wore glasses, which looked cute on her pointy little face, and she had scads of curly red hair. She came eye to eye with me, which meant she was tall. Her grey skirt suit was not all that flattering, but it was well made, and I assumed it was her uniform for funerals.

"You know, Vikki," I said. "Thomas here might have a point. Now that poor Stanley's gone, I probably should hire a new financial advisor." I smiled pleasantly. "Maybe I could meet with you sometime?"

"With me?" She seemed confused.

So did Thomas. I pretended not to notice and concentrated on Vikki. "You're an investment counselor just like Stanley was, correct?"

"Umm, sure. Jessica, is it?" Vikki tore her gaze from Candy and Evan, who were busy tasting each other's drinks, and glanced back at me. "Come down to Boykin and Dent anytime. I'll be glad to help you."

Thomas walked off in a huff. And when I noticed Margaret Sweetzer and Amanda Crawcheck coming toward us, teeth bared, I took Candy's glass from her, handed it to Evan, and insisted it was time for us to leave also.

***

Karen called me early that evening. "Turn on your TV, Jess. Like, now." Something in her tone made me obey without question, and I rushed over to the bedroom, where my twelve-inch, seriously outdated television sat on the dresser. "Channel 8," she instructed and hung up.

I clicked to Channel 8 and saw my face plastered across the screen. Lord help me—I had made the national news. I plopped myself on the edge of the bed and watched in horrified disbelief as Dee Dee Larkin, an anchorwoman even I recognized, reported to the whole wide world that I was under investigation for murder.

It got worse when she mentioned Stanley's job at Boykin and Dent and my supposed investments with the firm. Then she started describing my books, and Adelé Nightingale's penchant for heroes who bore an uncanny resemblance to Stanley Sweetzer.

"I am going to kill Jimmy Beak," I said to the TV screen.

Snowflake purred in agreement and started kneading the duvet cover.

Dee Dee Larkin concluded with some comment about 'borderline pornography,' and Channel 8 mercifully cut to a commercial for a new kind of pain reliever.

I turned off the TV and began plotting the demise of Mr. Beak. But then the photograph Channel 8 had used flashed into my mind. Only one person had that picture of me.

***

Louise Urko answered her phone after half a ring. "Wasn't that fantastical, Jessica?"

"You're fired," I informed her and hung up without further ado.

She called me back within seconds. "Fantastical!" she shouted again. "We're opening a bottle of Korbel up here! I mean, the whole staff insisted on a little celebration in your honor."

"My honor? Dee Dee Larkin has just informed the entire nation that I write borderline pornography, Louise." I started pacing. "Do you want to explain to me how she got that idea?"

"Because that's what I told her!" Louise screamed. "Isn't it just fantastical?"

I listened as my deranged agent took a gulp of champagne. Drinking did seem like a good idea. I paced over to the fridge and found a half-finished bottle of Korbel in the door.

"You see, Jessica," Louise was saying. "After we spoke yesterday, I got hold of some footage from that Timmy Beaky guy you told me about. The man is brilliant! I mean, beyond brilliant!"

I interrupted to inform her that his name is Jimmy Beak. "And he most certainly is not brilliant."

"And while I was watching Timmy Beaky's report on you and Adelé, it dawned on me. 'Louise!,' I said to myself, 'if only we could pull off getting this reported nationally. Just think of Jessica's sales figures then!'"

Another champagne cork popped in the background.

"So, how exactly did you pull it off?" I heard myself asking. "The national news? Adelé Nightingale is not that well known."

"Yet!" Louise screamed.

I closed my eyes and imagined my manic agent doing a manic dance to the commission gods in the middle of her office.

"Oops." Louise laughed. "I almost fell off my desk!"

Okay, make that the middle of her desk.

"We are so lucky, Jessica—I mean, sooooo lucky— that it was a slow news day. I only had to make twenty or thirty phone calls to get this thing rolling. Dee Dee was, like, sooooo interested! She asked if there were any latest developments that she could add. You know, to spice it up a bit? So this afternoon I called Timmy Beaky back!"

I gave up on my glass and drank directly from the Korbel bottle.

Louise continued, "Timmy told me you were the dead guy's prime investor! He said he had just learned about it today! From a confidential source, he said! So then I told Timmy the good news about Dee Dee Larkin, and he asked if I could finagle a job interview for him, and I told him I'd work on it, and then I called Dee Dee right back. And then I gave her all the details, and she said you would be the second to top story, right after that scandal in Congress about—"

"Stop!" I shouted and poor Snowflake jumped. I lowered my voice. "Please, Louise." I put down the bottle and rubbed my forehead. "Just, stop."

Geez Louise, of course, did not stop. "Can you imagine the sales figures from this, Jessica! This is going to catapult Adelé Nightingale into blockbuster status! Blockbuster, Babe!" Louise actually hesitated. "Oh, God," she said. "I think I need to sit down."

I listened while someone in the background helped her off her desk and into a chair.

"Borderline pornography," I reminded her while she hyperventilated into the receiver. "Dee Dee Larkin just told the world that I'm a pornographer with faulty finances."

"And?" Louise asked as I heard another champagne cork pop. "What's your point, Jessica?"

I thought about the faulty finances thing and decided to concentrate on the pornography angle instead. "I am not a pornographer," I said firmly. "I write historical romances, remember?"

Louise laughed. "Well, Jessica, you know that, and I know that, but trust me—the thousands, and thousands, and thousands of people who are right this very minute in the process of buying *Windswept Whispers* and your entire back list do not know that!"

"So my integrity as an artist means nothing to you?" I actually said this with a straight face.

"Mark my words, Jessica. This will put Adelé Nightingale on *The Times* bestseller list by Sunday. Blockbuster, Babe. Think blockbuster!"

"And just imagine how my sales would skyrocket if I actually got convicted of murder."

Louise didn't catch the sarcasm, since she was too busy planning the sale of the movie rights to *Windswept Whispers*. "I wonder if we could get Penelope Cruz to play Ava La Tellier," she mused. "Penelope would be a fantastical Ava—don't you think? All dark and sultry?"

Okay, so I could picture Penelope in that role. But I was not about to agree with my agent about anything right then.

"And your picture, Jessica! Did you notice?"

Indeed I had. Geez Louise had given Dee Dee Larkin the photograph of Adelé Nightingale scheduled for release with *Temptation at Twilight*.

"I suppose I should thank you for letting the entire world know exactly what I currently look like?" I asked.

"Oh, but, Jessica! You look so much better than you used to. With that little blond hairdo? You're looking downright perky these days!"

"Perky!?" I interrupted. "You know damn well I have never been perky a day in my life."

Louise giggled. "Well, Jessica, you know that, and I know that, but—"

I hung up before I fired her again.

Chapter 13

"Borderline pornography!" Ian screamed into the phone, and I wondered if I had been too hasty hanging up on Louise. "What the hell do you think you're doing?"

I informed my ex-husband I was listening to him have a hissy fit and poured myself more champagne.

"Not funny, Jessie. I am really, really, not in the mood."

I understood why when I heard Amanda shrieking "Borderline pornography" over and over again in the background.

"Amanda's very upset."

"So I gathered."

"You're way too old to be pulling these stunts." Ian increased the volume. "Amanda and I have our reputations to consider, even if you don't. I'm ashamed to be associated with you."

I reminded my ex that he no longer was associated with me, but he continued ranting anyway. Indeed, it was rather impressive, the way he could keep his train of thought, what with Amanda standing nearby, screeching something about my "stunts."

"First you go and get yourself arrested for freaking murder," Ian shouted. "Then you play it up for publicity. What the hell were you doing at Stan's funeral, anyway? And don't think I didn't notice you flirting with that cop all afternoon. The guy's got to be a good ten years younger than you, Jessie. You're making a fool of yourself."

"I'm making a fool of myself? In case you haven't noticed, Ian, your new wife is at least twenty years younger than you. And in case you're too stupid to realize it, her stellar reputation is a figment of your imagination."

"Amanda's reputation is none of your business."

"Excuse me? Didn't you just tell me—"

I stopped myself before I popped an artery. I even considered hanging up. But I am not that highly evolved.

I took a long, deep, breath and continued in an exceedingly calm voice. "My love life is none of your business," I said. "I will flirt with anyone I choose, anywhere I choose, anytime I choose. And I have not been arrested for murder, as you well know. Captain Rye—you remember Wilson Rye, Ian? The hunk you say is far too young for me? He thinks I'm innocent now."

"Jessica Hewitt has never been innocent." Ian may have snorted, but his voice was calmer, too. And I noticed the background cacophony had ceased altogether. Perhaps Amanda had tired herself out and left the room to go sulk in her coven.

"Getting this whole ridiculous saga on national TV was Louise's idea," I told my ex. "And you are right about one thing—she was after the publicity. The poor woman thinks of sales figures and loses all perspective."

"Geez Louise Urko." Ian groaned at the memory. "You should fire her, Jessie."

"Yeah, right."

We were actually sharing a slight chuckle when Amanda returned to the fray. This time she was shrieking something about the 'trash' I write.

"You might remind your new wife this trash she's so concerned with paid for that lovely house she's redecorating."

"How the hell do you know we're redecorating?"

"I'm a writer," I said. "I know these things."

"I'm warning you, Jessie. Get all this garbage straightened out, or else."

"Or else what? You'll cheat on me with that flagrant fool and then try to screw me in the divorce settlement?"

I waited while Ian huffed and puffed and found a way to change the subject.

"How's Snowflake doing?" he asked eventually.

I told him Snowflake was managing quite well and hung up in search of more champagne.

Lord knows I needed it, since Jimmy Beak had returned. He was banging on my door and shouting something about Stanley, Boykin and Dent Investment Services, and my bank account.

Presumably, he was speaking to the camera as he elaborated, "Jessica Hewitt now admits she invested her entire life's savings with Stanley Sweetzer. Every last penny! My confidential sources have verified it!

"Dee Dee Larkin, the nationally acclaimed investigative reporter, and I are collaborating," Jimmy proclaimed triumphantly. "Together, we plan to unveil the exact amount Jessica Hewitt entrusted to Mr. Sweetzer before his untimely demise right behind this very door!"

Banging on the very door.

"Dee Dee Larkin and I are working around the clock to prove Jessica Hewitt's guilt. Mark my words, Stanley Sweetzer's disgruntled client and elderly lover will not get away with murder! The public has a right to know. No!" he shouted. "The *nation* has a right to know!"

Elderly?

Snowflake and I stared at each other in dismay. "It's time for a sex scene," I told her.

"Sex scene!" That was Jimmy. "Who do you have in there now, lady!?"

***

It had grown dark while I was dealing with Jimmy, and my mood wasn't all that bright, either. But writing a sex scene always cheers me up. I switched from champagne to tea and sat down at my desk to write the climactic, and I do mean climactic, love scene between Rolfe and Alexis.

I can't say what so inspired me to new creative heights, and the lovers to new creative positions. But if the whole, wide, reading world was expecting borderline pornography from Adelé Nightingale, she was not about to disappoint them. I was thinking of another word for nibbling when someone else knocked.

"Grand Central Station," I mumbled and called toward the door, "Is that you, Sweetie?"

"It's Karen, Jess. I brought M & M's."

I scurried to let her in, and bless her heart, she had the cellophane package opened by the time she sat down at the counter.

"Sorry it took me so long to get these up here." She held out the package and poured a few Peanut M & M's into my outstretched palm. "Jimmy scared me away, and then I got busy with my electric sander."

I found a bowl for the candy and started the tea kettle while we discussed Jimmy Beak's latest foray into our building.

"I can't believe he came back so soon," she said. "Considering what's going on with the school board? The guy must work twenty-four—seven."

I poured some milk into Karen's teacup while she updated me on the elementary school desk debacle. It seems Superintendent Yates had been released from the hospital that morning and had decided to press charges against the people who had injured her.

"Jimmy barely even mentioned you tonight," Karen said. "He was too busy interviewing the entire school board, claiming the public has the right to know what every eyewitness saw. All the school principals weighed in on the issue, too. It started off as a panel discussion, but then the fists started flying." Karen shook her head. "It was mayhem, even before Jimmy started bopping everyone with his microphone."

"That explains his absence at the funeral," I said. "But clearly the Dee Dee Larkin thing got him all riled up again. I'd bet money he's hoping for a job with her. National TV and all that."

Karen studied me while I poured our tea and found the seat next to her.

"What?" I asked.

"Dee Dee said you invested with Stanley. I thought you said you didn't do that, Jess?"

"I didn't. But I have a hunch his job had something to do with the murder, so I've been lying to all and sundry about my supposed investments. You know, to get people talking?"

She raised an eyebrow, and I admitted to the sheer stupidity of my plan.

"What was I thinking?" I groaned. "Anyone who was at The Stone Fountain last night must have heard me spouting off. Which means anyone could have forwarded my lies to Jimmy. And then Jimmy told Dee Dee."

"And Dee Dee told the world."

I thanked Karen for reminding me and ate a yellow M & M.

"Oh well," I said with a shrug. "At least Captain Rye understands the truth."

Karen raised her other eyebrow, and I decided to move on. I described my harrowing day, starting with the funeral service and ending with a minor tirade against my ex.

"I still can't believe he and Amanda were at the service," I said.

"Who's Amanda?"

"Ian's new wife—the wannabe socialite."

"In Clarence, North Carolina?" Karen was incredulous.

"Insane, but that's Amanda for you." I imitated her society voice. "Seems she and Stanley's mother are simply the best of friends, don't you know. Why, Ian even plays cards with Stanley's father nowadays. Can you imagine such a thing?"

I sat up straight and hissed a four-letter word.

"What's up, Jess?"

Ian played cards with Roger Sweetzer. And according to Candy, Stanley played poker with his father every Thursday night. Which meant that Ian had played cards with Stanley? Which meant that—oh, my Lord—it meant all kinds of things. Not the least of which, I now knew how Stanley had learned the details of my net worth.

"Jess?" Karen asked. "Are you alright?"

"No," I said honestly.

"Do you need an Advil? I can go get the bottle?"

Dear Karen. I told her I must be tired. She took the hint and left soon afterwards.

I began some vigorous pacing, found the phone, and started dialing Ian. But then I changed my mind. Why subject myself to the Crawchecks three times in one day? And besides, Ian deserved nothing less than a face to face confrontation over this one. I would watch him try to squirm his way out of it, and then I would—I stopped short and looked down at Snowflake.

"What will I do to Ian?" I asked her.

She didn't offer any suggestions, but she did follow me as I paced over to the window. And that's when I noticed Captain Rye emerging from The Stone Fountain.

I stopped short again and turned off the desk lamp to get rid of the glare.

He and Lieutenant Densmore stood at the curb talking for a while before Densmore climbed into a nearby car and drove off. But Rye stuck around, apparently fascinated by the traffic at the corner of Sullivan and Vine. He looked up and caught me staring. I jumped back, but not before I noticed the grin.

I glanced down at the receiver still in my hand. It was time to call my mother.

***

"Of course I saw Dee Dee Larkin's report," Mother answered my first question. "I would have called you, Honeybunch, but I've been on the phone all evening. Everyone's been asking after you."

I may have whimpered slightly.

"I am sorry about that poor young man," she continued. "He was a good friend of yours?"

"Mother! Please tell me you didn't believe everything Dee Dee said. Yes, I knew the guy, but I did not have an affair with him, and I did not invest with him. And I most certainly did not murder him!"

"Oh, Jessie. You know I know that already. But isn't that agent of yours a clever girl? Clever, clever, clever."

I closed my eyes and prayed for strength while my mother sang Geez Louise's praises. Clearly, she had figured out how Adelé Nightingale's plight had ended up on national TV. I doubt she was dancing on her desk, but Mother was spouting off words like blockbuster and bestseller when I interrupted to ask the obvious. "You think this is good publicity?"

"Don't you? All my friends are so excited! They can't wait to see that new book of yours when it finally comes out. Vivian Mims says she's going shopping first thing tomorrow to buy all your old ones, too!"

Vivian Mims is a resident at the same retirement home outside of Columbia, South Carolina, where Mother moved after Daddy died. She and my mother are becoming fast friends.

"I promised Vivian you'd autograph them the next time you visit," Mother was saying. "You'll do that for me?"

I promised to pack an extra pen for that express purpose. "I take it Mrs. Mims isn't concerned about the borderline-pornography thing?"

Mother giggled. "Oh, Honeybunch. You write historical romances, remember? You can't help it if you're just better at it than everyone else."

I rolled my eyes, but chose not to argue.

"Have you spoken to Danny?" I asked. I was fairly certain my brother and his wife Capers would not be quite so enthusiastic about Dee Dee Larkin's report.

"Well now, Capers is a bit upset," Mother admitted. "But you know how she is. She worries about what other people think far too much."

"Mm-hmm." I wandered back to the window and noticed Rye had left.

"What else?" Mother asked. "Something else is bothering you, Jessie."

"Well," I began. "You know Ian?"

"My only daughter was married to the man for twenty years. Now then, what about Ian? Is that silly wife of his causing you trouble again?"

I told her it wasn't Amanda who was bothering me this time. And after getting her to promise to keep Mrs. Mims and the rest of her friends in the dark, I explained all I knew about Stanley Sweetzer's murder, the ensuing investigation, and my own involvement in the whole unpleasant mess. This took a while, but Mother is a night owl and was in no hurry.

"But what does any of this have to do with Ian?" she asked as I finished the saga.

"I'm ninety percent sure Ian's the one who told Stanley about my finances. They played cards together."

"Oh dear."

"Exactly. But that's not all. Captain Rye found twenty-seven thousand dollars in Stanley's house the night he died."

"He must have gambled."

"Exactly! At those poker games with Ian."

"Ian?" Mother sounded skeptical. "What are you saying, Jessie?"

"I'm saying Stanley could have won that money from Ian."

"From Ian Crawcheck? Oh no, Honeybunch. I can't imagine that."

I slumped. "You don't think Ian would gamble like that."

"Not with his own money. No, no, no."

On further reflection, I had to agree with my mother the wise-woman. Having been married to a professional gambler for close to sixty years, she has a sixth sense about these things. I trust her instincts almost as much as my father did.

"But enough about silly Ian," Mother was saying. "Let's talk about this Captain Rye of yours instead, Jessie. He sounds just darling!"

Chapter 14

Alexis Wynsome should never have been left unattended, not even for a moment. The following morning, while Rolfe Vanderhorn was distracted sharpening his sword, dear, sweet Alexis got herself kidnapped, yet again. The evil Maynard Snipe's even eviler step brother Derwin had carried her away when she ventured out of Rolfe's cottage to pick daisies. An unlikely plot twist, but there you have it.

At least the woman had sense enough to scream when the dastardly Derwin swept her onto his horse and galloped away. Rolfe looked up from his task just in time to identify the man who was stealing his lady love away this time.

What to do, what to do? Another man, one with less fortitude and far less libido, might have given up on the hapless Alexis. But Rolfe's memories of the previous night, of Alexis's trembling bosom, of her soft, fluttery lips, her tender caresses, and her trembling bosom, inspired our hero to action once again.

His challenge was daunting, indeed. For the older Snipe brother was a lot smarter than Maynard. Derwin rode a faster steed, lived in a better fortified castle, and actually knew which end of his sword to brandish in a duel.

Rolfe sighed in despair. He would need to think long and hard about how to tackle this latest crisis.

Thoughts of the dastardly Ian Crawcheck distracted me from Rolfe's latest quandary. I was closing my computer and planning a surprise visit to my ex when Candy called to inform me she was at the police station.

"The police station! For Lord's sake, what happened?"

"They arrested me, Jessie. Captain Rye says Carter and me killed Stanley."

The word I screamed into the phone didn't exactly relieve Candy's hysteria, but I recovered quickly and asked what had happened in only a mildly curious tone. Calm and serene—that's me.

Bless her heart, Candy also made an effort at inner fortitude, and managed to describe the basics of what had transpired since she last saw me. She had gone straight to bed after the funeral and had slept through the night. Supposedly, she did not even hear Jimmy Beak and his cameraman traipsing up and down the stairs, pounding on my door, etcetera.

"I felt a lot better this morning," she said. "But then Captain Rye showed up."

Her explanation got a bit muddled at that point, but apparently Rye and Densmore had hauled her off to the police station at about the same time Derwin Snipe absconded with Alexis Wynsome.

"They arrested Carter, too, Jessie. I think I forgot to mention he spent the night with me?"

I closed my eyes and prayed for strength.

"They said I could only make one phone call, just like on TV. I hope it's okay I called you?"

I assured Candy she had made a good choice. "I'll contact Rye and see what I can do. And I know a lot of good lawyers," I lied. "If I have anything to say about this, you won't be spending the night in jail. Ever."

"Oh, Jessie. I knew you'd know what to do."

"What about your parents?" I asked. "Should I call them, too?"

"Nooooo! Oh, Jessie! My mother will kill me if she ever finds out about this. And if my father hears I'm back with Carter? Oh, my gosh. Please, oh please, don't tell them!"

Okay, so I had no idea what that was about, but agreed not to contact the parents. Clearly, we had enough problems to deal with. Speaking of which, Jimmy Beak popped into my head. But I banished the thought and tried to convince myself and my neighbor that we would prove her innocence before the five o'clock news.

Yeah, right, I thought to myself, but Candy had faith in me. Indeed, she sounded almost confident by the time we hung up.

I, however, was more agitated than Rolfe Vanderhorn and Alexis Wynsome combined. With shaking hands, I rummaged around my desk until I found Rye's business card.

"So much for calm and serene," I told Snowflake.

***

"Rye here," he offered as a greeting.

"Why?" I snapped. "Why on earth are you sitting at your desk? When you should be out searching for the real killer. Candy Poppe? Candy Poppe? Get a grip on reality, Captain!"

"Good morning, Ms Hewitt."

"Good! What's good about it? What's going on?"

"We have your friend in custody—"

"No shit?"

He waited while I tried again. "I'm sorry," I said. "But I'm very upset right now. Do you understand?"

"Yep, I think I do."

Snowflake jumped onto her windowsill to stay out of the way as I started pacing.

"Okay, so what possessed you to arrest Candy Poppe?" I asked.

"Not that it's any of your business—"

"Any of my business?" I did an about face and paced faster. "The guy died on my couch! And Candy's my friend. Of course it's my business."

"Well then, why don't you be quiet and let me explain?"

I yanked the phone away from my ear and glared at it.

"Ms. Hewitt?"

I plopped myself into an easy chair. "I'm listening," I muttered into the phone.

"O'Connell admits to being at Ms. Poppe's apartment Saturday night."

"What!?"

"Candy's old boyfriend—Carter O'Connell. They're back together again. I assume you know about this?"

I remained silent.

"I'll take that as a yes," Rye said. "They're both claiming O'Connell was only over there waiting for her to get off work. She admits to giving him a key."

Rye waited, but I still said nothing.

"It gets worse," he warned.

"How exactly is that possible?"

"O'Connell admits to seeing Stanley Sweetzer just before the guy went up to your place to die. Seems old Stanley used his own key to let himself into Ms. Poppe's apartment."

I had to agree, at least silently, when Rye made some snide comment about Candy giving out the keys to her home a bit too readily. He then regaled me with yet another riveting dissertation about why we needed a lock on the front door of the building. When the phrase 'everybody and his brother' popped up, I suggested we get back to the murder thing.

Rye cleared his throat. "According to O'Connell, Sweetzer showed up in Ms Poppe's living room completely hammered and stumbled away in a great big hurry when he saw the new boyfriend. But I'm pretty sure that encounter between the boyfriends lasted a lot longer than O'Connell's claiming."

"Let me guess. Long enough to poison Stanley."

"Very good. O'Connell's denying it, but they must have argued about Candy, and then he slipped the Phenobarbital into Sweetzer's drink."

"So this guy Carter just happened to have a supply of Phenobarbital in his back pocket?" I hoped I sounded as skeptical as I felt. "Didn't you say the stuff's fairly hard to come by? And you think these guys just happened to sit down and have a drink together in the middle of their supposed argument? Doesn't this seem a bit farfetched, even to you?"

"Take a guess what O'Connell just earned his degree in. His PhD from NC State."

"Enlighten me. Please."

"He's a chemist. A pharmaceutical chemist to be exact."

"Oh, for Lord's sake!"

"Very good again. His past record with Ms. Poppe isn't helping any, either."

I sat up straight. "Past record?"

"Candy Poppe and Carter O'Connell managed to get themselves into a whole lot of trouble back in high school. They were in and out of juvenile court for years before Judge Sheppard finally came up with a solution."

I may have managed an 'Oh?'

"The judge ordered them not to see each other for ten years. O'Connell graduated and moved away soon after that. To his credit, he has stayed away from Clarence for the allotted time."

I was getting the mother of all headaches, but forced myself to continue the conversation, "I'm sorry, Captain, but I'm having serious trouble picturing Candy Poppe as a juvenile delinquent."

"Well, picture it. But I can see how this would be a shock to you. Poppe and O'Connell have been model citizens since Judge Sheppard's ruling. Until now, that is."

"But now they're back together again," I mumbled.

Rye took a deep breath. "There's one more thing I think I ought to mention."

"Oh?" I asked, the dread veritably oozing out of me.

"You yourself gave me a tidy piece of evidence against Ms. Poppe the night Sweetzer died."

I groaned as it dawned on me. "Stanley whispered her name to me," I said in a very small voice. "It was the last thing he ever said."

"I'm sorry, Ms. Hewitt, but it's likely he was telling you who was responsible for killing him."

I wiped away the tear that was traveling down my cheek.

"And I'm sorry, but it's also looking premeditated," Rye said. "Your friend had just found out she was the sole beneficiary of the will, so she gave her new guy a key to her place, and tricked Sweetzer into going over there. It was a set up, which makes her an accessory to murder. O'Connell's been booked on first degree murder charges."

I was sobbing by then, but held my hand to the phone as Rye continued, "I still don't know how they intended to get rid of the body. But O'Connell must have been thrilled when Sweetzer went up to your place to do his actual dying. He took the opportunity to slip out of the building and was probably long gone by the time you dialed 911."

He must have heard me crying. "Are you okay, Jessie?"

I took a deep breath and swallowed hard. "What can I do?"

"Find her a good lawyer. I have some suggestions in that regard, if you're interested."

I was. I found a scrap of paper and took down the three names he gave me.

"What else?" I asked.

"Well, you can also post bail for her, if you're so inclined. You know how that works?"

"I'm not Leon Hewitt's daughter for nothing, Captain."

***

Before doing anything, I called Sylvia Nettles. She was the only attorney I knew, and I knew she could fight like a bulldog. After all, this was the woman who had handled my divorce.

Sylvia reminded me she doesn't handle criminal cases and insisted Anthony De Sousa was the man to call. "This case sounds right up his alley," she said. "Tony's the best defense attorney in town. And he loves impossible odds."

I checked Rye's suggestions, and sure enough, Tony De Sousa was his first choice, too. I called the number Sylvia gave me and explained Candy's situation, impossible or not, to Mr. De Sousa's paralegal. De Sousa himself was in court, but his assistant assured me I would get a call from him before the day was through.

Next, I got things rolling with the bail bondsman.

Then I drove back home and waited for the phone to ring. I pretended to work, but ended up staring out the window and watching the lunchtime clientele come and go at The Stone Fountain. Days ago Rye had said Stanley was poisoned either in that bar or in my building.

I called Karen.

"Our little Kiddo in jail, Jess? What is the world coming to?"

Clearly Karen knew nothing about Candy's sordid past, and she had not known of Candy's arrest until I told her. But after hearing the news, she agreed that an evening at The Stone Fountain was definitely in order. We would meet in the lobby at eight.

I hung up and continued gazing out my window. "It had to have happened over there," I told Snowflake.

She shifted position on the windowsill, and together we stared at the bar.

***

"Your friend will be spending the night in jail," Anthony De Sousa informed me a while later. "Candy knows we're working to get her out, but these things take time. Especially in a capital case."

I suppose I should have been happy Candy's new lawyer had called me back as promised. And I suppose I should have been happy he had already scheduled her bond hearing for the following day. But I whined a bit anyway.

"I don't want you to worry over this, Ms. Hewitt. Candy says she'll be fine."

I forced some optimism into my voice and made sure to thank Mr. De Sousa for his efforts. "So, you've talked to Candy about all the supposed evidence against her?" I asked.

"I have. There's quite a lot of it, as I assume you already know."

I sighed dramatically. "I suppose I should be happy Captain Rye never arrested me when the evidence seemed to dictate."

"Must be the evidence didn't dictate." De Sousa chuckled. "Whatever Jimmy Beak is claiming."

"Excuse me?"

The lawyer again told me not to worry. "Everyone with a working brain knows if Jimmy Beak says it happened, it most likely did not. And Rye and Densmore both have working brains. You can quote me on that."

"But if I didn't do it, and Candy and Carter didn't do it, who did?"

"Who did?" He sounded as if I might know.

"Someone at The Stone Fountain," I said with conviction. "It's our neighborhood bar, and Stanley was there that night."

"Candy mentioned it."

"I intend to do some more sleuthing over there, starting tonight. Someone's got to figure this thing out."

"That would be the cops," De Sousa said. "You should leave this to the experts."

"You mean the experts like Wilson Rye? The genius who arrested poor Candy? No, sir, I don't think so."

"I've got to tell you, Rye had plenty of cause to arrest them."

I wondered if all defense lawyers were so all-fired willing to agree with the police as De Sousa continued, "It would have been nice if Rye hadn't found Carter O'Connell at Candy's apartment this morning—less than twenty-four hours after Sweetzer's funeral."

"She's young," I said. A lame excuse, but it was all I had.

"It would have been even nicer if O'Connell hadn't been there Saturday night. He ended up face to face with Sweetzer just moments before he died. Did Candy tell you that?"

I closed my eyes and prayed for strength. "Somehow, she forgot to mention it," I said.

Chapter 15

I had both a headache and a stomachache after hanging up with Anthony De Sousa. What better time to confront Ian?

In preparation, I dressed in my best don't mess with me black suit and donned a pair of heels which brought me close to six feet tall. Then I drove on over to the old homestead. It was only five o'clock, but tax season was months away, so I assumed my ex the CPA would be home from the office.

I parked at the curb and stared at what had once been my dream house. They had re-painted and changed the color from pastel yellow to beige. And for some reason all of my flower beds had been removed. So much for dreamy.

I climbed out of my Porsche, and was marveling at the vast expanse of solid lawn, when Frankie Smythe whizzed by on his skateboard. He did a double take, maneuvered a quick u-turn, and was suddenly standing beside me, skateboard in hand.

"Miss Jessie!" He smiled, and I noticed his braces were gone. "How's it going? How are you?"

I gave him a great big hug. "Exactly how tall are you nowadays, Frankie?"

He shrugged his incredibly lanky teenaged shoulders and I realized how much I had missed this boy. I had missed my house not at all. But Frankie?

We had a lot to catch up on, but we covered the lost time fast, especially since Frankie was too polite to mention the Stanley Sweetzer fiasco. He was also too polite to ask what I was doing in the neighborhood.

Frankie's big news was his impending driver's license.

"Two months!" He held up two fingers, and my mind flashed back to the day he had peddled up my driveway to show me his new tricycle. A few years later, it was his first bike. And a bit more recently he had strolled up the driveway hand in hand with his first girlfriend.

I was waxing way too nostalgic when Frankie dropped his skateboard and hopped on. He promised to visit me in my new digs sometime soon and started rolling away.

"I'll drive down to Sullivan Street," he called over his shoulder and pointed to my car. "Maybe you'll let me take that for a spin."

I winced at the idea and turned to face the beige door beckoning me from across the turf. I winced again.

***

"What do you want?" Amanda answered the door, her usual charming self. "I hope you know my life is ruined, Miss Borderline Pornography. All my friends keep asking about you. I may never be able to show my face at the club again."

Somehow, I didn't find Amanda's angst all that compelling. But I endured her tut-tutting for an entire minute before demanding to speak with Ian.

"What about?"

"I want to beg him to come back to me. What do you think?"

"I think you're a bitch."

I didn't argue, and Amanda informed me it was rude to show up unannounced. I didn't argue there either, but giving Ian fair warning before this visit had definitely not been an option.

Ignoring Amanda's less than gracious welcome, I walked inside. But I stopped short after only a step or two, overwhelmed by the new décor. Unlike the exterior, which had gone from cheery to dreary, the interior of my former home had changed from tasteful to tacky. Indeed, the foyer was veritably ablaze in exuberant colors.

I was staring aghast at the bold-print gold, green and purple—and I do mean purple—wallpaper, when my ex barged down the stairs.

"What the hell do you want?" he asked cordially.

"I need to talk to you." I tilted my head in Amanda's direction. "Privately."

What a shocker, Amanda stamped her foot and insisted she had a right to hear any conversation that took place under her own roof.

I uncurled my lip and turned back to Ian. "Trust me," I said. "You will want this to be private."

If I expected further argument, the hideous wallpaper saved me. Ian was staring at it as if he had never noticed it before, and he seemed not to have heard his new wife at all.

"The study," he said. He tore his eyes from the walls and led me down the hall.

I will spare you a description of what had once been my beloved writing room. Just think purple, and you'll get the basic idea.

"I need to ask you something about your Thursday night poker games," I said as Ian closed the door and pointed me to a chair.

"What about them?" He sat down in an exaggerated huff. "Get to the point, Jessie. I'm busy here."

"Who's the fourth guy? You played with Roger and Stanley Sweetzer and one other person, correct?"

"Who wants to know?"

I stated the obvious—that I would like to know.

"Why?"

"Come on, Ian. Just tell me." I hesitated, and decided I was just desperate enough to say it. "Please?"

He made me wait for a full minute before answering, "Neil Callahan. You remember him?"

Neil is the junior partner in my ex-husband's accounting firm. The man is not too bright, and I could easily envision him losing loads of money at a card game.

I thanked Ian for the info and moved on, "You're not going to like this next question, either."

"What, what, what?" He again reminded me how busy he was.

"Did you guys play for high stakes?" I asked.

Ian's head snapped in the direction of the closed door. I watched him watch the door and chose not to remind him of his pressing schedule. I also failed to point out that he had just answered my question.

Eventually, he remembered me. "My finances are none of your business," he said.

Perfect! I leaned forward and went in for the kill. "And my finances were none of Stanley Sweetzer's business."

Ian's mouth dropped open.

"But that didn't stop you from telling him all the details, did it?"

While my ex struggled to breathe, I reminisced about our divorce proceedings, which had dragged on for months while he fought me for the rights to my book royalties. We had finally settled, but only after he stopped listening to Amanda and conceded that I might actually deserve the income from my own writing. What a guy.

"You do remember our agreement, Ian?" I asked. "You got this beautiful house." I waved a hand in the air of what had been a beautiful house. "And I got the car, the cat, and a lump sum payment. A figure that was to remain confidential." I emphasized that last word. "Do you recall all those legally binding documents you signed just a few short months ago?"

He stuttered something about Stanley pressuring him for information. "Every Thursday night, Jessie. The guy was relentless."

"Stanley's file on me almost got me arrested for murder, Ian. The cops were quite interested in how he knew so much." I folded my arms and glared. "I was a bit curious about that, myself. Until now."

Ian squirmed but said nothing, and the full extent of his transgressions suddenly occurred to me.

"Oh, my Lord, Ian! It wasn't just me, was it?"

More squirming.

"You were feeding Stanley information on a lot of your clients, weren't you? Anyone with some extra cash lying around?"

He still refused to answer, so I relied on intuition and kept going. "Neil was in on it, too, I bet. What did you guys get in return? Some sort of kick back from Stanley?"

"Oh, and like you've always been such a fine, upstanding citizen." Ian sneered. "Remember who your Daddy was, Little Miss Cue-It."

I blinked twice. "I remember who you were, Ian. You used to have integrity. You used to care about professional standards."

"Yeah, and what are you gonna do about it? Report me? Remember Jimmy Beak, Jessie. Your credibility is shot."

I thought about Jimmy Beak. And there's a first time for everything—I actually smiled.

"You are so right," I agreed. "I am bound to run into Jimmy Beak again. Why, the man practically lives outside my door. And when I see him? I'll be sure to explain all the details about Stanley's poker games." I tapped my chin and pretended to think about it. "I'll mention your name, of course. And Neil's. And the name of your company." I batted my eyelashes. "I imagine the word 'fraud' is bound to pop up at some point, don't you think?"

I stood up and waited while my ex sputtered a string of obscenities. When he had finished, I bent over and grabbed the arms of his chair with each hand.

"After all," I said as he tried disappearing into the cushions. "The public has a right to know."

"Is that a threat?" he squeaked.

I winked and stood up.

"No need to see me out," I called over my shoulder. "I know the way."

***

"Mother was wrong for a change," I told Snowflake the moment I arrived home. I took off my heels and dropped them inside the door. "Ian did gamble a lot. So now what?"

Snowflake trotted over to her empty food dish and meowed.

"That's not what I was talking about," I told her. I walked over to the cupboard to find her crunchies while I pondered my latest discoveries.

I now knew my ex was complete slime and had broken who knows how many laws divulging privileged client information to the equally slimy Stanley Sweetzer. I also knew where that pesky twenty-seven thousand dollars had originated.

However, I still couldn't say who killed Stanley, and I could almost guarantee it wasn't one of the poker players. Ian might have lost all sense of decency, but he wasn't a murderer. And Roger Sweetzer was the guy's father, for Lord's sake. I gave Neil Callahan some thought.

"Nope," I said out loud. Neil might have been an extremely remote possibility, but I still couldn't quite picture it.

But then Amanda popped into my head. I stood there mesmerized, holding the box of cat food aloft.

What if Ian had lost that kind of money to her friend Margaret's son? What if Amanda had found out about it? And what if she had followed Stanley into The Stone Fountain last Saturday? Armed with Phenobarbital? Which she had obtained from—where?

Snowflake scolded me and wrapped herself around my ankles.

"Okay, so that's a lot of what ifs," I admitted as I recalled my main purpose in life. I bent down and poured some food into her bowl, and then I sat down at my computer and Googled Amanda Crawcheck.

For someone who was embarrassed to know me, Amanda sure was spreading the news about the borderline pornographer with a murderous streak. The woman had been tweeting about me several times a day. Indeed, she was practically campaigning for my imminent arrest.

I concluded, not for the first time, that Ian's new wife is at least as bitchy as his old. Then I moved on to Facebook, where I learned more than I ever wanted to know about the new Mrs. Crawcheck's social life. But I failed miserably in my main purpose, which was to find a photograph of her—something bigger than a postage stamp.

The *Clarence Courier's* web site proved more useful. I found her wedding announcement from earlier that year, but alas, no photo was attached. She and Ian must have decided a picture for his second, and her third, wedding might not be appropriate. But the announcement did remind me of Amanda's name before she had become a Crawcheck.

I searched further back and, lo and behold, found what I was looking for in a society page from five years earlier. It was grainy, it was in black and white, and she was wearing a big hat that hid at least half her face, but it was indeed a photograph of Amanda. She had attended a function at the Clarence Garden Club.

The Garden Club? I pictured the Crawcheck's new and definitely not improved front lawn, shook my head, and hit the print key.

Chapter 16

The usual suspects were in their usual places when Karen and I arrived at The Stone Fountain that night. While Bruce Springsteen reminded everyone where he was born, Matthew and Bryce concocted Long Island Iced Teas, Gina delivered Long Island Iced Teas, and Evan McCloy and the Dibbles drank Long Island Iced Teas. Meanwhile, over at the pool table, the gang waited patiently as Bernie and Camille Allen argued over who would shoot next.

Karen and I took our seats and Bryce pulled out the Corona and Korbel.

"Where's Candy?" he asked as he poured Karen's beer.

"You mean you haven't heard?" she said. "Candy's been arrested."

"What? What for?"

"Like, duh." Karen reached for her glass. "For murder."

"For accessory to murder," I clarified. "But surely Jimmy Beak has reported this by now?"

Bryce shook his head and made confused and bewildered faces while Karen explained that no, Jimmy had not reported the latest. "He showed that scene outside your door last night, Jess. When he had his panties in a bind about your bank account? But then he went right back to the school board scandal. No mention of Kiddo whatsoever."

I joined Bryce in bewilderment. "You mean Rye hasn't informed the media yet?"

"I'm guessing not," she said.

"But she's innocent." That was Bryce. "I mean, she's gotta be innocent, doesn't she?"

"Not according to Captain Rye." I waved him toward the Korbel bottle he had yet to open. "He's convinced she and Carter O'Connell killed Stanley."

"Who's Carter?" my neighbors asked together.

"Candy's new boyfriend."

"What?" Again, they spoke in unison.

"Perhaps I should say old boyfriend," I continued as Bryce finally handed me a drink. "They were high school sweethearts."

Labeling the delinquent duo high school sweethearts may have been a bit misleading, but did everyone really need to know the sordid details of Candy's past?

Unfortunately, I did know the details. After looking into Amanda in the *Clarence Courier's* web site, I had moved on to my neighbors.

A ten-year-old article confirmed what Rye had told me about Candy. It outlined the juvenile court's ruling against her and Carter and offered an extensive summary of the kinds of trouble they had gotten into—truancy, underage drinking, a couple of DUI's, disturbing the peace, and grand theft auto.

Grand theft auto. I whimpered slightly and decided to focus on the present. "Carter's moved back to town," I explained. "He and Candy have gotten back together."

"But she was engaged to Stanley," Bryce argued.

"Was," I repeated. "Believe it or not, she broke up with Stanley Saturday night. Right before he showed up here."

"So let me get this straight," Karen said. "Kiddo had two boyfriends at once?"

"When she was already engaged?" Bryce added.

I shrugged. "You did tell me Candy's love life is hard to keep track of."

"I guess I wasn't kidding." He knocked on the bar and wandered off to tend to some other customers.

I watched him create another batch of Long Island Iced Teas and recollected my research efforts in the Clarence newspaper's web site. I had found no mention of Bryce Dixon. This made sense, considering he had only moved to town a few years earlier, but it was still a bit disappointing.

I had better luck with Karen Sembler. I ran into her name several times since she was on the Board of Directors for our local Habitat for Humanity and helped build houses for the cause. The *Clarence Courier* had even provided a picture of her, clad in her tool belt, and hammering away on a small, but I am sure, well built roof of a Habitat house.

"Two boyfriends at once," she was mumbling as I glanced over.

"But that's not the issue, Karen. The murder is. According to Rye, Candy tricked Stanley into going to her apartment the other night. And supposedly Carter was lying in wait and somehow convinced the poor guy to consume poison."

"But why, Jess?"

"Money. Candy's the sole beneficiary of Stanley's will. And Carter's a PhD chemist. Convenient, no?"

"Oh boy."

"At least her lawyer comes highly recommended." I tried sounding optimistic. "He's working on getting her out on bail, and then we can get her side of the story."

"Two boyfriends." Karen twisted her beer in her hands. "Did you ever have that kind of luck when you were young?" She looked up to study me. "You must have been gorgeous—even prettier than Candy."

I harkened back to the good old days and sighed. "I never had Candy's charm," I said. "And Lord knows I've never been sweet. Guys fall for sweet."

"It must be nice."

I tilted my head. "So, like, you've never dated two men at once?"

"Are you kidding? I've seldom dated one guy at once. In case you haven't noticed, girlfriend, I'm not exactly a beauty queen."

I quickly, and sincerely, disagreed. Okay, so Karen doesn't exactly dress like a beauty queen, and her mop of auburn curls might look like she cuts her hair with a chainsaw. But somehow it works. On Karen anyway.

"You have great skin, and great cheekbones," I insisted. I glanced at the top of her head. "And fascinating hair."

"Great cheekbones?" She laughed at me. "I'm guessing guys don't much care about cheekbones."

"Well they should."

I watched my neighbor shake her head and recollected Rye's ridiculous theory about my own motivation for killing Stanley. Could Karen be the older woman who was jealous of Candy's love life?

"Speaking of threesomes," Karen was saying. "You should have seen that four-poster bed when I got done with it. The thing was big enough to throw a small orgy on. We barely got it onto the truck this morning."

She went back to sipping her beer and I dismissed my silly suspicions. If Karen Sembler were going to kill someone, she would do it with a power tool.

***

Bryce returned and asked what he could do to help Candy. "There must be something?" He rocked back and forth and looked at me for an answer.

Lo and behold, I actually had one. I pulled out the picture of Amanda I was harboring in the back pocket of my slacks and handed it to him.

"Have you ever seen this woman in here?" I asked. "Think hard, okay?"

Karen stretched herself over the bar to take a peek, and the two of them studied the photograph.

"I must need glasses," she said as she sat back down. "That woman could be sitting next to me right now, and I wouldn't recognize her from that."

I admitted the picture was a bit blurry, and the dim lighting of the bar wasn't helping any.

"How about you?" I asked Bryce. "I think she might have been in here Saturday."

He continued squinting at the picture. "Who is this?"

I avoided that pesky question, and asked Bryce to show the photo to the regulars. "Just see if anyone recognizes her. Can you do that?"

He jerked his head in Matthew's direction. "I'll try, Jessie. But I hope you aren't expecting much."

I assured him whatever he could do without jeopardizing his job would be appreciated.

"What about me?" Karen asked. "What can I do?"

I looked around and spotted Evan McCloy. He didn't seem particularly busy, and he frowned only slightly when I caught his eye.

"Evan." I hit the bar with the palm of my hand. "Get him over here, Bryce."

Bless his heart, Bryce bounced off on his appointed mission, and I quickly told Karen what I knew about Stanley's colleague.

"He's already lost his patience with me," I said. "But use your charm and get him to tell you all the dirt about Stanley's job. Can you do that?"

Karen finished her beer in one gulp and tossed her hair back, Alexis Wynsome style. "Oh sure," she said. "I'll just flash these cheekbones at him and the guy will be putty in my hands."

She pointed at me. "Meanwhile, what will you be doing?"

I finished my glass in one gulp also and motioned toward the Dibbles. "I'll tackle Audrey again. She promised to get back to me after she consulted with her astrologer."

"You are one brave woman, Jessica Hewitt."

I stood up. "Tell Bryce to send over some fresh drinks when he gets a chance."

***

"So much news!" Audrey exclaimed as I approached. She removed a canvas sack of who- knows-what from the spot next to her and patted the seat.

"Things have gotten a lot more serious," I said as I slipped into the booth. "Candy's been arrested."

"Oh, but it wasn't her," Audrey said. She plopped the bag onto the table, and I heard a loud thunk. "Ezekiel said so. I had my consultation this afternoon."

Gina delivered a round of drinks, and as Jackson grunted a thank you in my direction, Audrey reported the details of her inquiry.

"Unfortunately, I didn't have Stanley's time of birth," she said. "So poor Ezekiel was at a severe disadvantage, as you can imagine. But even so, he was real helpful."

"Oh?"

"Oh, yes!" Audrey clapped her hands and her jewelry jingled accordingly. "I told him all about Stanley, and

Ezekiel consulted his library and astrological charts to see what he could discover. It took us hours of hard work, but this was important, right? It was worth the extra money?"

She appealed to me with her bulbous eyes. I turned away and watched Jackson gulp down his drink.

"What did Ezekiel discover?" I forced myself to ask.

"Jealousy," Audrey declared. She leaned in with another meaningful look. "Someone was jealous of that boy, Jessie."

"Jealous of what? His money, his job, his girlfriend?"

"Oh, now Ezekiel couldn't tell me that. We didn't have Stanley's time of birth, remember?"

"But did Ezekiel mention exactly who was jealous of Stanley?"

"Jessie!" Audrey scolded. "I just told you—Ezekiel didn't have all the vital facts. The poor man did the best he could, under the circumstances."

I sighed dramatically and tried again. "What about Stanley's job?" I asked. "Did Ezekiel have any insights there? I'm still trying to figure out who invested with him."

Jackson harrumphed. "Other than you?"

I rolled my eyes. "Yes," I said. "Other than me." Perhaps I should have set the record straight on that issue, but the Dibbles weren't exactly sticklers for accuracy, so why bother?

Audrey had suddenly turned quiet, but Jackson became almost verbose. "We didn't invest with him," he said proudly. "Mr. Astrology ordered us to, but I refused. Tell her about it, Audrey." He removed his hand from his glass long enough to wave at his wife, and Audrey reluctantly admitted to getting some bad advice from the legendary Ezekiel.

"He told me to go ahead and make those investments Stan was so keen on," she said. "But Jackson wouldn't let me. And after hearing what's happened to you, Jessie? I guess I'm glad we didn't do it."

I mumbled something about Jimmy Beak's exaggerations as Audrey dropped the mysterious canvas bag onto my lap.

"Ouch!" I looked down. "What is this?"

"Crystals," Jackson answered. "My brilliant wife's decided to give you a bunch of stupid rocks. Aren't you gonna thank her?"

I peeked into the bag, and sure enough, it was filled with rocks—at least a dozen of them. They weren't exactly boulders, but they were significantly larger than any of the baubles hanging from Audrey's neck, wrists, and earlobes.

"Umm," I managed. "Thank you, Audrey."

She smiled broadly and began rummaging around in her purse. "After seeing all those TV reports on you and your troubles, I just knew your chakras needed a boost, Jessie. I packed that with only the bare basics, mind you. But place those crystals around your house and I guarantee your chakras will be back in balance in no time."

She pulled out a rather lengthy handwritten note and handed it to me. "Follow these instructions carefully and your chakras will thank you for it. You wait and see."

I placed Audrey's notes inside the canvas sack. I still had no clue what my chakras were, but perhaps the notes would enlighten me.

"Now then, what about your couch?"

I lifted my head out of the sack and registered the look of grave concern on Audrey's face.

"You haven't allowed it back in your home, have you?"

"No," I answered and watched helplessly as Jackson beckoned to Bryce for another round. A quick tabulation of my bar tab for the month was causing me far more anxiety than my demon-possessed couch. I informed Audrey that the police still hadn't returned the sofa.

"Thank goodness!" she exclaimed. "You mustn't allow all that bad karma back into your home or your chakras may never recover. Promise me?"

I was deciding how to answer when I sensed a tall, angry presence hovering at my right. Captain Rye, I presumed, and looked up to verify.

"You got a minute?" he said and stepped away without waiting for a response.

I whispered something about Captain Rye's excess of angry chakras to Audrey, hefted the canvas bag over my left shoulder, and excused myself from the Dibbles.

***

"What are you doing here?" Rye asked as I approached.

"It's a pleasure to see you, too," I said. "What time was Stanley Sweetzer born?"

"Excuse me?"

"His birthday, Captain. Do you happen to know what time of day Stanley was born?"

Rye glanced up at the ceiling. "Call me lax, but I haven't come across that vital piece of information."

I shrugged my right shoulder. "Never mind," I said. "It probably doesn't matter."

"Okay, let's try this again." He directed his gaze back at me. "What are you doing here?"

"I might ask you the same question."

"You do remember our conversation the other night?" He managed to raise his voice, even though he was whispering. "Didn't we agree you'd stay away from this place until the case was closed?"

"Noooo," I said. "I don't recall that at all. And besides, I thought the case was closed. The ever malicious Candy Poppe and company are behind bars tonight, correct?"

He ignored me and looked around the room until his eyes landed on Karen. Bless her heart, she had Evan McCloy deep in conversation. Apparently, Evan was a cheekbone man after all.

"I see you brought backup this time," Rye said.

"Karen and I came over to have a drink together." I tried sounding innocent. "Is there a problem with that?"

"Oh, probably."

Rye left me to join Karen and Evan, likely interrupting an informative and helpful conversation about Stanley.

I refused to follow, and instead walked past the Dibbles' booth to thank Audrey again for the crystals. The more I thought about it, the more touching her gesture of friendship seemed. Then I made my way over to the pool table. I plopped the bag of crystals at my feet before I threw my back out, and leaned against the wall to watch the game between John the New Guy and Gus.

Kirby saw me forthwith and asked for the next available game. I was about to accept when Rye spun around from Karen and Evan and declined for me.

"Ms. Hewitt was just leaving," he said firmly.

"Excuse me?" I was about to argue more vehemently, but Karen's wild gesticulating behind his back stopped me.

I promised Kirby some other time and bent down to pick up my rocks. Rye reached over, took the canvas sack, and led us away.

"I absolutely hate obeying this guy," I told Karen as we approached the door.

"But I think I got something," she whispered. "We need to talk."

That conversation would have to wait, however, since Rye insisted on seeing us home. Indeed, he and Karen made all matter of small talk as we crossed Sullivan Street, and by the time we were standing at her doorway, she was even promising to install a lock on our front door within the week.

I myself was a bit less cordial. I huffed and puffed my indignation, but Rye didn't seem to notice the melodrama. He wished Karen a pleasant night and turned toward the stairwell.

Karen held me back. "Call me," she whispered and shut her door.

Chapter 17

What a shocker, Rye was frowning when I turned around.

I folded my arms and glared. "I really can make it all the way up to the third floor by myself, you know?"

"We've been through this before." He opened the stairwell door and waved me forward.

I resigned myself to the inevitable and followed him up the stairs, but he stopped and turned on the second floor landing.

"What the hell do you have in this thing?" He pointed to the bag he was carrying.

"Rocks," I said honestly.

Rye blinked twice. "You're a little scary, you know that?"

I didn't argue, he hoisted the bag onto his other shoulder, and kept climbing.

We made it to my doorway, but the man still wasn't in the mood to leave and insisted we needed to talk. "We've got a problem," he informed me.

"Why am I not surprised?" I unlocked my door. "I am tired, Captain. I've had an extremely busy day."

"I'm sure you have. May I come in?"

I thought about it. "Upstairs," I said. I called to Snowflake, told Rye to leave the crystals in my doorway, and led the two of them toward the roof.

"At least if we sit up here, you won't expect me to serve you tea," I said over my shoulder.

He told me there was no need to be testy.

"Yeah, right," I responded testily.

***

We sat down, and Rye was once again enamored with the garden. I, however, refused to let the pleasant breezes and almost-full moon dissuade me from my bad mood. I interrupted a question about watering the daisies and demanded some answers.

"Why hasn't Jimmy Beak been informed of Candy's arrest?" I began. "Aren't you required to keep the media posted on these things?"

"Beak knows. We briefed the media this afternoon."

"What? Then why hasn't he reported it?"

Rye raised an eyebrow. "You're really not that naïve, are you? The public doesn't always have the right to know, Ms. Hewitt. Not if the facts aren't likely to boost Beak's ratings."

I folded my arms and glared. "Are you telling me Jimmy's sitting on Candy's arrest because it makes for better ratings if I'm the killer?"

"Yep, that's what I'm telling you. And remember his fixation with Dee Dee Larkin? If you're not the killer, there goes that supposed partnership. Beak's been trying to go national for years."

I mumbled a four-letter word, but Rye told me not to worry.

"Larkin didn't even mention you in tonight's broadcast, whatever Beak was hoping," he said. "And you'll be off the hook around here by tomorrow. The *Courier* will run an article on Poppe and O'Connell in the morning paper—front page, most likely. After that, Beak will be forced to tell his adoring public what's really going on. Which is exactly what I want."

I myself was a bit confused about what exactly I wanted. I wasn't thrilled with the idea of Jimmy latching on to Candy's arrest, but his continued harassment of yours truly wasn't all that appealing either.

"Beak could end up helping your friend's cause." Rye interrupted my thoughts. "That's what I'm hoping, anyway."

"How in the world can Jimmy Beak help Candy?"

Rye studied me, the baby blues more intense than ever.

"What?" I asked impatiently.

"I'm trying to decide how much I should trust you."

"I'm a trustworthy person," I said.

"Maybe. But you're angry with me as it is, and you're really not going to like what I'm about to tell you."

I rolled my eyes. "I do know how to control my temper, you know?"

"Mm-hmm."

"What is it, before I decide to kill you, Captain?"

"We have every reason to assume your friend is guilty—"

I jumped up and reminded Rye of my terrible temper.

He glanced up. "You want to hear this, or not?"

I sat back down.

"As I was saying," he continued, "we have a good amount of evidence against Poppe and O'Connell, and I've officially closed the case."

I sat on my hands so as not to slug him.

"But I'm still looking into things. Unofficially." Again the intense stare. "You get it?"

I did not.

"Well then, I'll explain," he said. "I'm still not completely satisfied that something didn't happen in that bar on Saturday." He pointed down toward The Stone Fountain. "Which is why I still insist you stay clear of the place. Stop stirring things up, until we're sure."

There, you see? I knew I had a right to be testy.

"Are you actually telling me," I hissed, "you have Candy in jail, and you're not absolutely, positively, one hundred percent sure she's guilty?"

"I'm ninety percent certain she is guilty." Rye remained his incredibly aggravating, calm self. "But I'm also keeping an open mind, and I'm still investigating some other possibilities. Unofficially."

"And I'm supposed to sit here and let you take your sweet time about it? While Candy rots in jail?"

He shook his head. "Ms. Poppe is not about to rot in jail, okay? She'll be out tomorrow morning. I had to call in a few dozen favors, but I convinced the DA not to fight too hard at the bond hearing."

"And her friend Carter? What about him?"

"He stays in jail. Don't even try to argue with me about that."

"And you think I'm the scary one? You're impossible, do you know that?"

"Listen to me carefully," he said and waited until I did so. "Once Ms. Poppe is released tomorrow, you have got to let her think—let everyone think—I'm finished with the investigation. If Poppe and O'Connell aren't the culprits, then the real murderer is still on the loose. If they think I'm done looking, they may get complacent. You get it now?"

I did. "That's where Jimmy Beak comes in, correct? He'll report the news on Candy and Carter, and the killer will think he's gotten away with it?"

"He or she."

"And then maybe he'll do something stupid to tip us off," I concluded.

"Us?"

I watched Snowflake chase a moth and considered Rye's plan.

"If you really think Carter's innocent, it's wrong of you to hold him in jail. There are laws about that." I tried to remember which of Carter O'Connell's civil rights Rye was violating.

"Can you trust me on this?" he asked. "Just this once?"

I was mumbling a reluctant agreement when he reached into his suit pocket and pulled out a sheet of paper. I cringed as he unfolded the picture of Amanda and held it up for me.

"Now then, you want to explain this?"

I studied the photograph as if I had never seen it before. "Where did you get that?" I asked ever so innocently.

"As if you didn't know. Bryce Dixon was flashing it to everyone and his brother until I confiscated it." Rye frowned at me. "Do you actually hate the new Mrs. Crawcheck so much you're willing to accuse her of murder?"

"I haven't accused her. Yet." I crossed my arms and glared. "But she did have a motive, you know? And since you're still looking into the possibilities, you might just take a peek at dear Amanda."

"Already have."

"Oh?"

"I'm not an idiot, Ms. Hewitt. I know all about your ex-husband's poker games with the Sweetzers."

I bounced a bit. "I think that's where Stanley got all the money you found. I'm thinking he won it from Ian, and then Amanda got mad. Don't you see?"

"It's already been covered. First of all, those guys never played for anywhere near that kind of cash—"

"That's not what Ian told me," I interrupted. "They played for high stakes."

Rye raised an eyebrow. "You two have been talking?"

I raised an eyebrow back. "Trust me, it was not that fun."

We had ourselves a little stare down before Rye broke the silence. "There's high stakes, and there's high stakes," he said. "Those guys never played for anywhere near that kind of money. You'll also be happy to know, I think, that the Crawchecks were out of town last weekend. They were in Savannah visiting her sister. Densmore's verified it."

I watched as he crumbled up the picture and put it back in his pocket.

"You have to admit it had possibilities," I mumbled.

"Mm-hmm."

I thought about the other information I had garnered from my ex that afternoon. Did Rye really need to know all the details of those stupid poker games? And if so, did he really need to hear it from me?

Snowflake hopped into his lap and meowed encouragement. Rye stroked under her chin and she purred accordingly.

I took a deep breath and blurted it out, "I've figured out how Stanley knew so much about my finances."

"From Ian Crawcheck."

I jumped. "You knew about that? For how long?"

"Since Densmore questioned him—right after we searched your place the other day."

"What? Why didn't tell me?"

Rye grinned. "By that point I was ninety percent certain you weren't a murderer. Call me foolish, but I kind of wanted to keep it that way."

"Believe it or not, I haven't fantasized about killing my ex for months." I sat back and frowned. I might be the forgiving type, but if any of Ian's other clients found out what he'd been doing, one of them might not be so understanding.

"You don't have to report him." Apparently, Rye was reading my mind. "Densmore and I will take care of it."

"So," I said slowly. "You know all about those poker games?" I emphasized the all.

"I know enough. It isn't my area of expertise, but your ex-husband's arrangement with Sweetzer will be investigated. Divulging confidential financial figures like he did constitutes fraud."

"Ian insists Stanley practically forced him into it."

Rye nodded. "Sweetzer was good at getting what he wanted out of people. He knew lots of secrets, but that doesn't let your ex-husband off the hook."

Oh, Ian. I held my face in my hands and shuddered.

"He used to be a good guy," I said eventually. "Once upon a time he had standards."

Rye waited until I glanced up. "I can see that," he said.

***

Snowflake yowled for no good reason and jumped from Rye's lap onto Karen's safety railing. She sat staring at us, her white coat shimmering in the moonlight.

"I hate it when she does that," I said. "She knows it makes me nervous."

"Cats like heights." Rye tapped my knee with his fist. "So, we have a deal, right? You'll keep your mouth shut and trust me, and I'll keep looking into the murder. Deal?"

"I hate this," I agreed. "But I'm still going to The Stone Fountain. It would actually look more suspicious if I stopped hanging out in there."

"Well, at least stop it with the sleuthing. And don't be over there alone, or late at night."

Speaking of late at night—I leaned back and closed my eyes to better enjoy the breeze.

"Tell me about your mother," he said the moment I got comfortable. "What did she do?"

My mother? I kept my eyes closed and told him I was sick of discussing my private life. "Let's talk about you for a change, shall we?" I sat up and pointed to Snowflake. "You must have a cat, for instance?"

"Two of them. Wally's jet black, the exact opposite of yours. And Bernice is the fattest calico on Planet Earth."

I smiled. "And parents?" I asked. "Do you have any of those?"

"Two of them."

"What do they do?"

"They're retired. My mother was a dispatcher with the force in Raleigh."

"The police force? Like the woman who answered my 911 call the other night?"

"Yep. And my father was a cop."

"Children?" I asked. "Do you have any of those, Captain Rye?"

"You're very nosey, you know that?"

"I've been taking lessons."

He held up an index finger. "I have one of those. My son Chris is a sophomore at UNC, Chapel Hill. What about you?" he asked. "No kids, right?"

I shook my head and swallowed a sigh. "So, where exactly do you live?" I changed the subject. "Not downtown?"

He raised an eyebrow. "You plan on paying me a visit, Ms. Hewitt?"

I told him not to flatter himself and waited until he informed me he has a place out on Lake Lookadoo. "Below Belvidere Mountain," he said. "You know the area?"

I tilted my head toward the mountains in the distance, outlined under that spectacular moon. "You live in the boondocks."

"Yep." Rye stood up. "And I think I'm done answering questions."

"One more." I pulled him back down. "Where did you learn to shoot pool. You're very good, you know?"

"Gee thanks."

"Just answer the question."

"My commanding officer in the Air Force taught me."

Again he got up to leave, and we walked downstairs.

"You still haven't told me about your mother," Rye said as we made it to my door. "What did she do?"

"She was a bank teller." Snowflake and I walked inside. "Daddy used to joke that they both liked the feel of cold hard cash between their fingertips."

"And you ended up a writer?"

"Mother read a lot. Daddy was away most nights, so she read romances to while away the time. She still does."

"She's still alive then?"

"Yes, Captain. And her name is Mother."

I picked up my sack of rocks and shut the door.

**

I erased a message from Louise Urko without bothering to listen and called Karen.

"Good Lord, Jess. Did he finally leave?"

"Finally. And if I'm expected to stay awake any longer, I must have chocolate."

"Anything specific?"

"Surprise me."

Five minutes later, Karen was at my door armed with a package of Hershey's Kisses, and the tea kettle was whistling on my stove.

"Should I even ask what you and Rye were doing all that time?" She gave me a Candy-like look and took a seat at the counter.

I turned away to find the tea cups. "We were talking about the murder."

"Yeah, right."

"The three of us were up in the garden. Ask Snowflake if you don't believe me."

"And?"

"And I wish that she would stay away from the edge. She especially loves to torment me by sitting on your railing."

"It'll hold her." Karen bent down to acknowledge Snowflake. "But what about the murder, Jess? What did Rye say about Kiddo?"

Nothing I'm allowed to share, I thought to myself. I avoided the question and worked on pouring the tea.

"I'm more interested in what you learned from Evan," I said. I walked our cups over to the coffee table. "It looked like you guys were having a real heart to heart."

"He's looking to put a gazebo in his backyard." Karen followed me to the easy chairs, candy in hand. "When Bryce told him I build stuff, he got interested."

"Oh?"

"So I lied. I quoted him a ridiculously low price and promised I'd be able to get it done within the month. Then I got down to business and asked about Stanley."

"But that's fantastic, Karen. What did he say?"

"We talked about the company they work for— Something Or Other Dent. And then I asked how business was, and Evan got kind of nervous. So I kidded him a little about whether he could afford this gazebo he has planned."

"Believe it or not, I really don't care about that gazebo."

"Hey, it kept the guy talking."

"Good point," I agreed and unwrapped a Kiss.

Karen continued, "It sounds like the office politics at Something Dent are from hell." She shook her head. "Man, I don't miss that."

"Don't tell me you ever worked in an office?"

"For ten years. I was a bookkeeper at Mountain Top Real Estate."

I scowled. "I can't quite picture you at a job that doesn't require a tool belt."

"Try picturing me at a job that required pantyhose."

I glanced at her work boots.

"Like, every day," she said. "I hated it."

"And Stanley's office?"

"Get this." She sat up and Snowflake jumped from her lap to mine. "Stanley got a promotion to senior something or other right before he died. According to Evan, there were lots of people in the company who weren't too happy about it."

"Jealousy," I said, remembering Audrey and Ezekiel.

"I guess maybe. Stanley was a lot younger and hadn't been there as long as some of the others. Evan says there was a lot of back stabbing going on."

"Any names? Anyone I should pay particular attention to?"

"Huh?"

"I met a few of Stanley's colleagues at the funeral," I explained. "Lord help me, I even told a woman, Vikki, that I need some advice on my investments. You know, now that Stanley's gone?"

Karen's eyes got wide. "Don't tell me you're actually going down there?"

Yes, I suppose I actually was. Snowflake gave me a disapproving look, and I remembered my promise to Rye to stop sleuthing. But that was only at The Stone Fountain, correct?

"I'll just poke around and see what I can learn." I tried sounding confident.

"Man, I wouldn't have a clue how to snoop around like that."

Neither did I. But surely I would think of something.

"Any insight from Audrey's astrologer?" Karen asked as she went for another Kiss.

"Jealousy," I said. "Ezekiel the Astrologer says someone was jealous of Stanley. But, alas, he didn't have Stanley's time of birth, so he couldn't be more specific."

"Jealousy," Karen repeated after swallowing. "At least we've got ourselves a theme."

Chapter 18

"Are you awake?"

"Barely."

I rolled over to check the clock on my night stand and wasn't surprised to see it was after eight o'clock. I seldom sleep past five, but the past few days had wreaked havoc with my normal routine.

Normal routines. I groaned quietly, rolled out of bed, and made a bee line for the coffee pot.

"Why the hell are you calling me at this hour?" I asked Rye.

"Are you always this pleasant in the morning?"

"Wouldn't you like to know." I pressed the on-switch and opened some blinds to another beautiful day. "And no, actually. I'm usually up and writing way before this."

"Candy Poppe's bond hearing is first thing on Judge Singh's docket this morning," Rye informed me. "She should be released by ten o'clock."

"Thank you," I stopped mid-blind. "Really, Captain. Thank you."

"I thought you might be interested."

"There's still no chance of Carter O'Connell getting out?"

"We been over this already, Ms. Hewitt."

"Well," I whined. "If you're willing to admit Candy might be innocent, then maybe Carter is, too."

"Have you ever even met the guy?"

I blinked at Snowflake. "Umm, no."

"But you still insist he's innocent? Based on what?"

I gave up. Arguing with Wilson Rye before my morning coffee was far too challenging. I thanked him again for his help with Candy and promised to be there at ten to pick her up.

"I thought that might be the case." He stayed on the line while I chose a coffee mug.

"Is there anything else, Captain?"

"We're still in agreement, right? You're going to keep quiet about the continuing investigation?"

I rolled my eyes and promised not to mention it to anyone, but he still didn't hang up.

"Anything else?" I held the coffee pot aloft, waiting for who knows what.

"Well," he sang. "I'm just a little curious is all."

"Oh?"

"Last night when you were asking about my family— my parents and kids and cats?"

"What about them?"

"I'm wondering why didn't you ask about my wife?"

"What!?" I spilled the coffee and burned my hand.

I did some quick thinking as I sucked on my index finger. Hadn't Candy assured me ages ago that Rye was single?

"Ms. Hewitt? Are you still there?"

I closed my eyes and prayed for strength. "Okay." My voice was exceedingly calm. "What about your wife?"

"I don't have one of those," he said and hung up.

***

Why me?

But I had too many other things on my mind to worry about whatever it was Rye wanted me to worry about. I showered and dressed, promised Alexis and Rolfe I would get them out of their current fix as soon as I got Candy out of hers, and drove to the police station.

I was trying to figure out where to go when a uniformed officer took pity on me. She directed me to a narrow hallway lined with straight backed chairs reminiscent of the one Alexis Wynsome had rested her curvaceous bottom on in Maynard Snipe's turret.

I sat my own skinny butt down and waited, staring at the closed door, through which I imagined Candy would emerge. Lord knows, there was nothing else to stare at. The drab beige hallway had no windows, no pictures, no outdated magazines piled up on an ugly end table. I almost felt like I was the one imprisoned.

I checked my watch occasionally, and by 10:15 had begun to worry something had gone wrong at the hearing.

When Lieutenant Densmore came out to join me, I was sure of it.

"The captain told me you would be here," he said. "How are you, ma'am?"

"I've been better, Lieutenant." I invited him to sit. "Is Candy okay?"

"The paperwork's taking a little longer than usual," he said as he took the chair next to me. "It's not every day we let a suspect in a first-degree murder out on bail."

Now, how exactly was I supposed to handle that statement? Especially since I had no idea how much Rye confided in this guy? I mumbled something about getting a headache and resumed careful watch of the door.

Densmore watched with me. "You know," he said after a few minutes. "I just can't figure it out."

I looked up. "What's that?"

"Who murdered Stanley Sweetzer. Can you?"

"All I know is Candy's innocent." I caught myself. "No matter what your boss says."

"And you're innocent?"

I blinked twice. "You don't happen to have an Advil on you?"

"I think we should keep looking."

I blinked again. "For the murderer? But Captain Rye has closed the case, correct?"

"Yes, ma'am. Once we get your sofa returned, we'll be finished with this one until the trial."

My couch. Here was a problem that might actually have a solution. I asked the lieutenant when I might expect to get it back.

"We can probably deliver it this afternoon. Would that be convenient?"

"Fine with me. Just don't tell Audrey Dibble."

"Let me guess, she has some weird problem with your sofa?"

"Apparently it's hazardous to my chakras."

Densmore chuckled. "Interviewing the Dibbles all week has been pretty entertaining."

"Audrey thinks it was jealousy, you know? She thinks someone was jealous of Stanley—either of his love life, or his job, or his money." I studied the lieutenant for a reaction, but he stared at the door and refused to catch my eye.

I leaned forward and tilted my head, blocking his view of the stupid door. "Is that what you think, sir?"

Densmore looked at me. "I think it's about the money we found. The Captain's told you about that, right?"

"He has. And if Stanley didn't win it from my ex, I would love to hear your theory."

"That money got him killed," Densmore said firmly. "Think about it, ma'am. Stanley Sweetzer was a fairly average guy. He had a good job and a pretty girlfriend. A nice apartment, some friends. Nothing out of the usual, except the load of cash in his apartment—"

"Jessie!" Candy teetered in the doorway.

I jumped up and ran to greet her.

***

"Can we have tea?" Candy asked for the third time in a row.

I stopped at a red light and once again assured her tea was on the way. "But let's get you home first, okay?"

No answer. She stared out the passenger window and chewed her knuckle. The light turned green and I hit the gas.

We repeated the same, not so compelling conversation several more times before we made it into our building, where I steered her toward the elevator. But the thing never works, and while I was busy throwing a few bad words at it, Mr. Harrison popped his head out of his door. I could have sworn the man was actually smiling, but I had too much on my mind to worry about the peculiar mood swings of Peter Harrison. I waved politely, guided Candy into the stairwell, and up to my place.

Bless her heart, Snowflake made a to-do the moment we entered. She purred and purred, and wrapped herself around Candy's ankles, making it almost impossible for her to walk.

Despite the cat, Candy followed me into the bathroom where I handed her my coziest, plushiest terrycloth robe.

"Take a shower," I told her. "It'll make you feel better, and then we can talk." I held up a hand before she could ask again. "With tea." I closed the door and waited to hear the water running before moving to the kitchen.

As I puttered around the stove, I noticed another message from Louise Urko blinking on my answering machine. This time I pushed the button and listened.

"Jessica!" Geez Louise's scream startled poor Snowflake. She jumped up and hissed at the phone jack as Louise informed us she had news. "Call me!"

I braced myself and dialed.

"Jessica!" She answered on the first ring. "I have fantastical news! I mean, beyond fantastical!" I held the receiver about a foot away from my ear as Louise continued, "Adelé's made *The Times* paperback list! *Windswept Whispers* will be number four by the weekend! And don't even get me started on your e-book numbers. Off the freaking chart! Blockbuster, Babe! This is it!" she shrieked. "It!!"

Oh, my Lord. Making *The New York Times* Bestseller List really is 'It!!' I did a little dance of joy around the kitchen counter, twirling a teaspoon over my head, and singing 'Blockbuster, Babe,' while Louise chanted a few thousand 'Fantasticals.'

Who knows how long we would have gone on like that if Louise hadn't gotten a grip.

"Gotta go," she chirped as we both came up for breath. "I'm off to Three P to do the lunch thing." Three P is our affectionate nickname for Perpetual Passions Press, my publisher.

"They're looking to re-negotiate your contract," Louise continued. "They want to release *Temptation at Twilight* in hardcover! Can you even believe it, Jessica? Hardcover!"

I allowed myself one resounding 'Hardcover, Babe!' before returning to sanity. I reminded my agent that our good fortune might be short lived. "I'm no longer making the evening news," I said. "And, of course, I did not kill Stanley."

"Oh, who cares?" Louise scolded. "Haven't you been listening to me? *The New York Times* Bestseller List!"

I laughed. "Okay, okay. But can't I still be grateful I won't need to finish *Temptation at Twilight* from a jail cell?"

"Don't be ridiculous, Jessica. Everyone knows you wouldn't hurt a fly."

***

Candy emerged from the bathroom and dumped the rather sad, beige, and totally un-Candyish skirt suit Anthony De Sousa had her wear for her court appearance at the front door.

"You're smiling," she told me as she padded over in her bare feet.

"It's good to have you home."

I pursed my lips and tried to stop my smiling, but images of *Temptation at Twilight* in hardcover were making me positively giddy. I pictured a deep blue jacket, with Adelé Nightingale's name imprinted in metallic gold…or perhaps silver. And with Alexis Wynsome sitting atop a glowing white stallion, a full moon in the background…

I looked up and scowled. Where in the world was Rolfe?

"Your couch?" Candy spoke loudly and I realized she had been standing before me, asking after my couch for who knows how long.

"Couch." I glanced at the empty spot where she was waving. "Lieutenant Densmore promised to bring it back later today."

"He's really nice, isn't he?"

I shook my head. Who else but Candy Poppe would consider one of the cops who threw her in jail 'really nice?'

"I do believe Densmore thinks you're innocent." I directed her toward the easy chairs and carried over the tea. "No matter what his boss insists," I added dutifully.

"And you think I'm innocent, right?"

"I do." I sat down across from her. "So let's try to figure this out."

"But how?" she whined. "I don't know who killed Stanley. I've been thinking about it all the time, and I really, really don't know."

"Lieutenant Densmore thinks it has something to do with all the money they found in Stanley's apartment," I suggested. "Have you given any more thought to that?"

"Didn't we decide it came from his poker games?"

"Apparently the cops have ruled out that out."

Candy started chewing her knuckle, which looked like it had taken quite a bit of abuse the past few days.

"What about Stanley's job?" I asked. "I understand he had gotten a promotion?"

"Gosh, how do you know about that, Jessie? It just happened."

"When?"

"A couple of weeks ago. Mr. Dent made Stanley a Senior Investment Analyst. Stanley was, like, super excited about it."

"Was anyone at his office not so super excited?" I asked. "Was anyone jealous?"

"Thomas Fell," she answered without hesitation. "You remember him from the funeral? Thomas was the one who's almost as old as you are."

I thanked her for the reminder. "He was anxious to get my business, correct?"

"That's Thomas alright."

"He was angry about Stanley's promotion?"

Candy looked down and studied her tea. "I know what you're trying to do, Jessie, but I don't think so, okay? I don't like this—blaming people for killing Stanley."

I gently reminded her that someone was to blame. "And unless we figure out who, you and Carter are in worse trouble than ever befo—"

Oops.

She looked up. "You know about Carter and me?"

"Umm." I swallowed. "Captain Rye might have mentioned something."

Candy tilted her head, waiting for more.

I took a deep breath. "I'm sorry, Sweetie, but I thought I should know the details if I'm going to try to help you. So I checked for you and Carter in the *Clarence Courier's* web site.

She wrinkled her nose. "Did you find that article about Judge Sheppard?"

I nodded.

"It was awful, huh?" Candy looked like she was about to cry. But she quickly recovered, sat up straight, and looked me in the eye. "I've been really, really good since then, Jessie. I swear to God, I have."

"I know that, Sweetie."

We shared an awkward silence.

"I looked up all of our neighbors while I was at it," I said eventually.

That perked her up. She sat forward and asked what I had learned. "Has anyone else ever been arrested?"

I shook my head. "Not that I know of. The *Courier* had nothing at all on Bryce."

"Why not?"

"Well, the guy's only lived in Clarence a couple of years. It's probably a good thing he hasn't been in the news." I sipped my tea. "I didn't find much on Karen, either. The web site doesn't go back to when she was in school."

"I wonder what she was like in high school," Candy said. "I wonder if she ever got in trouble."

I shrugged. "I have no idea. But what she did—what anyone did—in high school really isn't the issue, is it?"

"Why did you look her up then?"

Okay, good question.

I shrugged again. "I must be turning into a nosey old lady."

For some reason Candy didn't argue. I sipped my tea and thought about our other neighbor.

"I looked up Peter Harrison, too," I said.

Indeed, my research into our most reclusive neighbor had yielded surprising results. The *Clarence Courier's* web site had a plethora of articles on him. It seems Mr. Harrison had enjoyed a successful career teaching music and band at Clarence Central High School. He had been named Teacher of the Year on a regular basis, and his star students were forever earning this or that music scholarship or award.

"Did you know him in high school?" I asked.

"Mr. Harrison?"

I summarized my research and Candy's eyes got wide. "You mean, our Mr. Harrison." She pointed downward. "Is *that* Mr. Harrison?"

"Apparently so. The last article I found was about his retirement party. It was from the same year you and Carter—" I stopped.

"The same year we went before Judge Sheppard?" she asked.

"I take it you were never one of Mr. Harrison's students?"

"Carter and me didn't do any school activities like that. I was never in the band or chorus or anything." Candy scowled, apparently recollecting the old band teacher from her school days. "He looks a lot different than he used to."

"He's been sick," I reminded her.

"I wonder when he got so grouchy."

"I wonder about Karen," I said. "Maybe she knew him when she was at Clarence High." I frowned at Snowflake and made a mental note to ask Karen about it.

"What about you, Jessie?"

I looked up. "What about me?"

"What were you like in high school?"

Oh, good Lord. It was one thing to ponder everyone else's ancient history, but why bring up mine?

"Fair's fair," Candy said. "Tell me."

"I was tall and unpopular. Not many kids were interested in shooting pool. And other than basketball, that's all I cared about."

"Boys must have liked you."

I shook my head. "Like I said, I was too tall. And too competitive. Boys didn't like losing to girls back then."

"I bet you were smart, though. I bet you got straight A's."

"Well, yeah."

"And you never got into trouble."

I smiled to myself. "Not in high school, anyway."

"Not ever," Candy insisted. "I bet you've always been good."

I took a deep breath. "Umm, Sweetie?" I asked. "Have I ever told you how I paid for college?"

Chapter 19

After learning about my own sordid past, Candy told me I'm a little scary and went home to rest. She may have agreed to stay inside and hide, but I was not so inclined. Talk about a little scary—I was planning a visit to Boykin and Dent Investment Associates.

Thus I donned hose and heels for the second day in a row. "So much for my Huck Finn impersonation," I complained to Snowflake as I added pearls to the silk blouse and skirt ensemble I pulled from the back of the closet. This was my typical book-signing outfit, and I hoped it would make me look like a professional woman of means.

I ate a quick lunch and headed down to Stanley's place of employment before I had time to change my mind or contemplate the consequences. If Captain Rye ever found out what I was up to, my cat would likely be orphaned.

I found the building, one of the few skyscrapers in Clarence, and hopped on the elevator to the top floor. Perhaps by the time I arrived at the Boykin and Dent offices, I would have some small clue as to what exactly I planned on doing.

An impressive wall of floor-to-ceiling windows overlooking the Blue Ridge Mountains greeted me from across the room as I stepped off the elevator. I ventured forth over the plush carpeting and stood before a huge S-shaped desk, where I gave my name to the receptionist—one Roslynn Mayweather, according to her desk plate.

She, too, was impressive in a formal, business-like way. She wore a suit which was probably even more expensive than my own outfit, and had an equally expensive floral print scarf expertly arranged around her neck. Her makeup had also been expertly applied. And her hair? Well, you get the picture. Unlike Karen and me, Ms. Mayweather was a woman born to wear pantyhose.

"Welcome to Boykin and Dent Associates, madam. How may I help you?" was her pat greeting, which matched her pat smile, bright white teeth beneath bright red lipstick.

I gave my name, but when I mentioned I was there to see Vikki, I realized I didn't even remember Vikki's last name. Perhaps I should have planned this a bit more.

"Fitkin."

I glanced down at Ms. Mayweather and blinked.

"You want to see Vikki Fitkin," she repeated.

She pursed her perfect lips and directed me to a row of leather chairs. I sat down and obediently waited, trying to ignore the receptionist's almost incessant stares. She wasn't hostile, per se, but she did seem more curious than necessary. I checked my hose for runs. Finding none, I feigned interest in the decor.

Boykin and Dent's reception area was much more posh than the Clarence Police Station, but no less uncomfortable. I listened to some odd background music destroy a perfectly good Bob Dylan tune and wondered whether Karen Sembler might have built Ms. Mayweather's desk. No one entered, no one left.

I was back to admiring the view of the Blue Ridge when Vikki finally came out from behind the formidable looking door at Ms. Mayweather's right. As she crossed the expanse of carpeting, I noticed she was not nearly as well groomed as the receptionist. Although she, too, wore a business suit, Vikki's hair was tied back in a sloppy pony tail, her shoes were scuffed, and her nails were unpolished.

"Jessica Hewitt, right?" She extended her hand and then turned to the receptionist. "Ms. Hewitt was a client of Stan's, Roslynn."

I swallowed a cringe as Vikki guided me through the big, bad door.

***

Another huge and intimidating space loomed before me. But I barely had time to orient myself before Vikki came up from behind and veritably propelled me across the central space. We moved along at a rapid clip, but I still managed to peek around a few open doors. I noticed the offices to the left boasted floor-to-ceiling windows similar to those in the reception area. The offices to my right seemed much more humble, which I verified when Vikki directed me into hers.

She ushered me to a chair and took her seat behind the desk. "Now then," she said. "You're interested in some new investment opportunities?"

No, that was not at all what I was interested in. But I kept up the pretense and nodded eagerly.

Vikki cleared her throat. "You do have the—how should I say this—the means to continue investing, Jessica?"

I giggled and waved a hand, and told Vikki not to let Jimmy Beak's reports worry her. "I have plenty of money to keep going," I lied. "And I'm keen on trying again. I'm quite sure that's what Stanley would want me to do." I smiled brightly. "By the way, Vikki. Do you happen to have my file?"

"Pardon?"

"Stanley's file on me," I elaborated. "I'd love to see it if you do?"

Vikki frowned and informed me the police had confiscated Stanley's files. "That African American guy took them all," she said. "I understand yours was of particular interest."

She was still frowning, but I myself wanted to stand up and give a great big cheer for Lieutenant Densmore. If he had my file, that meant Vikki did not. And that meant I could likely bluff my way through this whole interview with no pesky repercussions.

I sat back and relaxed, and encouraged Vikki to tell me all about the financial opportunities still awaiting me at Boykin and Dent.

Unfortunately, she did just that. Thus I endured a mind-numbing explanation of the various and sundry ways I might invest my remaining fortune. With each new option, she set before me a mound of brochures and forms. I kept my eyes on the paperwork, hoping she wouldn't notice my yawns.

"What would you say are the riskier options?" I asked when she came up for breath. "Like the ones Stanley had me in?"

Vikki skipped a beat. "Pardon?"

"Oh, I know I've lost some money so far." I flung an arm into the air to demonstrate my devil may care approach to personal finances. "But Stanley promised we would make it up the next time around. I'm interested in making as much profit, or interest, or whatever, on the money I have left, as fast as possible." I crossed my legs and waited while Vikki wiped the scowl off her face.

"I'm not sure how to put this politely," she said to my knees. "But I wouldn't advise a woman your age to do anything that risky."

"Oh?"

"You see, Jessica." She folded her hands and carefully placed them on her desk. "As people get older, we usually suggest investments on the safer side, even if it does mean smaller returns."

"We?" I asked. "Does that mean all your colleagues would offer the same advice?"

She shifted slightly in her seat. "Not necessarily. But that would be my approach."

"Oh, dear." I furrowed my brow to demonstrate my perplexity and confusion. "I was so certain Stanley had the right idea for me. But then, of course, he died."

"Stanley didn't just die, Jessica," Vikki scolded. "Your friend Candy Poppe killed him. It was all over the paper this morning."

Well, darn. I sighed dramatically and feigned interest in the various brochures littering the desk while I thought of what to do next.

Eventually I looked up. "Candy didn't kill Stanley," I said in passing. "She was way too proud of him."

"Of Stanley?"

"Oh, yes." I nodded vigorously. "She was proud of the work he did here at Boykin and Dent."

Vikki actually snorted. And when she regained her voice she informed me that Candy Poppe had no idea what she was talking about. "She's not exactly a financial whiz kid, is she?"

I pretended to pout as Vikki continued, "Listen to me, Jessica. I know you were friends with the guy, but you don't want to waste any more of your hard earned cash investing in anything Stanley Sweetzer was pushing. In fact, I won't even discuss those options. It wouldn't be ethical."

I gasped in dismay. "Are you implying Stanley wasn't ethical?"

She offered yet another stern frown and pointed to her stupid brochures. "Let's see about actually improving your portfolio, shall we? How much money did you say you're looking to invest?"

I hadn't said, and did not intend to.

"I'm sorry, Vikki." I sat forward. "But if Stanley was unethical, why did he get that big promotion?"

She began tapping a pencil on her desktop as I continued, "Candy told me he had just been named Senior Something Or Other. Wouldn't that indicate he knew what he was doing?"

The pencil was moving a mile a minute. I waited patiently for an answer.

"Have you ever worked in an office like this?" she asked eventually.

I answered no, telling her the truth for once.

"I didn't think so." She grabbed who knows what tedious form out of the pile and poised her pencil above it. "Now then," she said. "What about your bank balance?"

What about it? I again resorted to honesty and told Vikki I had not brought any financial records with me that day.

"I suppose I'll just have to come back some other time." I stood up to leave. "When I have the information you require."

Vikki sighed and stood up also. She gathered her beloved brochures into one tidy pile and handed them to me. "In the meantime, be looking at these."

She opened the door and seemed about to escort me back to the reception area, but I assured her I could find my own way out.

"I've wasted enough of your time for one day," I said brightly.

She did not disagree, and shut her door behind me.

***

Okay, now what?

I stood for a moment before spying Stanley's name on a closed door on the left side, the posh side, of the big room. Hmm. I also noticed Thomas Fell's name on the door nearest Vikki's. Unfortunately, that door was closed, too.

But maybe that wasn't so unfortunate? No one was watching as I glided across the room to Stanley's office and tried the doorknob. Lo and behold, it was unlocked. I entered his office and closed the door.

***

Okay, now what?

The desk, of course. I scurried over and sat down in what had been Stanley's chair. I dropped all the garbage Vikki had given me in the waste basket and stared at his computer. It was turned off, and I dared not try it out. First of all, it would probably sing to me as it booted up, and I certainly wasn't about to make any noise. And what the heck would I do with it even if I did get it turned on?

I had no idea, so I started rifling through Stanley's desk instead. Lieutenant Densmore might have absconded with all the important stuff, but there was still a plethora of paperwork in those drawers. And lo and behold, I found a little black address book wedged into a stack of stupid brochures.

It was a small address book, I noticed. Small enough, in fact, that it would fit quite easily in my purse. I swiveled the chair around to admire the gorgeous mountain view as my right hand dropped the address book into my purse, which just happened to be open.

Suddenly less interested in the view, I stood up and headed to the file cabinet. I had just gotten the top drawer open when the door behind me squeaked. I pushed on the drawer and twirled around as it banged—and I do mean banged—shut.

I flinched hardly at all and smiled at Thomas Fell, who hovered in the doorway. I do believe I have never bared so many teeth in my life.

"Where do I know you from?" he demanded.

I walked forward with my right hand extended, at the same time reaching over to close my shoulder bag with my left. "Jessica Hewitt," I reminded him. "I'm a friend—excuse me—I was a friend of Stanley's. We met at the funeral?"

I kept smiling but put my hand down when Thomas ignored it.

"What are you doing here?" he asked. "And especially, what are you doing here?" He waved both hands, indicating Stanley's office.

"This is a bit embarrassing," I said. Well, that certainly wasn't a lie. "But I just finished a meeting with Vikki Fitkin, and then I saw Stanley's office on my way out, and, well, I'm sorry, but I just had to have a peek." Surprisingly, none of that was a lie either.

Thomas stared and frowned.

I kept talking, all too aware that he was blocking the pathway to my escape. "And once I got in here, I noticed this glorious view." I swung around and waved my hand with a flourish at the glorious view.

Proof that there is a God in heaven, someone else joined us before Thomas could bombard me with any more pesky questions. An old man came up from behind and literally pushed him aside to approach me.

"May I help you, madam?" he asked.

His sinister smile reminded me of the vile Maynard Snipe. But this guy still seemed far less hostile than Thomas, even if I now had two bodies to wrestle before I could ever make it out that door.

I stalwartly ignored the way my face was starting to ache and kept on smiling.

"Hello, sir," I said. "I was just telling Thomas here that I came to see Vikki Fitkin. But I'm an old friend of poor Stanley Sweetzer." I opened my eyes wide. "And I just had to see his office when I had the chance. And then this view." Again, I fluttered an arm toward the Blue Ridge. "Well, sir, I'm afraid I was in here admiring it a bit too long, wasn't I?"

I took a step toward the door. "Thomas was just showing me the way out."

"Arnold Boykin." The old man stepped up and extended his hand. I shook it and told him my name.

Mr. Boykin shooed away Thomas Fell—now my smile was genuine—and turned back to me. "You've been talking to Miss Fitkin, you say?"

"Oh, yes, sir. Vikki has been most helpful."

Mr. Boykin studied me. He didn't seem in any hurry to kick me out, and he hadn't grabbed a phone to call the cops either. I took the opportunity to conjure up my latent skills at flirting with old coots. Lord knows I had gotten enough practice back in my pool-hustling days. Lord also knows I had been three decades younger and prettier back then.

"May I be honest with you, Mr. Boykin?" I smiled demurely.

Boykin bobbed his bald head. "Oh, please, Miss Hewitt."

I batted my eyelashes, Alexis Wynsome style, and gave Boykin the basic lie about my investing with Stanley, yadda, yadda, yadda. "Before he passed away he was encouraging me to try again," I said. "That's why I met with Vikki today. But she gave me just the opposite advice, sir. And now I don't know what to do."

I sighed forlornly. "I do so wish someone with a bit more experience would help me."

Boykin blinked. I waited.

"You know, Miss Hewitt," he said eventually. "I was just heading out."

"Oh?" I murmured as he gave my legs some serious consideration.

Eventually his gaze made it up to my eyes. "May I be so bold as to buy you a drink?" He chuckled. "It must be happy hour somewhere?"

I giggled, veritably channeling Alexis Wynsome. "That would be lovely, sir."

I took his arm and refused to acknowledge Thomas Fell's glare as Arnold Boykin led me out of Stanley's office and toward the exit. By the time we rounded Roslynn the Receptionist's desk, Arnold and I were on a first name basis.

161

Chapter 20

"Stanley Sweetzer." Arnold Boykin shook his head and squeezed my knee. "Such a terrible, terrible, tragedy."

We had settled ourselves into a booth at the bar on the ground floor of the office building. And instead of sitting across the table, like any normal human being, Boykin had sidled in next to me. The better for groping, apparently.

I was deciding how much pawing I was willing to tolerate when the waitress came over to take our order.

"The usual, Mr. B?" She spoke to Boykin but had her eye on me.

Mr. B enquired as to whether I liked champagne, and I murmured very much. But when he mentioned his usual preference, I coughed out loud. The waitress waited until I could nod a silent approval before she left us.

Oh my Lord, the old coot had ordered a bottle of the French stuff—the hundred dollars a bottle stuff. Now I was going to have to drink, and sleuth, and flirt, and be charming. All at the same time.

I took a deep breath and resorted to honesty. "Stanley died on my couch, you know?"

Boykin jumped. "Oh, my God! I mean, oh, my dear. Oh, you poor thing." He blinked his watery eyes. "You're the one who's been on the news, aren't you?"

I nodded solemnly. "I do hope you haven't been listening to Jimmy Beak, Arnold?"

"Oh, no, Jessica," Boykin assured me. "Jimmy had it all wrong after all. According to the *Courier*, Candy Poppe is to blame." He moved his hand an inch northward, and I smiled weakly.

"Is it warm in here?" I asked and unbuttoned the top two buttons of my blouse. No, it wasn't the sweet and charming Alexis Wynsome whom I was channeling. It was Ava La Tellier, the brazen hussy from *Windswept Whispers*.

Finally, our champagne arrived. We watched the waitress pour, and as she stepped away, Boykin offered another Snipe-like leer. "To Stanley," he said.

"To his memory," I added and took a dainty sip of my beverage. Good God, it was perfect. I fortified myself with another sip and got to work, reminding Boykin of my utter confusion about personal finances.

"I was so hoping Vikki would set me up in more of those whiz-bang investments Stanley was so fond of." I sighed for effect. "But she refused to do any such thing."

I fluttered my eyelashes, all woebegone and perplexed, but Boykin barely noticed the melodrama. He was too busy concentrating on his drink and my right thigh.

Okay, time for Ava La Tellier tactics. "You know, Arnold." I leaned in close. "Vikki may have even implied Stanley was unethical. But how can that be?"

"Be?" Boykin squeaked. He looked away and spent a moment wiping the sweat off his brow. Then he noticed his empty glass and worked on refilling it. This took a while, since he had only one free hand, and it was shaking.

"Am I making you nervous?" I asked gently.

"Oh, no, no, no."

I tapped his shoulder. "Oh, yes, yes, yes. What is it, Arnold? You can tell me."

The hand wandering around on my thigh had turned cold and clammy, but I contorted the cringe on my face into a smile as the old coot finally got around to answering me.

"Oh, Jessica," he said. "The sad fact is, Stanley's investment strategies weren't always so lucrative. You learned that the hard way, I'm afraid."

"But, Arnold!" I exclaimed, as aghast as can be. "My losses were just temporary, weren't they? Stanley promised I would do better next time."

Boykin shook his head, his eyes wide with fake sympathy.

"Oh dear." I sighed dramatically in yet another attempt at the demure, forlorn, perplexed act. "I must not understand these things very well. If Stanley wasn't doing a good job, well then, why did he get such a grand promotion? Wasn't he just named a Senior Investment Analyst?"

I tilted my head and watched as Boykin poured himself another glass of champagne. He gulped it down and suddenly remembered his wife was expecting him home early that afternoon. With one last grope for good measure, he excused himself and scurried out the door.

***

I breathed deep of the Boykin-free air. Another woman might have lamented her less than stellar sleuthing skills. But I looked on the bright side—a half-finished and fully paid for bottle of French champagne stood before me. I poured myself another glass and sat back to enjoy it in blissful, grope-free solitude.

I buttoned up and contemplated my latest findings. Okay, so Stanley was dishonest and disreputable. But I think I already knew that. I also knew he hadn't deserved a promotion. The mere mention of it got these Boykin and Dent people all atwitter. But why?

I hadn't a clue, but I did have Stanley's address book. I pulled it out from where it was lurking in my purse and began looking for anyone I might know. Clarence is a small enough city that this seemed likely.

Very likely, apparently. Right there under the A's was Camille Allen. So she had invested with Stanley after all. I moved on and searched for more familiar names. Lord forgive me, I looked for Bryce, and Karen, and the Dibbles. Not there. The Stones were missing, too.

I blinked at the champagne bottle. Hadn't Bryce told me the Stones had lost some money with Stanley? In fact, it was a real sore spot with Matthew, wasn't it?

"Curious," I whispered to the bottle and went back to my reading. I rifled my way backwards from the S's and noticed Candy's name in the P's. Candy Poppe had been one of Stanley's clients? Okay, now I was really confused. Something was odd about this little black book.

Little black book.

I sat up straight and started back at the A's. Why a young guy like Stanley would keep an old fashioned address book instead of a Blackberry for this sort of thing was beyond me, but I had far more interesting questions to ponder at the moment.

Such as Camille Allen. Her name glared up at me, and I groaned out loud. Camille wasn't one of Stanley's clients, she was one of his girlfriends.

I fortified myself with a bit more bubbly and studied each and every name in Stanley's book. Sure enough, they were all women. Forty-six of them. Fortunately or unfortunately, the only two names I recognized were Camille's and Candy's.

Okay, now what?

Upon further reflection, I realized I had missed an opportunity by not engaging Roslynn the Receptionist in conversation when I had the chance. I tossed Stanley's book into my purse and hastened back to the elevator.

***

"Hello again!" I chirped as I stumbled out of the elevator and brushed a non-existent stray hair from my brow. After consuming a fair amount of champagne mid-afternoon, acting a bit flustered wasn't all that difficult.

Roslynn Mayweather was unfazed, of course. All perfectly groomed and professional, she looked up from her computer screen.

"I'm sorry," I said, "but I think I left my keys here." I made a show of searching around the chair I had sat in earlier, where clearly there were no missing keys.

Exasperated, I sat back down. "Now where do you suppose they went?"

Roslynn squinted at me. "Did you leave them inside?" She pointed a red talon at the door leading to Boykin and Dent's inner sanctum.

I ignored her question and searched my purse instead. "Can you believe it?" I pulled out the keys. "I always do this. I drop them in here somewhere, and then have fits when I lose them in all this junk." I jiggled the keys like an idiot while Roslynn continued frowning.

"That Mr. Boykin sure seems like a nice fellow!" I smiled like an idiot. "This must be a nice place to work?"

"What are you doing here, Ms. Hewitt?"

Apparently Roslynn the Receptionist had gotten sick of playing games. She held my gaze until I looked away—not a common occurrence.

I slumped and gave up on all the exceedingly exhausting acting. "Stanley Sweetzer died on my couch last week, as you probably already know from Jimmy Beak. I'm here trying to figure out who killed him."

"Oh, my God."

"I was hoping to pin it on someone at this company," I continued baring my soul. "Since I really don't want it to be one of my friends or neighbors. And I especially don't want it to be Candy Poppe."

Roslynn cringed. "I read about that in the *Courier*," she said. "I'm really sorry."

"Do you know Candy?"

"She used to visit Stan here. And, of course, I shop at Tate's."

I was offering Roslynn what may have been my first genuine smile of the afternoon when Vikki and Evan barged out of the big, bad door. So much for smiling. I swallowed a scream and quick knelt on the floor, key searching in vain once again.

"Jessica?" Vikki stopped short. "Are you still here?"

"Jessie?" Evan McCloy sounded even more confused. He scowled down at me, and I was busy devising who knows what response, when Roslynn answered for me.

"She's lost her keys," she told them. "You guys go ahead. I'll help her look."

They hesitated, but she waved them toward the elevator. Once we heard it make its way downward, Roslynn came out from behind her monstrous desk and sat down with me.

"I could really use some help getting Candy out of this mess," I told her. "What do you know?"

"I know you're Adelé Nightingale!"

"Excuse me?"

"I'm a big fan, Adelé!" Roslynn was positively beaming. "I write romance stories, too, and you're my inspiration!" She leaned forward.

"Oh?" I managed as I leaned backward. I glanced down to make certain Roslynn the Wannabe Novelist wasn't clutching a dog-eared manuscript to her chest.

"I knew about you even before Jimmy Beak and Dee Dee Larkin," she was saying. "Candy told me all about you—that you actually live in her building."

She sat back and sighed. "I kept asking Stan about a million times to introduce me to you, but he was always too busy to bother with my problems."

"What else do you know about Stanley," I asked.

"Nothing more than you do. He loved Candy and he worked here."

I was certain the woman knew more than that and told her so. "Talk to me," I demanded and gave her one of the stern looks I usually reserve for Candy. "Candy's in serious trouble."

Roslynn pursed her lips and stared out the window, obviously calculating a deal. "If I tell you what I know," she said slowly, "will you do something for me?"

I took a wild guess at what was coming. "I can't get your book published for you," I said firmly.

"Oh no!" Her face turned almost as red as her fingernails. "I wouldn't ask anything like that!"

"Oh?"

"No," she insisted. "But I'm just dying to have an editor or an agent at least read my stuff. Couldn't you put in a good word for me with someone you know? Please, oh please?"

I thought about Geez Louise and decided she owed me one.

"Okay," I said. "You tell me, and the police, anything and everything you know that might help Candy, and I'll read what you have."

Roslynn stood up and started pacing in her perfectly polished pumps.

"And if I think your work has any merit whatsoever," I continued, "I'll send it along to my agent Louise Urko. Deal?"

"Deal!" Roslynn shrieked and started jumping up and down. "Louise Urko!" She held her fists up in victory. "She's, like, the absolute best!"

"If I ask you to sit back down, will you promise not to hug me?" I asked.

She dropped her arms. "Sorry." She sat back down. "But I'm just so excited. I mean, this is beyond fantastic!"

It occurred to me that Roslynn Mayweather and Louise Urko were made for each other.

"Okay, so start talking," I ordered. "What do you know about Stanley that I don't?"

Roslynn took a deep breath. "I know he was blackmailing Billy Joe Dent."

Now I was the one to get excited. "Dent, not Boykin? Over what? Do the police know?"

"Dent," she answered. "Over me, and no."

I blinked twice. "Keep talking, Roslynn."

"I had an affair with Billy Joe Dent." She waited while I let that sink in. "And in return, he gave me this cushy job in this nice building and pays me a fortune to do virtually nothing all day."

She appealed to me, "You understand, Adelé? I'm a writer. I need time to write, but I also need to make a living." She tilted her perfectly coiffed head toward the desk. "So I get to sit there, earn a fantastic salary, and write my stories all day."

"And Stanley found out?" I asked.

"Stan had a way of finding out about everything," she said. "It was kind of uncanny."

"How did he learn about this?"

"I'm not sure, but he threatened to tell his mother."

"Excuse me?"

"Mrs. Sweetzer would have told Mrs. Dent, since Mrs. Dent used to babysit her. The families are, like, this close." Roslynn held up her crossed index and middle finger.

I stared at her manicure and pondered the other babysitting connection I had recently learned of. Stanley's mother used to babysit Amanda. Who else in Clarence was part of this odd, babysitting circle of weird women, I wondered.

"Billy Joe gave Stan a promotion to keep him quiet," Roslynn was saying.

"And some cash, presumably."

"Huh?"

I thought better of discussing the money Rye had found in Stanley's apartment. I shrugged and said something vague about Stanley demanding some cash, too.

"It wouldn't surprise me," Roslynn agreed.

I took a deep breath. "And the police weren't informed of this affair?"

She shook her head. "I have no idea what anyone else around here told them, but I sure didn't say anything." She again indicated her desk. "Call me shallow, but I like this arrangement."

I stared at her desk and thought about the arrangement.

"Umm, Roslynn?" I asked casually. "Could Billy Joe Dent have something to do with it?" I emphasized the 'it,' hoping she would get the implication.

She did. She asked exactly what time Stanley had died.

"Around nine," I answered, and her shoulders relaxed.

"No." She spoke with confidence. "Billy Joe was with me. His wife thinks he plays poker on Saturday nights."

I ignored the headache I was getting and continued clarifying, "This relationship is still going on then?"

"Like I said, call me shallow."

Speaking of which, I pulled Stanley's little black book from my purse.

"What about Stanley's love life," I asked and handed her the book. "Do you know any of these women?"

Roslynn paged through the thing. "This is Stan's?" she asked. "Where did you get it?"

"I kind of found it in his office." I shrugged. "It, umm, practically jumped into my purse."

"You actually got into Stan's office?" Roslynn stared at me in wide eyed amazement. "That's been locked ever since he died."

"Not today. I walked right in."

"Well, that's really strange." She glanced over at the big, bad door. "The cops told us to stay out of there until further notice."

"Maybe someone needed a file or something," I suggested. "Thomas Fell caught me, by the way. He asked a lot of pesky questions about what I was doing."

"You should have asked him the same thing. He had no right to be in there, either."

An intriguing observation. But I decided to think about Thomas later and tapped Stanley's address book. "Were any of those women important to Stanley? Was he fooling around on Candy?"

"Absolutely not." Roslynn seemed certain of that. She took a cursory look at a couple of names before handing the book back to me. "I mean, Stan was pretty popular. But once he met Candy, the guy was a goner. It was L-O-V-E, love."

I opened to the A's and pointed to Camille's name. "What do you know about her?"

"Camille Allen." Roslynn read the name out loud. "Never heard of her."

Well, darn.

"Okay, so what about Stanley's clients?" I tried. "Was anyone mad at him about their investments? I get the impression they should have been."

Roslynn swore she had no idea. "I pay, like, zero attention to what goes on back there." She waved impatiently at the stupid door. "Sorry I can't help you more."

"Are you kidding?" I argued. "You've been an amazing help."

Because of Roslynn, I now understood the logic behind Stanley's promotion, and I was fairly certain where all that money had come from. Finally.

I patted her knee and stood up. "E-mail me your book." I found a card in my wallet and handed it to her. "And once this fiasco with Candy blows over, I'll be glad to take a look."

Roslynn stood up and started jumping around again. "I think you're going to like it, Adelé! It's really sexy. I mean, really, really, sexy. Just like your stuff!"

"And meanwhile, you're going to call the cops and confess all," I reminded her. "That's the deal, correct?"

"When?" she asked.

"Now wouldn't be too soon." I headed for the elevator. "Captain Rye and I have become good friends," I lied. "I'll find out if you don't call him."

Roslynn shuffled some papers around on her desk until she found his business card. "Captain Wilson Rye!" she read and waved the thing enthusiastically. "I'm calling him right now, Adelé!"

Chapter 21

Lieutenant Densmore had delivered my couch while I was busy at Boykin and Dent, and it was waiting for me outside my condo when I arrived home. That was the good news. The bad news? Jimmy Beak and his cameraman were also waiting for me, resting their sorry butts on said couch and looking altogether too comfortable.

"Go away," I said as the cameraman stood up and got his equipment in gear.

Jimmy patted the cushion beside him and invited me to join him for a chat. Mighty gracious, considering it was my couch. I reminded him of this fact and again demanded he go away, not much caring that the camera was rolling.

"Now, now, Jessie," Jimmie scolded. "Let's remember our southern hospitality, shall we? Just set a spell and tell me all about your best friend Candy Poppe." He gave the camera what must be his standard meaningful look. "The mastermind of the plot to murder Stanley Sweetzer."

I rolled my eyes and waited as Jimmy continued on his merry way, "Sweetzer died right behind this very door!" He sprang up and pounded on my door for the benefit of his more forgetful viewers. "And on this very couch!" He waved frantically, and the camera scanned my couch accordingly.

"You guys must be having a really slow day," I said. "Isn't there some crisis with the school board you should be worrying about?"

Jimmy curled his lip. "I'm surprised a divorced and childless woman such as yourself would care about such things, Jessie. You're not exactly PTA material, are you? And besides," he continued before I slapped him. "The parties responsible for the unpleasant incident at the school board have decided to let bygones be bygones. They're getting married, and they've asked Superintendent Yates to be the matron of honor."

While I let that unlikely news sink in, Jimmy assured his viewers they could depend on Channel 15 to cover the impending nuptials. He then remembered that his more immediate purpose was to annoy me.

"I have in my hands a note from Officer Russell Densmore of the Clarence Police Department." He waved a slip of paper at the camera. "A note authorizing Jessica Hewitt to take her couch back, now that the Sweetzer case is closed, and the killers are safely behind bars."

As I reached out to grab Lieutenant Densmore's note, Jimmy held it up over his head. This might have kept it out of my reach under normal circumstances, but he didn't account for the heels I was wearing. I snatched it from him and mumbled something about trespassing on private property.

Undeterred, he faced the camera. "In fact," he continued ominously, "Channel 15 has just verified Captain Wilson Rye has left town. Now that Candy Poppe and her ilk are behind bars, he's decided to take an extended vacation."

"What!?"

"That's right, Jessie. Captain Rye is that sure your best friend is a cold-blooded murderer!" Looking like the Grim Reaper dressed in plaid, Jimmy lifted a long and crooked index finger and pointed it at my face.

Of course, the camera was also pointed at my face while he recited a thorough litany of Candy and Carter's past transgressions. Reminding his viewers that they had a right to know, he took pains to describe Candy in the most unflattering terms.

"How long have you known Candy Poppe was a convicted felon, Jessie?" Jimmy didn't wait for an answer. "And how about Carter O'Connell? And what about that charge of Grand Theft Auto? What possible explanation can you give for your best friend's, shall we say, interesting past?"

He shoved the microphone at me, but I am proud to say I remained stalwart and silent. I could have asked him how he got the idea that Candy is my best friend, since I don't even believe in the notion. All my friends are a blessing, and I would never label one as more important than another. And I could have informed him Candy Poppe was not behind bars, as he was so gleefully reporting, but I am not an idiot. And I certainly did have an opinion about Rye taking off at such a critical juncture, but I wasn't about to share that either.

Jimmy sneered as only Jimmy can sneer and tapped my nose with the microphone. "Don't you have anything to say, Jessie? Now's your big chance."

Well, if he insisted.

I ever so delicately took the microphone being offered. "Where's Dee Dee Larkin?" I asked.

Jimmy stumbled backwards and landed on the couch.

"How's that partnership coming along, Jimmy?" I stepped closer and gently bopped his nose with the microphone. "Has Dee Dee invited you to join her national team yet?" I turned to the camera. "After all," I said, "the public has a right to know."

Jimmy bounded to his feet and made a cutting motion across his neck until the cameraman finally shut off his stupid equipment. They packed up, and the microphone was veritably torn from my hands as they hastened to the stairwell.

I reminded myself of my non-violent nature and resisted the urge to give Jimmy's backside a good, solid kick to expedite the departure.

***

I waited until I heard the front door close before plopping down on my couch. Resisting the urge to take a good, solid nap, I read Densmore's note, which was far more polite than Jimmy had implied. The lieutenant apologized for keeping the couch so long and informed me that Captain Rye had gotten it cleaned. Bless his heart, Densmore even offered to come over and help me move it into my condo if I needed assistance.

I hoped that wouldn't be necessary and went downstairs to see if Bryce were home. He answered the door quickly, but the smile on his face disappeared when he saw me.

"Oh, hi, Jessie."

"Are you expecting someone else?"

He looked past me into the hallway. "I guess I was hoping to talk to Candy before I left for work."

"Shhhh!!" I hissed and pushed him back into his apartment.

"Jimmy Beak's on the prowl again," I said as I shut the door. "He doesn't know she's over there. If I have anything to say about it, no one will find out she's over there."

I frowned. "How the heck did you know she's over there?"

"I heard her in the hallway this morning." Bryce seemed startled, and I apologized for being so bossy. He continued, "I went out to see if the cops were back again. You know, searching the place or whatever? And there was Candy, standing around in her bathrobe."

"My bathrobe," I corrected him. "She had just gotten home from jail."

"That's what Candy said. She said you helped her a lot, Jessie. I was really glad she made bail, but she told me she wasn't in the mood to talk and went inside."

"She needs to hide, Bryce. And we need to let her."

He agreed with my wisdom and swore he wouldn't mention her whereabouts to anyone.

I told him about my couch. "Would you come help me with it?"

He nodded and went to find some shoes while I waited in his atrocious living room. Like all the apartments in our building, Bryce's had amazing high ceilings, a few brick walls, and some nice windows. But his decor of packing-crate tables and picked-up-at-the-side-of-the-road furniture ruined the elegant ambience. The electronics, on the other hand, looked way more elaborate than my own humble stereo system.

Bryce came out from his bedroom shod in sandals. Not exactly safety shoes, but I led him up the stairs and to my couch.

"How's Candy doing?" he whispered as he grabbed one end.

"She had a rough night." I struggled with my side of the thing and apologized for it being so heavy, but Bryce was unfazed. He's one of those tall, gangly young men whose strength can be surprising.

"This is better," I said once we had it in place and were sitting at opposite ends. Without the couch, my living room had looked rather forlorn. But now everything was back the way I liked it.

"Your apartment is so much nicer than mine." Bryce, too, was admiring the decor. "I guess it pays to buy actual furniture."

"My offer still stands, you know? I'll help you decorate anytime you're ready."

We both knew this would never happen, even though my preference for sleek furniture in soft grays and whites would probably suit a man's taste. But Bryce had other priorities to spend his money on—like rent and tuition.

I got up to start the tea kettle as Snowflake hopped up to inspect the couch. She paced along the back, sniffing daintily here and there, as if she had never seen the thing before.

Once she decided the couch could stay, she settled down near Bryce's head and started swatting at his pony tail. Bless his heart, he ignored his allergies, and offered her the requisite pat and three sneezes before moving to a barstool at the counter.

"So what's the deal with Candy?" he asked. "She's gonna get off, isn't she?"

I said I certainly did hope so, but was quick to point out Captain Rye had closed the case. "He's off on vacation, and meanwhile Carter O'Connell's still stuck in jail."

"Rye's on vacation? You're kidding?"

"I wish I was." I pushed our tea cups across the counter and sat down. "But don't worry. I'll prove Candy's innocence myself if need be."

"I've got something to confess, Jessie."

"Oh?"

Bryce picked up a teaspoon and stirred it around the sugar bowl, creating a lovely whirlpool design. "Rye caught me with that picture you gave me last night. He was kind of mad about it."

He winced as if he expected a scolding, but I assured him Rye is always angry about something. "You did your best."

"Which wasn't too good." He scooped two teaspoons of sugar into his cup, completely ruining his artwork. "How about you? Have you learned anything useful?"

I shrugged. "I've learned all kinds of things. Who knows what might be useful."

"Did Karen get anything out of Evan?"

I perked up. "She did great, actually. She found out Stanley got a promotion right before he died. So I paid a visit to Boykin and Dent today."

"You went over there?" Bryce was clearly impressed. "What'd you find out?"

"Stanley had some enemies at work. Believe it or not, he was actually blackmailing his boss."

"I can believe it. Did the boss kill him?"

I said I doubted it, and gave a brief summary of the other employees, while Bryce used the teaspoon to tap out a tune on the edge of his cup.

"Of all the Boykin and Dent people, Thomas Fell seems the most suspicious," I concluded. "Do you know him, Bryce? Maybe he was with Stanley the other night?"

He shook his head and insisted he had no recollection of any Thomas at The Stone Fountain.

"Well then, I probably wasted my whole afternoon." I sighed dramatically. "I'm getting nowhere."

Bryce put down the spoon. "Come on, now. What about all the people at the bar you've been talking to? You've had to learn something?"

"Like from the Dibbles? Other than drinking me into bankruptcy, they've been completely useless. And don't you dare tell Audrey I have my couch back."

We turned to observe my sinister couch, where Snowflake had settled down for a nap.

"Let me guess," Bryce said. "It's got cooties?"

"Who knows what it's doing to my chakras, even as we speak."

"The only thing dangerous about that couch is the cat hair."

We turned back to our tea. "Umm, Bryce?" I said as he returned to his tapping the teacup. "What do you know about the Allens?"

"What about them?"

"They remind me of the Dibbles." I shrugged and tried sounding nonchalant. "They seem kind of unhappy."

"Kind of? What's up with the Allens?"

"I don't know," I lied. "But I'm getting so nosey. I'm wondering if they'll stay together."

"I think so—they like fighting with each other." Bryce tapped faster. "But then again, I thought Stan and Candy would stay together. Until this Carter guy came along." He stopped tapping and the spoon froze in midair.

"What?"

"I have an idea, Jessie. But you're not gonna like it."

I rolled my eyes and told him he was starting to sound like Rye. "Spit it out."

"Maybe it was Candy's new boyfriend after all."

"What? How can you say such a thing, Bryce? We don't even know Carter O'Connell."

"That's what I'm getting at." He held my gaze. "We don't know him."

"But Candy knows him," I argued. "She's known him since high school." I frowned at my own words—emphasizing Candy and Carter's history together wasn't exactly the greatest defense.

"Maybe Carter's not as nice as she thinks he is," Bryce was saying. "Stanley sure wasn't."

Okay, good point.

The phone rang, and we jumped in unison. I hopped up to answer.

"What the hell do you think you're doing?" Captain Rye was his usual cordial self.

"Well," I said slowly. "I'm having a cup of tea with Bryce Dixon."

"Excuse me?"

"Tea, Captain." I winked at Bryce. "Bryce takes his with sugar."

Rye took a deep breath. "Get rid of him, Ms. Hewitt. We need to talk."

Chapter 22

I would have refused to kick out my guest so rudely, but Bryce was already leaving. I held my hand to the receiver. "Remember, Bryce. Mum's the word on Candy being home?"

He put an index finger to his lips and shut the door behind him.

"Okay," I said into the phone. "You've successfully scared away poor Bryce. Now what's this about you being on vacation? Are you insane?"

"Vacation?"

"Don't mess with me, Captain. I've had a very long day, and then came home to find Jimmy Beak camped out on my couch. He took great pleasure in informing me you've skipped town."

"My whereabouts aren't the issue, Ms. Hewitt. It's yours we're talking about."

"Mine?"

"Yes, yours. Tell me about this long day you've had. Starting with your visit to Boykin and Dent. I thought we agreed you would leave things to me."

"Nooo," I argued. "We agreed I wouldn't go around announcing you're still working on the case." Rye started to protest, but I continued, "I never said I would stop looking. I have uncovered a few interesting facts, by the way. That is, once you decide to return from vacation."

While Rye did some deep breathing exercises on the other end of the line, I joined Snowflake on the couch and took off my shoes.

"Captain Rye?" I asked as I rubbed my feet. "Are you still there?"

"I just got off the phone with Roslynn Mayweather. That name sound familiar?"

"Roslynn the Receptionist? Oh, yes, sir. I spoke with her this afternoon and insisted she call you."

Rye may have whined.

"Aren't you even interested in what I learned?"

"Do I tell you how to write your love scenes?" he asked.

"Excuse me?"

"Do I tell you how to do your job? Did you really think Ms. Mayweather's affair with Billy Joe Dent would be news to me?"

I sat forward. "You knew about this?"

"Densmore's been questioning Dent for days. I will say Ms. Mayweather's finally coming clean about it was," he hesitated, "satisfying."

"That's where the money came from, correct? Stanley was blackmailing Dent?"

"It accounts for some of it, yes. What isn't accounted for is Dent's whereabouts Saturday night."

"He was with Roslynn," I said.

"Not such a great alibi. At least he's stopped lying about the non-existent poker game, but his claim about being with his mistress has almost as many holes."

"But Roslynn can corroborate for him. She told me point blank Dent didn't do it."

"And you believed her?"

"Intuition tells me she wasn't lying."

"You're kidding, right? For someone who's so eager to find a murderer, you're way too willing to let people off the hook." I tried to defend myself, but Rye was on a roll. "Listen to me, Jessie. If Candy Poppe isn't the killer, someone you know and trust is. You need to be careful.

"Speaking of which, what's this about you rifling through Sweetzer's office? You're a little scary, you know that?"

I had to admit it had been a little scary in Stanley's office. I cringed at Snowflake. "Did Roslynn mention that, too?"

"She says you found an address book?"

I described Stanley's little black book, expecting to get a stern lecture about stealing, snooping, and minding my own business. But Rye surprised me by showing some sincere, non-angry interest.

"I can't believe you found something my own officers overlooked, but I want it."

I told him he could pick it up anytime. "Believe it or not, I am trying to help."

"Yeah, right. And don't you dare start calling any of those women and harassing them. You understand me?"

"What about Camille Allen?"

Rye skipped a beat. "What about her?"

"She's in the book," I said. "I'm no expert, as you keep reminding me, but it appears she had an affair with Stanley."

"Do not, I repeat, do not go over to that damn bar and ask her about it. You got that?"'"

"Are you through issuing orders?"

He cleared his throat. "Please," he said quietly. "Just let it go. I'll have Densmore check into it."

I promised not to harass Camille. "Although it sounds like Lieutenant Densmore could use some assistance. What with you being on vacation."

"Will you stop it with the vacation? I may be out of town, but I am not on any vacation. Not that I couldn't use one—after dealing with you all week. Which brings us to another point."

"Oh?"

"What did you think you were doing with Boykin?"

"Do you mean Arnold Boykin?" I do believe I was starting to enjoy myself.

"Yes, Ms. Hewitt. The old letch you were cozying up to all afternoon. Roslynn Mayweather mentioned that, too."

I winked at Snowflake. "Are you jealous, Captain Rye?"

"Don't flatter yourself."

I swallowed my smile and reported the pertinent details of my conversation with the old letch. For the sake of the poor Captain's sanity, I omitted the channeling of my heroines thing, and the groping hand on the thigh thing.

"Let me get this straight," he interrupted. "You and Arnold Boykin shared a bottle of champagne?"

"French champagne," I elaborated and Rye groaned. "And between Vikki Fitkin's insinuations about Stanley's unethical business practices, and how nervous Boykin got when I asked about Stanley's promotion? Well, I knew something wasn't right."

He groaned again. "So you just happened to ask Rosylnn Mayweather about it."

"Exactly! All this mischief at Boykin and Dent must have some significance. For instance, it seems likely Stanley had quite a few irate clients."

"Believe it or not, Ms. Hewitt, we've already checked that angle. Densmore's a genius at this kind of thing. He's spent hours tapping into Sweetzer's computer files and questioning his clients."

"And?"

"And if he comes up with anything, you can learn about it from Jimmy Beak and the Channel 15 news crew, how's that?"

I ignored the sarcasm and moved on. "What about Thomas Fell?" I asked. "He was jealous of Stanley's promotion, and he was about to go snooping around Stanley's office when I caught him this afternoon. He had no right to be in that office, you know?"

"And you did? You're not just a little scary—you're a lot scary."

Again, I ignored Rye's tone and politely asked if Thomas Fell had an alibi.

Rye was back to the deep breathing exercises. "Believe it or not," he said, "reporting to you is not in my job description."

"Well, it should be. It's pretty annoying the way I keep giving you all these great ideas and you keep poo-pooing them."

"Pretty annoying about sums it up. Now, if you'll excuse me, I'm kind of busy."

"Oh?"

I swear I actually heard Rye roll his eyes. "Yeah, you know?" he said. "Trying to clear Candy Poppe, trying to nail the murderer, trying to keep you safe and out of trouble. All, of course, while I'm on this magnificent vacation."

"Oh?"

"Good-bye, Ms. Hewitt."

***

I once again resisted the urge to recline on my couch, put my shoes back on, and went downstairs to warn Candy.

"Who's there?" It was Karen's voice behind Candy's door, and she didn't sound all that hospitable.

"It's just me, for Lord's sake," I said. The door swung open and Karen yanked me inside. "What are you doing here?" we asked each other.

Karen looked me up and down. "Another funeral, Jess?"

"No. I paid a visit to Boykin and Dent this afternoon."

She smiled approvingly. "Did you get anything?"

"Apparently not."

Camille Allen popped into my head, but with one glance at Candy I decided to follow Rye's advice and let it be. Poor Candy was huddled in a corner of her pink—and I do mean pink—couch and absently munching on an Oreo. She was still in the bathrobe I had loaned her earlier, and she clearly did not look up to a discussion of her dead fiancé's other women.

"Nothing Rye didn't already know," I added and sat down on the couch.

"Well, darn!" Karen stomped a work boot and did an about face toward Candy's kitchen.

"Did you meet Roslynn?" Candy asked, and I told her we had an interesting conversation about writing.

"Publishing, actually," I corrected myself.

"She's real ambitious, huh?"

I nodded and then explained I hadn't had time to change my clothes since I got home. "But I wanted to get up here to warn you about Jimmy Beak, Sweetie. He's back."

"We know." Karen had returned from the kitchen. She handed me a glass of milk and sat down opposite us. "I came up to see how Kiddo was doing after what he did to her in his five o'clock report."

"She brought cookies and milk and everything." Candy waved an arm at the spread on her coffee table.

"I figured Kiddo needed some comfort food."

Karen pushed the Oreos in my direction, and while I ate a cookie, they took turns describing Jimmy's latest segment. Other than how quickly he had gotten the segment on the air, none of it was news to me. He had reported from my hallway, and on my couch, after all.

I grimaced. "I was actually hoping he wouldn't air it."

"No such luck," Karen said. "But at least he didn't bother Kiddo, personally. He must not know she's home yet."

Candy sat forward. "That's good. Huh, Jessie?"

"Very good. The fewer people who know you're here, the better."

"Even my parents must think I'm still in jail. My phone hasn't rung all day."

"How exactly did you know she was home?" I asked Karen.

"Hey, it's a small building."

I raised an eyebrow. "And?"

"And I heard her up here. What are you getting at, girlfriend?"

I shook my head and admitted I had no idea. "I'm a bit on edge, okay? But as long as everyone in the building can keep a secret, I think we'll be fine."

"Say what?" Karen faced Candy. "Don't tell me Bryce and Old Man Harrison know you're back?"

"It's a small building," Candy reminded her and took two more Oreos. "They saw me."

Karen groaned. "Not good, Kiddo."

"Don't worry," Candy said. "Mr. Harrison never talks to anyone."

"And Bryce promised me he'd keep quiet, too," I added.

Karen slapped her forehead. "You guys! You can't pay Bryce Dixon to keep a secret. He blabs to everyone over there." She waved haphazardly in the direction of The Stone Fountain and I had to admit she had a point.

Candy, however, didn't seem at all concerned. She grabbed another cookie and mumbled something about the icky jail food. I, too, ate a cookie and drank my milk. It wasn't the most nutritious dinner I've ever had, but it was convenient.

"Umm, Karen?" I said eventually. "Did you happen to know Peter Harrison when you were in school?"

"Say what?"

Just my luck, Candy stopped eating and explained. "Jessie's been learning all about everyone's past on the *Clarence Courier* web site," she said. "Wasn't that smart of her?"

Karen folded her arms and glared. "Say what?"

"Umm," I answered brilliantly as she continued frowning. I took a deep breath. "I'm getting desperate to figure things out, so I did a little research. I'm not proud of it, okay? And I hope you'll forgive me for being so nosey, but—"

"Are you going to tell me what you found out or not?" Karen interrupted.

"Well, if you insist," I said and gave her the gist of it. "Peter Harrison's stellar teaching career at Clarence Central High was news to me," I concluded. "Sweetie here says she was never in the band. But I thought maybe you were?"

"I was."

"What?" Candy and I spoke in unison. Do not ask me why we found this revelation so fascinating.

"What was Mr. Harrison like back then?" Candy asked. "He wasn't nearly as mean as he is now?"

"Why didn't we know about this before?" I asked. "You've never mentioned it, have you? What instrument did you play?"

Karen held up her hands to stop the onslaught of questions. "I played the clarinet, if you must know. And yes, Kiddo, Old Man Harrison wasn't mean at all back then." She turned to me. "And I'm sorry, but I didn't realize being in my high school marching band twenty years ago was all that noteworthy. You want we should discuss my old locker combination next?"

I mumbled that probably wouldn't be necessary and stood up to leave.

Karen got up also. "If Jimmy Beak starts bugging you, call me," she told Candy. "I'll run up here with my electric drill a-buzzing. That should scare anyone away."

***

Snowflake was sleeping on top of my computer when I arrived home. She opened one eye and glared, and I had to admit I had neglected *Temptation at Twilight* far too long. I shooed her to the windowsill and sat down to see how Rolfe and Alexis were faring without me.

Ever-resourceful, Rolfe Vanderhorn was busy re-shoeing his horse and planning his next dare-devil rescue of Alexis Wynsome. Meanwhile, our hapless heroine, now at the mercy of the evil Lord Derwin Snipe, sat fretting away in Derwin's dungeon, a space even more miserable and damp than his brother's turret.

But, lo and behold, when Derwin's maid came down the steep and treacherous staircase to bring her a cup of water and a stale crust of bread, Alexis recognized an old friend from childhood! Why, it was none other than Annabelle Goodloe!

An exciting moment, indeed, but I yawned and left Alexis and Annabelle to catch up on old times while I checked my e-mail.

A message from Roslynn Mayweather made me groan out loud. I braced myself and opened her attachment. "*Lush and Tender* by Roslynn Mayweather," I read on the title page. At least the woman had a good romance author-sounding name.

Roslynn the Romance Writer also had some talent. In fact, I was well into Chapter Four before I even noticed that the Channel 15 News vans had returned to Sullivan Street. They were parked in front of The Stone Fountain, but of course.

"Cross your fingers Bryce can keep quiet about Candy," I told Snowflake as I closed my computer.

I did twenty minutes on my exercise bike, took a very hot and extended bath, and crawled into bed.

But just as I was about to doze off, Captain Rye's ominous warning flashed through my mind. "If Candy Poppe isn't the killer," he had said, "someone you know and trust is."

"At least that rules out Jimmy Beak," I mumbled into the dark.

Chapter 23

Energized by a full hour of yoga, and armed with a full cup of coffee, I was at my desk by six a.m., working my way toward the exciting and unexpected conclusion of *Temptation at Twilight*. Indeed, the conclusion was so unexpected, even Adelé Nightingale didn't know what it might entail.

Rolfe Vanderhorn spent an exasperating morning trying to learn the layout of Derwin Snipe's castle. He spoke to the groundskeeper, the game warden, and the gardener. Although all three men were eager to help out, none of them had ever set foot inside the castle, and thus were no help whatsoever. And when Rolfe scanned the perimeter of the castle, he found nary a trace of a white hanky or anything else that might indicate where Alexis was being held.

Duly chagrined, he returned to his cottage to plan some more, little knowing that at that very moment, Alexis was enjoying an elaborate repast of roast pheasant with all the fixings which Annabelle Goodloe had sneaked down to Derwin's dungeon. The clever and resourceful maid also smuggled in some cushions and blankets. She plopped her ample self down on a pillow next to Alexis and reported what she had learned while eavesdropping on her employer.

The previous evening Alexis had explained her unfortunate plight to Annabelle, and the two women debated why oh why the Snipe brothers had taken such profound interest in her. After all, Alexis told Annabelle, she had nothing to offer these men that other women didn't have. Annabelle took a not so subtle gander at the more than ample bosom of her friend, but Alexis insisted there must exist some other, more substantial reason to explain the Snipes' behavior.

Annabelle had vowed to learn the truth before the cock crowed, and sure enough, she succeeded. It seems that Alexis, who believed herself to be an orphan, was in reality the long lost daughter of the king! How King Percival had managed to lose his baby girl twenty years earlier was a long story which Annabelle chose not to relate. And how the Snipe brothers had managed to learn the true identity of Alexis Wynsome also remained a mystery. But once they figured it out, the evil duo devised their dastardly plans to kidnap the lovely lady.

Annebelle warned her friend of the brothers' evil intentions. For that very day they planned on flipping a coin to determine which of them would marry Alexis, and hence, which of them would someday inherit King Percival's entire realm! Annabelle expected Alexis to be upset at the idea of a forced marriage to one of the vile Snipe brothers, but Alexis only smiled serenely.

"Rolfe will make a fine king someday," she mused.

***

Alexis may have been certain of the future, but I had no idea what twists my plot would take before it arrived at its inevitably happy ending. And Snowflake was insisting on lunch. I fed her, and myself, and went for a walk.

Between thinking about Candy Poppe and her problems, and Alexis Wynsome and hers, I walked up and down the streets of downtown Clarence, barely noticing where I was going. I had found my way back home, and was in the lobby sorting through my mail when Peter Harrison poked his head out of his door. He held his position and stared at me until I had to look up.

"May I interest you in some iced tea?" he asked, and I dropped my mail.

Not the most gracious response, but I hurriedly accepted his invitation, collected the papers I had dropped, and crossed the threshold into Peter Harrison's home. It may have been the most surrealistic moment of my week.

He waved me toward the couch, but the piano caught my eye. I walked toward it, not even bothering to hide my curiosity. "I like your place," I said as I glanced unabashedly at the manifold photographs, placards, and certificates lining the walls. I also noticed the furniture, all of which looked like expensive family heirlooms and antiques. But the piano took center-stage.

"This is a grand piano, isn't it?" I asked.

"A baby grand, yes. Do you take sweet tea?"

I looked up. "Whatever you're having, Mr. Harrison. Thank you."

He told me to call him Peter, and when I dropped my mail again, I do believe the man actually giggled. He invited me to take a seat, and this time I obeyed, settling myself and my stupid mail on the couch while he went to retrieve our beverages.

"You say you've never played, Miss Hewitt?" Mr. Harrison tilted his head toward the piano as he came back into the room.

"It's Jessie," I said. "And, no. I have no musical talent."

"Oh, I doubt that." He set the iced tea on front of me and sat down. "Just look at those hands." He pointed to my hands, and I looked at them as if they were brand new.

"You have very long fingers," he explained. "Perfect for the piano. You could reach more than an octave without even trying." He leaned forward. "May I?"

I blinked twice as Peter Harrison gently grasped my right hand and stretched it wide open.

"You see!" He peeked at me from between my outstretched fingers. "An octave and one. No doubt about it!"

Okay, so maybe *this* qualified as the most surrealistic moment of my week.

"Are you feeling well, Mr. Harrison?"

"Peter," he reminded me and let go of my hand. "And yes, actually. I'm feeling better than I have in years." He threw his own hands into the air and laughed out loud. "Fit as a fiddle, Jessie!"

I blinked again.

"Oh, dear," he said and calmed himself down a bit. "Have I really been behaving that badly?"

"Umm, you do seem to be in a better mood than usual."

"It was all the medication!" he exclaimed. And with that my new and improved neighbor offered an extensive list of this, that, and the other prescription drug in his former pill-popping regimen. Trust me, I did not take notes, but I did stay alert for the word Phenobarbital. It never came up.

"I've gone cold turkey," he said proudly. "On four of them, anyway. And Doctor Trotter—he's my new physician—has cut my dosage of all the rest in half!" Peter clapped his hands. "He told me I was poisoning myself. Can you imagine?"

I think I could. My neighbor's personality had apparently transformed overnight.

"But enough about me," he said. "I wanted to ask after Ms. Poppe."

I cleared my throat. "Oh?"

"I was so relieved when I saw you two in the lobby yesterday, Jessie. I assumed the *Clarence Courier* had been wrong after all. But then I watched Jimmy Beak." Peter waited until I would look at him. "May I ask what's going on?"

He cocked his head and smiled, and I had to think fast. Was all this newfound friendliness just an act to trick me? Was the old man some sort of spy for Jimmy Beak?

"Candy's been released on bail," I admitted, since he already knew she was home. "But apparently the media have not been informed. We're hoping to keep it that way, Peter."

"Oh, absolutely. Whatever Jimmy Beak insists, the public does not need to know." He sighed dramatically. "I've often worried her past transgressions would come back to haunt her."

I sat up straight. Of course Peter Harrison would know about Candy's sordid high school career!

"Has Ms. Poppe ever mentioned I worked at her high school?" he asked, and I nodded mutely. "She was a little hellion back then. But I've always believed in giving young people a second chance."

I studied my neighbor. "So you rented her an apartment?" I pointed at his ceiling and towards Candy's place. "Even though—" I stopped myself.

"Even though I was in such an unpleasant mood?" he helped me out. "I may have been cranky, but I still had my principles. Candy Poppe deserved the benefit of the doubt."

"She still does," I said. "She's innocent."

"Oh, absolutely. I'm counting on you to keep me posted, Jessie. Will you do that?"

I offered the vaguest of nods and changed the subject. "I understand Karen Sembler is one of your former students?"

"Now there was musical talent!"

"Excuse me?"

"Miss Sembler!" He clapped his hands gleefully. "She played clarinet, she sang, she danced. Oh, my!"

Oh my, indeed. Karen Sembler singing? And dancing?

"She has a lovely soprano voice," Peter continued. "It was such a shame, really."

"A shame?" I prompted.

But bless his heart, the new, downright chatty Peter Harrison needed no prompting as he delved on in to Karen's ancient history. It seems she had auditioned for the lead in her senior class play, but had not gotten the part.

"We did *The Sound of Music* that year," he said. "Karen Sembler should have been our Maria. She knew it, too."

"Why wasn't she?"

"She auditioned perfectly. I was there, of course, being the band director." He sighed dramatically. "But I wasn't in charge of casting. And the lady who was? Well, she insisted Maria should be beautiful."

My face dropped. "And Karen wasn't."

Peter nodded. "She was offered only a minor part— one of the children, if I recall. She quit after that."

"Karen's a high school drop out?"

"Oh, no, no, no," he hastened to correct me. "She dropped out of the band, though. And chorus."

I shook my head in dismay. "You are a font of information, sir."

"Do forgive my gossiping, Jessie? I suppose I've been so unfriendly for so long—"

"You're making up for lost time," I helped him out. "Fine with me." We giggled in unison as I got up to leave.

"Have you ever spoken to Karen about what happened?" I asked at the doorway.

"We never have discussed old times. I suppose my cranky mood hasn't encouraged confidences." He glanced across the lobby at her door, behind which who knows what power tool was humming along. "But I'm sure Miss Sembler has moved on," he added. "After all, it was twenty years ago."

***

Twenty years ago, I reminded myself as I climbed the stairs to Candy's. I reached out to knock on her door. "It has nothing to do with Stanley," I said firmly.

"What has nothing to do with Stanley?" Candy asked.

I swear she had answered before I even knocked. I took in the figure—and I do mean figure—before me. Candy stood in her doorway, resplendent in a pink sequined mini dress.

"You haven't been out, have you?" I pointed to the silver stilettos adorning her feet.

She gave her shoes a brief glance. "Gosh, no" she said. "But I'm going stir crazy sitting around and hiding all day, so I got dressed up to make me feel better."

She waved me inside and tottered over to her ridiculous pink couch, which provided a perfect backdrop for her outfit. I shook my head and took a seat.

"Can't we please go out tonight?" Candy was saying. "Pretty please. Just over to The Stone Fountain, okay? Just for a few minutes?" She held her palms together, appealing to me.

"Jimmy Beak was over there last night."

"Yeah, but I bet he'll be somewhere else tonight. He gets bored just working on one story."

"No," I said in no uncertain terms.

"I feel like I'm in jail all over again," she whined.

I folded my arms and glared.

"It's Friday night and everything," she tried.

I kept glaring.

"I'll go alone, then," she said and gave her head a defiant toss. "Or I'll get Karen to go with me. Someone has to figure out who killed Stanley. You've said so yourself, Jessie. Lots of times."

Okay, so the girl did have a point. I gave up on glaring and noticed the triumphant smile on Candy's face.

"If we are actually going to do this," I said, "I am going to need some Advil.

Candy bounded off the couch and scurried to the phone. "I'll tell Karen eight o'clock, okay?"

"Lots and lots of Advil," I muttered.

"Don't worry, Jessie." She tapped out Karen's number with a silver fingernail. "If Jimmy Beak shows up, we can always hide under the pool table. Just like last time!"

***

"Number two!" Louise Urko screeched from her end of the line, and I lamented not getting that Advil from Candy. "Blockbuster, Babe! *Windswept Whispers* is selling like hot cakes. Hotter than hot!"

"Speaking of hot, I have something for you."

"Fantastical! Please tell me you have finally, finally, finished *Temptation at Twilight*?"

"Almost," I answered. "Once I get a few details ironed out about King Percival's past—"

"I thought his name was Ralph?"

"Ralph?" I scowled at Snowflake and attempted to think like Geez Louise. Ah, yes. "You mean Rolfe," I told her. "He's the hero, but King Percival's the father. It seems he's been harboring some deep, dark secrets for the last twenty years. One of which is his long lost daughter, Alexis Wynsome—"

"What-everrrr," Louis interrupted. "I know you'll come up with something fantastical, Jessica. Just be sure there's plenty of sex scenes. Sex, sex, sex!"

I rolled my eyes and assured my agent I would e-mail her the completed manuscript, replete with assorted sex scenes, sometime the following week.

"While I'm at it, I'd like to send along someone else's work." I told Louise about Roslynn Mayweather and *Lush and Tender*. "Roslynn has great potential." I smiled to myself. "And I think the two of you will really hit it off."

"Well then, by all means send me *Lush and Tender*! You know I'm always on the lookout for fresh talent."

I tolerated a few further fantasticals before I reminded Louise it was Friday night and she shouldn't still be at the office.

"Thanks for reminding me, Jessica! I'm meeting Dee Dee Larkin for drinks. I'm working to land you a segment on her morning program!"

I groaned, but Louise didn't notice. "What about you," she asked. "Any plans for the night?"

"I plan on catching a killer and/or growing the mother of all migraines."

"Fantastical, Babe! Gotta go!"

Chapter 24

"What, no power tools?" I asked Karen as I emerged from the stairwell that evening.

She pointed across the lobby to her door. "They're charging up, girlfriend. Just let Jimmy Beak try bothering us."

"You guys," Candy pleaded. "Will you forget about all that? Let's have some fun, okay?"

Candy certainly was dressed for fun. As if her pink and silver outfit from earlier weren't festive enough, she had added an impressive collection of rhinestone jewelry to the ensemble and applied some silver eye shadow for good measure.

Karen, too, had risen to the occasion of a Friday night out after a long and difficult week. She still wore her basic uniform of jeans and work boots, but she had combed her hair, and may have even put on some lipstick.

I admired them both, and sweet Candy complimented me on my own outfit as she teetered her way out the front door. "That sweater is very sexy," she told me as we crossed Sullivan Street. "I bet Captain Rye would like it."

I bet Captain Rye would never see it, what with that stupid, stupid, vacation he was taking.

Bless her heart, Karen volunteered for the Jimmy Beak look out detail. Once she announced the coast was clear, we entered The Stone Fountain. The place was packed, but at the sight of Candy the crowd parted and let us pass to our barstools unhindered. I tried to convince myself it was the outfit that had everyone's attention, not the accused murderer wearing it.

Oh well. At least it was Pink Floyd night. While I enjoyed the ditty about needing no education, Bryce fetched our drinks, and Gina brought over a platter of nachos.

"The food in jail was awful," Candy said as she helped herself to a huge glob of nachos. "I couldn't eat hardly anything."

Bryce watched her shove the chip into her mouth. "Food's on the house tonight," he said. "How's that?"

She mumbled a thanks, and after swallowing, began to describe some sort of turkey-roll thing they served in jail.

Karen and I both dropped the chips we were holding.

"I still don't get you being in jail at all, Kiddo." Karen looked around impatiently and turned to me. "Where are the cops, Jess? Why aren't they in here solving this thing?"

I was busy shrugging when Candy answered for me. "I guess Captain Rye thinks he's done," she said quietly and licked some guacamole off her pinky.

"Well that's ridiculous," Karen argued. "Just because you got into trouble back when you were sixteen, doesn't give him the right to pin this thing on you."

Again she looked at me. "And what's up with you?" she asked impatiently. "I thought you had some influence with the guy. Can't you use your sex appeal or something?"

I told her to keep dreaming. "Wilson Rye makes a point of not listening to me."

"Don't be mad at Jessie." Candy actually put down a chip to defend me. "She's been real helpful, okay?"

"She's been snooping around in here almost as much as the cops," Bryce added.

I looked around the cop-free bar and told Karen she had a right to be frustrated. What was Rye doing anyway? And what was I doing for that matter? Sitting around, sipping champagne, apparently just waiting for Jimmy Beak to show up and wreak more havoc.

I ate a nacho for sustenance and stood up. "Send some drinks over to the Dibbles," I ordered Bryce.

"You go, girl!" Karen cheered me on as I courageously marched away.

***

Jackson gazed forlornly into his empty glass as I approached their booth.

"It's coming," I grumbled and took what was becoming my usual seat next to Audrey.

"I see they let Candy out," she said.

I looked back at the bar, where Candy was talking with John the New Guy, who had helped himself to my barstool. "For the time being," I said. "The cops still think she did it, though."

"But how are you feeling, Jessie?" Audrey looked concerned, and for a moment I wondered if she knew my couch had been returned. "How are the crystals working for you?"

"Umm. I just put them out a couple of days ago, right?"

"And you followed my instructions about placement? That's so very important." She studied me, waiting for a response, and I assured her I had followed her notes explicitly.

She patted my knee. "Well then, we need to be patient. There's so much negative energy in your home after Stanley's death, it will take time to get your chakras back in balance."

"Sorry, Audrey. But if Captain Rye keeps insisting that Candy did this terrible thing, I think my chakras are doomed forever."

"Not to mention Candy's." Jackson wiggled his empty glass at me.

"But I have told Captain Rye, over and over again, it can't be Candy," Audrey insisted. "Ezekiel says that's just impossible."

Our conversation stopped momentarily as Gina placed fresh Long Island Iced Teas on the table. "Your tab?" she asked me, and I nodded.

"Jealousy," Audrey said absently as she watched Gina scoot away. She turned back to me. "I spoke to Ezekiel again this afternoon. It was all crystal clear once he figured out Stanley's time of birth."

"How did he do that?"

"Don't you remember, Jessie?" She seemed a bit impatient with my ignorance. "Ezekiel promised that given enough time, he could trace Stanley's time of birth by going backwards from his murder. If you know enough about a person's life, you can figure these things out, you see."

I didn't, but nodded anyway.

"Ezekiel was kind enough to consult his planetary tables and study the question extensively."

"Kind enough for a fee," Jackson grunted. "How much did he overcharge you this time?"

"When was Stanley born?" I asked.

"At three a.m., on November thirteenth, on the dot." Audrey announced with confidence. "Ezekiel was simply beside himself. Poor Stanley was destined to be murdered from the moment he was born!" She twirled her right hand over her head. "It was written in the stars."

I sat back and contemplated the ever-informative Ezekiel Titus. If possible, the man had an even more active imagination than I. Perhaps I should consult him on how I might guide *Temptation at Twilight* to its rightful conclusion.

Audrey interrupted my thoughts. "I've been reading up on the latest research on Tarot cards," she said brightly. "Oh, it's fascinating, Jessie. Just fascinating!"

I closed my eyes and prayed for strength. "Tarot cards?" I said weakly.

"I'm so disappointed, though. I've misplaced my set from college."

"Ain't that a doggone shame," Jackson muttered.

Audrey pursed her lips and gazed over at the bar. "The cards would be real helpful in identifying who killed Stanley. I could do a basic three-card reading for everyone associated with him and find out exactly what happened."

"Oh?"

"Oh, yes! I could just ask the simple question about who killed Stanley as I laid out each person's cards. We'd have the answer in no time."

She turned to her husband. "Get me a new set for my birthday, Jackson? We can order them off the internet. They're not expensive."

Jackson grunted.

"When's your birthday?" I asked.

She sighed dramatically. "I'm a Libra. So we'd have to wait a whole month that way. And Candy needs our help right now, doesn't she?"

Alas, yes.

I took a deep breath and tried again. "Let's just think about exactly what happened here on Saturday, okay? Maybe if we piece together Stanley's every move, we can come up with something." I looked at Audrey. "Even without Tarot cards."

Audrey insisted using the Tarot would be far more straightforward, but I reminded her she didn't have a deck handy. "So!" I plowed forward. "Stanley showed up here around eight, correct?" I looked back and forth between the two of them.

Jackson glanced over his shoulder at the bar. "I'm not sure when he got here. But he was over there talking to Bryce and Evan when Audrey here hollered at him to come join us."

"Great," I said sincerely. This was the most help Jackson had offered all week. "Did he seem upset to you guys?"

Jackson said no, but Audrey fondled her earrings and considered it.

"Think hard," I said. "If we don't figure this out, Candy is going back to jail."

Much to my surprise, Jackson responded again, "Stan seemed about the same as he always did."

I looked at Audrey. "Do you agree? Did anything seem odd to you?"

She sipped her drink. "You know what was strange, Jessie? Stanley let me read his palms."

"Arrgh," Jackson groaned and rolled his eyes while I contemplated banging my head on the table.

"No, Jackson, you know that was odd." Audrey turned to me. "It was kind of a running joke between Stanley and me. I asked him every time I saw him if I could read his palms, and he would always say 'No thanks.' But that night he said 'What the hell!' and told me to do my worst."

"Worst is the way to put it," Jackson said. "Ask her what she told the guy, Jessie. Go ahead, ask her."

Audrey bit her lip. "The light in here must not have been good enough to get an accurate reading."

"What did you tell him?" I asked.

"I told him he had the longest life line I've ever seen," she mumbled and Jackson burst out laughing.

"My brilliant wife told Stan Sweetzer he'd live to be a hundred, if he lived to be a day."

"But we got interrupted!" Audrey appealed to me. "I couldn't concentrate as well as I needed to."

"Interrupted by what?" I asked.

"Well, by Bryce," she said. "He came over with our drinks just as I was getting started." Audrey jumped. "Let me read your palms, Jessie? It's awful fun. And real informative!"

Now, I ask you, how could I refuse awful fun and real informative? Thus I endured my first, and one can hope, my last palm reading. Confident despite her recent failure concerning Stanley, Audrey told me all about my life, past, present and future.

My friends at the bar must have sensed my plight. They sent Gina over with the champagne bottle to refill my glass, and I sipped slowly while Audrey studied what she ascertained to be my heart line.

She traced her index finger across the top of my palm and explained that the 'feathering' indicated a difficult childhood filled with much, much, pain. She stopped and looked up at me for verification. My childhood had been pretty darn happy, actually. But I didn't argue and let her continue on.

"But just look at your head line!"

I looked down at where she indicated.

"It's so long and pronounced." She looked up at me, impressed. "You're very smart. Very intelligent."

"Oh?" I asked. Believe it or not, I wasn't feeling all that brilliant.

Audrey went back to my hand in order to study my fate line. Apparently whatever she saw there was most alarming.

"Oh, Jessie!" She kept a firm grip on my right hand and looked deep into my eyes. "I see pain." She squeezed harder. "Much, much, pain!"

I blinked dumbly until she returned to my palm.

"But now, if I look a little closer, most of the pain is in the past."

"That's a relief," I said, relieved.

"Have you suffered a recent trauma?" Audrey asked eagerly.

"Maybe that's referring to my divorce?"

"Divorce! It was painful, wasn't it?"

I insisted my marriage had been far more painful than my divorce and suggested she move on. Meanwhile Jackson waved to Bryce to send over another round of drinks, and I wondered if anything on my palm might indicate my diminishing cash flow.

Audrey abruptly dropped my right hand, my dominant hand as she called it, and took up my left. She traced another line or two on that palm with her index finger.

"Your life right now is also painful, isn't it?" she asked without looking up. "Oh, but no need to worry. It looks like this new problem is only temporary."

"Maybe that's about Stan's murder?" Jackson had leaned over the table to get a closer look at this telltale palm of mine.

"What about the future?" I heard myself asking.

Audrey kept her eyes on my palm. "Oh my! Oh my, oh my, oh my!"

"What's it say, Audrey?" Jackson asked.

She looked up at me, thoroughly alarmed. "Now, I don't want you to be alarmed, Jessie. But you're in danger!" She hovered over my hand. "You poor thing!"

"Keep looking," I ordered.

"Oh, but it all works out." She tapped the middle of my palm. "See here?"

I did not see anything.

"There's an ever so faint fork in this line."

I looked harder and must admit I was a wee bit happy to see the fork.

"Everything will be alright," Audrey assured me. "As long as you make the right choices."

Bless his heart, Kirby came over to rescue me. "We need you at the pool table, Jessie. Bernie's got a question."

I thanked Audrey for her expertise, reclaimed my hand, and scooted out of the booth.

"Don't you worry, Jessie," she called after me. "You're going to re-marry. I saw that in your fate line also."

I resigned myself to a future of pain—much, much, pain—and followed after Kirby.

Chapter 25

"If you concentrated more on the pool table, and less on Miss Pink's outfit, you'd probably do better," Camille Allen was harassing her husband as I approached the table. She saw me and smirked. "You friend's outdone herself," she snapped.

"I don't dress her," I said quietly and asked what the issue was. "With the game," I clarified, pointing to the table where Bernie and John the New Guy were waiting for my verdict.

"Scrap," Kirby said and explained that Bernie had knocked the nine ball into the corner pocket. "He got the eleven, just like he said he would, but then the nine went in, too. He can't do that, right?"

I agreed. "If you were playing league rules, it would count. But in casual barroom eight ball, you're required to take out any of your own balls that drop accidently. Sorry, Bernie."

He shrugged and apologized to John, who put the nine ball back on the table and continued the game.

I returned to my barstool, but could still hear Camille making a scene behind me, as she scolded poor Bernie for making a scene. Yadda, yadda, yadda. The woman yammered on and on, but Candy was busy staring at John and didn't seem to realize she was the 'Miss Pink' to whom Camille kept referring.

Indeed, Camille was in a worse mood than usual, which perhaps indicated she had recently been interrogated by the Clarence police as to her involvement with Stanley. Not that anyone was keeping me posted on these things.

Bryce caught my attention. "Anything new from Audrey?"

"Nothing." I frowned. "Unless you care to know Stanley's time of birth, or the results of his palm reading?"

Candy peeled her eyes away from John the New Guy. "Stanley never let Audrey read his palms."

"He did Saturday night, Sweetie."

"Audrey told him he'd live long and prosper." Bryce shook his head. "How'd it go for you, Jessie?"

"Not so well. My past was painful, my present is equally so, and my future will be filled with danger." I glanced at Karen. "So much so that I'm destined to re-marry."

She patted my shoulder and poured me more champagne.

I sipped my warmish beverage. "I'm still trying to retrace Stanley's steps," I said to no one in particular. "I'm wondering who he spoke with after the Dibbles?"

"Don't look at me." That was Karen. "I was home that night, remember?"

I asked Bryce.

"I think that's when he left, Jessie—when he went to see you."

"After making a stop at Kiddo's," Karen added.

We turned expectantly to Candy, but she was still concentrating on John, who was now shooting a game against Gus. Karen's attention soon drifted back to her beer, and Bryce wandered off to work on the next batch of Long Island Iced Teas.

Perseverance, I told myself. My neighbors might have shorter attention spans than Snowflake, but I was not ready to give up. Not yet.

I focused on the other end of the bar, half-expecting to see Jimmy Beak walk through the door. No Jimmy—thank you, God—but there were plenty of people down there, closer to the doorway. People who might have seen Stanley leave that night. People I had not yet harassed.

And speaking of people I had not yet harassed, what about the Stones? I had promised Bryce not to bother them, but that was days ago.

"Times change," I said and stood up, but Karen was the only one who noticed.

"Where to now?" she asked.

I tilted my head toward Matthew Stone. "Wish me luck."

She grimaced. "You'll need it, girlfriend."

"Bryce not taking good care of you?" Matthew seemed pleasant enough as I elbowed my way to his end of the bar. "What's up, Jessie?"

"Stanley Sweetzer's murder," I said.

He slammed down the beer he was pouring, and everyone in the vicinity flinched. Then he whipped his towel at the sink and called over to Bryce, "Take care of things," he ordered. He stormed out from behind the bar and glared down at yours truly. "I have something else to take care of."

Oops.

***

"Outside," Matthew demanded as he guided, or rather pushed, me through the door.

"You're angry with me?" I asked stupidly as he kept us moving down Sullivan Street.

He stopped short and dropped my elbow. "Have you even thought about how all this nonsense about Stan is affecting the bar's reputation?" he asked. "Better yet, do you even care?"

I blinked twice and stared at his chest. Matthew was a rather large person, up close like that.

"Answer me!"

I looked up and assured him that I did care about The Stone Fountain. "I don't house my pool cue just anywhere, you know?"

He put his hands on his substantial hips and glared some more.

"Although I suppose I haven't been thinking about your business," I said quietly. "I'm sorry."

"Those cops have been over here night after night, not to mention Jimmy Beak." Matthew pointed to the Stone Fountain sign. "Take a wild guess how many times that's been plastered on the five o'clock news."

"It hasn't been good publicity?"

"Publicity?" he bellowed. "Every night now we get a crowd of looky-loos coming in to gawk at the place."

"But isn't that good?" I asked, and the poor guy almost popped an artery. "No, really," I continued. "I'm not being sarcastic. It seems like the crowds would be good for your business?"

"Good for business? Gina and I spent years making our bar a place people can feel safe in, and now this?" He waved his hands around, and I instinctively ducked. "People being poisoned, TV reporters, cops."

"I'm sorry," I said again.

"And if the cops nosing around for days on end aren't bad enough, I've also got you to contend with every other night."

I waited until his hands were back on his hips before replying. "I never meant to annoy you," I said honestly. "But Candy's in trouble, Matthew. She could end up in prison, for Lord's sake."

"Oh, so blame it on someone from my bar instead. That's just great!" Again he threw his hands in the air, and again I flinched.

"I'm just trying to learn the truth," I said.

Matthew huffed and puffed.

"Come on, Matthew," I said. "Try to calm down, and I'll try to be good, okay?"

He shook his head, but he did seem to lose the hostility. "I feel sorry for that poor cop," he mumbled.

"Rye? Why?"

"He'll be dealing with you for all eternity."

"Rye's closed the case. He's finished dealing with me."

"Yeah, right. I'm a bartender, Jessie—a student of human nature. And believe me, you and that poor cop are in it for the long haul."

It was my turn to glare, but when Matthew actually smiled, I thought it a good idea to smile back.

"Would you just cool it?" he asked. "Stop bugging my paying customers and let your new boyfriend handle things?"

"Wilson Rye is not—" I closed my eyes and tried again. "Okay." I opened my eyes. "If I promise not to bother anyone else, will you at least answer a few questions for me?"

"Do I have a choice?"

Before he decided he might, I quick counted out my questions on my fingers. "Who did Stanley talk to that night after the Dibbles?" I asked. "When did he leave? Did you and Gina invest with the guy? And do you know anyone else who did?"

"Other than you?"

I reminded Matthew I was the one asking the questions, and he again mumbled something about feeling sorry for Rye. I waited patiently.

He sighed dramatically and stuck a beefy thumb in the air. "One—I didn't notice Stan leave that night, but Gina did. She told the cops it was after he talked to Audrey." His index finger appeared. "Two—yes, we invested a little with Stan." His middle finger. "But other than you, I don't know anyone else who wasted their money with him."

"You lost it all?"

"It wasn't much, and we didn't kill him over it. We're not idiots."

I assured him I knew that. "But maybe some other disgruntled client did kill him," I suggested. "It's one of my theories anyway."

Matthew tilted his head and studied me.

"What?" I asked.

"Gina and I have been thinking the exact opposite."

"Excuse me?"

"We think it was someone Stan wouldn't take money from. One of the poor slobs who still believed his lies about returns on investments and portfolios and all that crap."

He pointed to the bar and reiterated what I already knew—that lots of the regulars at The Stone Fountain didn't have the financial wherewithal for Stanley to be interested. "He called them 'The Little People' right to their faces, Jessie. Said they weren't worth his effort."

"He humiliated people," I said quietly.

"Guys his own age mostly—my bartender, all your friends at the pool table. Just about every guy in there was insulted by that pompous—"

"Girlfriend!" Karen called out, and Matthew and I both jumped.

She hurried down Sullivan Street to join us. "We were worried you'd been kidnapped by Jimmy Beak. Bryce and Gina are looking for you, big guy." She punched Matthew's bicep and turned to me. "And John the New Guy is looking for you."

"Me?" I asked as the three of us walked back to the bar.

"Everyone wants him to shoot a game against you, Jess. No one's beaten him all night."

***

Bryce handed off my cue stick as I rounded the bar, and Candy clapped her hands in glee. "Gosh, Jessie," she said, "John's been winning right and left." She bestowed a smile on the guy and he actually blushed. "But I told him no way he could beat you!"

"She also told him she'd go out with him if he did," Karen whispered from behind me.

Gus racked the balls, and John invited me to break, but I declined and watched while he did the honors. Not too impressive, but certainly better than anything Kirby Cox had ever managed.

I assessed the table and decided on the stripes. I pocketed the nine ball and made one of my rather brilliant bank shots off the ten ball to down the thirteen. Amid murmurs of appreciation, I prowled around the table.

I love my hobby. The sound of cue balls clinking and clanking into pool balls is good for my heart and soul. And mind. I purposely flubbed on the twelve ball so as to give John a turn.

He stepped up to the table and set to work on the solids. But I barely had time to enjoy a bit of Pink Floyd's "Dark Side of the Moon," before he missed a shot at the two ball.

I frowned at the table, which was mine for the taking. "Would you like a lesson?" I asked, and he nodded eagerly.

"Okay then. My daddy taught me never to ignore the leave." I pointed to my next, very easy, shot. "It's important to think about where the cue ball will end up after each shot. Never leave it easy for your opponent."

John frowned at the fifteen ball. "I'm about to lose, aren't I?"

I shrugged and bent over the table. The fifteen ball disappeared, as did the ten. But Candy was having so much fun watching John, and John was having fun, and I was having fun, too. Shooting pool was way more rewarding than sleuthing. I smiled to myself and missed on that pesky twelve ball once again.

While John took another turn, I stepped away and Karen handed me my glass. The champagne was incredibly warm and flat by then, but I took a sip or two anyway and set my glass down next to where Bryce was concocting some more Long Island Iced Teas.

John missed on the one ball and again it was my turn.

This time I really couldn't help but clear the rest of the stripes. I did so, called the shot, and took aim for the eight ball. But just as I was in mid-swing, Bryce hollered out to Gina to come pick up some more drinks for the Dibbles.

And suddenly, it all made sense.

Chapter 26

Looking back, I'm surprised my stick even made contact with the cue ball. But it did. In fact, I hit it way too hard and scratched.

"Holy shit!" I heard Kirby and Gus hiss through the ringing in my ears.

I stood upright and faced the bar. Karen and Candy stared at me, identical expressions of disbelief on their faces. Bryce was behind them, mouth agape and eyes wide. I sensed John at my side, but my vision had blurred.

"Good game, Jessie." He was holding out his hand to me. "I guess I really am having a streak of luck tonight."

I shook his hand and mumbled a 'Congratulations.'

"Are you feeling okay, ma'am?"

"What?" I gazed blindly at the wall behind him. "Oh, yes. I'm fine." I blinked until I could focus again. "Umm, John," I said as calmly as possible. "Why don't you play a game with Candy?"

I managed the three steps to the bar and handed Candy my cue. "John's going to teach you how to play," I told her. "I'm going home now."

"Are you okay, Jess?" Karen still had a stricken look on her face, but I venture to guess it wasn't nearly as stricken as the look on mine.

"I'm fine," I lied. "I guess I just lost my concentration."

"Say what? At pool?"

"No, really." I caught sight of Bryce. "But I have a terrible headache. I need to go home now."

Candy and Karen both insisted on leaving with me, but I declined. "No, no." I backed away. "I'll be fine once I take an Advil."

I turned and headed for the door. Karen called out something about me being out of Advil, and Roger Waters was insisting he'd meet me on the moon, but I was not inclined to stay and argue with either of them.

***

I stumbled out to the sidewalk and into Jimmy Beak and the entire Channel 15 News crew. Jimmy asked some snide question about how I had managed to get a known killer out on bail, but I was not inclined to argue with him either. I kept going and had made it halfway across Sullivan Street before I realized he was following me.

I swung around and promptly got knocked over by the cameraman who hadn't stopped in time to avoid me. Of course, he didn't bother to help me up—he was too busy filming.

"Why the hell are you following me!?" I snapped at Jimmy as I struggled to my feet. I turned him toward the bar and gave his bottom that swift kick I had been fantasizing about all week. "The killer is in there with Candy, you idiot!"

I was about to kick him again, but Jimmy was already off and running, flailing his arms and shouting out orders. "Corner her! Blockade the pool table this time! Don't let her get away!"

With a great deal of pushing and shoving, and a few exclamations of "Candy Poppe! Candy Poppe!" the entire Channel 15 News crew followed their fearless leader and disappeared into the bar.

Horns blared and I almost fell down again. Apparently, I was still standing in the middle of the street. Waving apologies to various cars, I ran toward my building. Candy would just have to deal with Jimmy Beak without me.

I needed to call Captain Rye.

***

But whatever adrenaline had given me strength out on Sullivan Street vanished the moment I entered the lobby. My knees were shaking so badly I actually tried using the elevator. No luck there, so I straggled all too slowly up the stairs and into my condo.

Even Snowflake was concerned when she saw me. She followed after me, meowing loudly, as I practically crawled to the bathroom to be sick. Afterwards I splashed cold water on my face and brushed my teeth.

I looked in the mirror and willed myself to stop shaking. "Please let me be wrong," I whispered to my reflection. But I knew I wasn't.

Snowflake continued yowling.

"Fresh air," I told her. I grabbed my cell phone and Rye's business card and she followed me up to the roof.

I didn't expect to find him at his desk at that time of night, and I was right. I left him a message to call me no matter what the time and tried his cell phone.

"Rye here," he answered.

Thank you, God. I plopped down on the nearest bench.

"It's Bryce, Captain."

Chapter 27

"Where are you?"

"Didn't you hear me? It's Bryce Dixon!"

"Answer me, Ms. Hewitt."

"Who cares where I am? Where are you?" I noticed some background noise on Rye's end. "It sounds like you're in your car. Don't tell me you're still on that stupid, stupid, vacation. I need you here!"

"I'm on my way. But where are you?"

I stared at The Stone Fountain, and for no good reason, noticed the lovely full moon hovering over the building. "I was at the bar—"

"Shhhit!"

"Was," I repeated. "But I'm home now."

"Thank God. Now stay put," he ordered. "I mean it this time."

"Don't you even want to hear why I know it's Bryce?"

He must have driven another mile before answering. "We need three things," he said eventually. "Motive, means, and opportunity. What do you got?"

"Opportunity, definitely," I said. "That's how I figured it out. Bryce served Stanley his drinks that night. All of his drinks. Even when he was sitting with the Dibbles."

"And?"

"And," I said impatiently, "Bryce and Matthew never venture out from behind the bar to deliver drinks. That's Gina's job."

I waited for Rye to tell me how brilliant and clever I am. When he didn't, I continued, "I'm guessing Bryce started poisoning Stanley's drinks when he was sitting at the bar with Evan. But remember you told me it would take a whole lot of Phenobarbital to kill someone that young?"

"Mm-hmm."

"So it must have thwarted his whole plan when Stanley up and joined the Dibbles. Bryce had to keep the poison flowing. And he had to be sure it was put in front of the right person."

"Very nice, Ms. Hewitt."

I was about to pat myself on the back when Rye mentioned motive. "You got that, too?"

"Matthew has an interesting theory," I said.

"You've been talking to Matthew Stone? You really are brave."

"He was a bit grouchy," I admitted. "But he gave me an idea. This wasn't about Stanley's clients at all. It was about the people he ignored. Matthew thinks Stanley insulted someone one too many times about their lack of funds."

"Bryce Dixon was one of the 'Little People.'"

"Exactly!" I said, thrilled that Wilson Rye was finally beginning to appreciate my logic. "You've heard about those insults? Bryce must have been tired of the humiliation."

"Enough to kill?"

I blinked at Snowflake, who was sitting on Karen's railing staring at the moon. "Okay, maybe not. But Ezekiel Titus was on to something, too."

"The astrologer?" Rye was incredulous.

"He insists it was jealousy." I thought a second. "And you said it yourself. That first morning you accused me of murder, remember?"

Rye groaned.

"Jealousy," I repeated. "Bryce was jealous of Stanley's love life. He's infatuated with Candy Poppe." I shook my head. "I can't believe I never noticed it."

"You mean, your intuition failed you?"

"Okay, be sarcastic. But Bryce is so jittery around her. And he's always giving her free food. However," I added, "he's just about the only guy in that bar Candy's never dated. Yet another blow to his ego."

"Now do you see why we've kept Carter O'Connell behind bars?"

I sat up straight. "To keep him away from Bryce?"

"More like the opposite. When things started falling into place with Dixon, I convinced O'Connell to stay in jail for a couple extra nights. It would keep him safe in case Dixon went even further off the deep end."

I whimpered, and bless her feline heart, Snowflake sensed I needed support. She hopped down from the railing and into my lap.

"Anger, humiliation, jealousy." I petted the cat and frowned. "Even I have to admit, it all seems a rather flimsy excuse for murder."

"Maybe, but he's done it before."

"Excuse me?" I squeaked.

"You know anything about Dixon's past?"

I closed my eyes and prayed for strength. "Why am I guessing not?"

"He's not from Missouri like he's told you. He's from a little town in Tennessee. His real name is Keith Webb. And he killed a kid when he was in high school."

I was starting to shake again.

"For the same reason," Rye continued. "Jealous of his love life. It appears he wanted the poor kid's girlfriend for himself. She still swears Webb—that's Dixon to you— asked her to the Junior Prom not two hours after her boyfriend was found dead."

I had to ask, "And somehow it's clear Bryce killed this boyfriend?"

"Clear if you know what you're looking for. But they could never prove he stole the Phenobarbital from his mother."

I shook my head. "You're losing me."

"Remember, Ms. Hewitt—motive, means, and opportunity. Have you given any thought to means?"

I gave some thought to means. "Umm," I said slowly. "Do veterinarians use Phenobarbital?"

"Densmore did the research. It's used to treat canine epilepsy."

"The poor dogs."

"The poor kid, you mean. Webb's mother's denied he took the Phenobarbital from her clinic, and the records back then weren't always computerized. It couldn't be proven. And he had the right connections. One grandfather was a judge and the other was best friends with the mayor."

I thought about dear, sweet Bryce. Okay, so maybe not so dear and sweet after all. I took a deep breath. "Can we prove it this time?"

"Yep, I think we can." Rye emphasized the 'we.' "It's been frustrating, but that's what's taken so long. First, we had to figure out who Dixon really was. Densmore did a great job on that."

"Candy and I think Lieutenant Denmore's really nice."

"I'm thrilled. But he's also really smart. He identified Webb, and then we could start digging into his past. He got away with murder once before. This time we wanted hard and fast evidence to convict the bastard."

"And?"

"And I'm driving back from Tennessee with proof. These days there's computerized records for tracking pharmaceuticals. They're much harder to tamper with."

"So Bryce got the poison from his mother again? I'm still having trouble picturing this, Captain."

"Picture it," he said. "Webb took the drugs from his mother's office a couple weeks ago. But she couldn't cover for him this time, since she knew nothing about it until I showed up with a search warrant. I got some fingerprints, too. It will help."

I remembered Bryce had taken a trip home right before his new semester began. "When do you arrest him?" I asked.

"Soon. I should make it to Clarence by midnight. In the meantime, Densmore's on his way to the bar. He and John Chavis might even make the arrest before I get there."

"Oh, my Lord. John the New Guy's a cop, isn't he?"

"Yep."

"John the New Guy's a cop," I told Snowflake. She yawned and moseyed over to the opposite end of the bench.

I spoke to Rye. "He just beat me at pool, by the way."

"What!?"

"I scratched on the eight ball."

"What!?"

"I was distracted, okay? I figured out it was Bryce just as I took the shot."

"Oh, for God's sake. Did anyone notice?"

"What do you think? Poor Kirby Cox may never recover."

"Please tell me you didn't explain why you got so flustered."

"Would you give me some credit? I mumbled some lame excuse and came home to call you."

"Well, thank you." Rye sounded calmer. "Now stay put behind locked doors until we nab the guy. You got that?"

I looked at Snowflake. "Umm…"

"Umm, what?" When I didn't answer, Rye started shouting at me, "You are at home? You just told me that you're home, Ms. Hewitt!"

"I'm sort of home." I stood up and gathered up the cat. "I'm on the roof."

"The roof! For God's sake, Jessie! Go downstairs and lock yourself in. That's an order!"

I promised I would and hung up.

And that's when I noticed Bryce Dixon blocking the stairwell.

Chapter 28

I dropped Snowflake. She scolded me and hopped back onto Karen's railing.

"Who was that on the phone, Jessie?"

"Phone?" I stared at my cell phone, searching for an answer. "Umm, I was talking to my mother."

"At 11:30?"

"Mother is a night owl," I said and set the phone on the bench. For some reason I wanted my hands free.

"You think you're pretty smart, don't you?"

"Smart?" I repeated. Audrey had told me the same thing earlier, but I still wasn't feeling all that brilliant. "What are you doing home so early, Bryce?"

"I told Matthew I'm sick. I lied, just like you did."

Much to my dismay, he had moved out from the stairwell and was coming closer. I backed up, relieved to have the bench between us.

"Lied?" I said and cringed at my own stupidity. Parroting words was likely not the best strategy to get me out of this mess.

"Would you stop it with the games, Jessie? I know you know."

We began doing a bizarre dance around the bench. Bryce took a step forward. I, a step backward.

"It took me a while to realize it," he said. "Since Jimmy Beak came in right after you left and caused all kinds of trouble. But you figured it out at the pool game."

I continued backing away. "How could you do such a thing, Bryce?"

"Easy. I could dump a whole gallon of bleach into those disgusting drinks and no one would know the difference."

"But why?" I already knew why, but I was stalling for time—my new, and I hoped, improved strategy for getting out of this mess. "Why did you kill poor Stanley?"

"Poor Stanley, my ass. I hated the guy."

"Because of Candy?"

"He didn't deserve her. And he didn't deserve all that money. I'm free now."

"Free from what?" I asked on reflex, and Bryce stopped short. In fact, I do not believe I've ever seen Bryce Dixon stand so still.

I, too, stopped. Perhaps even time stood still for that moment or two, but my intuition kicked into overdrive.

"He was blackmailing you."

Bryce blinked and I knew I had nailed it.

"Over what?" I asked as we started moving again.

Who knows how many times we rounded that stupid bench, as bits and pieces of conversation floated back to me.

"Stan had a way of finding out about everything. It was kind of uncanny," Roslynn Mayweather had said. "The guy was relentless," Ian complained. "Sweetzer was good at getting what he wanted out of people. He knew lots of secrets," Rye had told me.

Why, even Bryce had insinuated some such thing. It was when I told him about Billy Joe Dent. Bryce said he wasn't surprised Stanley was blackmailing him.

We rounded the bench for the umpteenth time.

"Stanley found out who you really are." I was more or less sure of myself. "You let it slip somehow. Maybe when he was belittling you? Maybe you bragged about," I hesitated, "about your secret."

Bryce was breathing heavy now, and he was moving faster. I kept backing away. If I could make it back to the other side of the bench, I would have a clear path to the stairs.

"Did he threaten to tell the cops?" I hesitated again. "No," I corrected myself. "He threatened to tell Candy."

"You bitch!" Bryce lunged forward.

I ducked and made a run for it.

The stairwell wasn't that far away. I would make it there. And then I would run all the way downstairs, and out to Sullivan Street, and back to The Stone Fountain—

And then Snowflake howled.

I froze. And time stood still again.

"I've always hated this cat," Bryce said from across the roof.

I blinked at the stairwell looming before me and tried to breathe.

"Didn't you hear me, Jessie?" He lowered his voice. "I said I hate this cat."

I turned slowly and forced myself to look.

Bryce was holding Snowflake around her middle and was dangling her over the edge of the roof.

"Noooo!" I screamed.

But he dropped her anyway.

He dropped Snowflake.

And she screamed, and screamed, and screamed, the whole way down. But it was more horrible when she stopped screaming.

I stared into the abyss where my cat had been.

And then I bounded over two benches and who knows how many plants and went for his throat.

Not a good idea. Within a second he had wrestled me into submission and held me, hands behind my back, and leaning backwards, way the hell over the railing.

"God, Bryce!" I choked, or whatever it was I could do with my neck yanked back at that angle. For one brief, terrifying second, my feet were actually lifted off the roof. "Killing me won't help."

"Like hell it won't."

"Rye knows," I said. "He's on his way."

"Yeah? Like when?"

Okay, good question.

I stopped arguing and gasped for breath as Bryce rocked me back and forth. Maybe he was thinking about his choices. Believe me, so was I.

Then I heard the sirens.

"They're headed here," I managed.

"Yeah, right," he said, but he stopped rocking me and listened.

"They're headed here," I repeated, and sure enough, the sirens stopped below us. I could even see flashing blue lights. Or maybe that was the blood rushing to my head.

Bryce mumbled a few obscenities, but I was too busy rejoicing over the sounds of someone running up the stairs to care. I still couldn't see a darn thing with my head tilted back at such a distressing angle.

"Oh, my God." That was Lieutenant Densmore—I was almost sure of it. I was about to feel relieved when I heard a heavy thud.

Bryce snickered and glanced over the railing. "Too bad for you, Jessie. Densmore's out cold."

If I could have cried, I would have, but I was discovering that crying upside down is near impossible.

But now more people were on the stairs. I was about to feel relieved when I heard Jimmy Beak.

"I want this on film," he shouted, and a lot of people began running around the roof. Someone tripped and landed in Karen's fountain with a splash and a curse, but Jimmy kept yelling, "Get as close to her as possible! Now, people! This is gonna get me a national spot if it kills me!"

Suddenly things got much brighter—someone must have aimed a spotlight at me as Jimmy started reporting something about Adelé Nightingale finally meeting her match. I tried crying again.

But now there really was more help arriving. Sirens blared and whistles blew on the street below, but I concentrated on what sounded like the entire Clarence police force hurrying up the stairs. I was about to feel relieved when I noticed how everyone kept stopping far, far, away.

Bryce noticed also. He kept warning people to keep their distance. Several people instructed us to remain calm. Perhaps that would have worked if Candy Poppe hadn't arrived.

"Oh my gosh. Oh, Jessie!" she squealed from somewhere near the stairwell, and Bryce almost dropped me.

I slipped even further backwards amid a lot of screaming, some of which I assume was my own.

But Lord help me, could this position from hell actually be better? My foot had snagged hold of one of the rails as I slipped. I twisted my right ankle around the baluster as far as it would twist and held on for dear life as Karen encouraged me to hang in there.

"We're with you, Jess," she said. "We're all right here with you."

Several people offered a casual hello, as if we were meeting over a bottle of Korbel, and it occurred to me that all the regulars from The Stone Fountain had joined us.

"Jealousy," Audrey Dibble said with confidence, and Jackson grunted accordingly.

Meanwhile the Allens were actually arguing, within my earshot, about whether or not I would survive the fall. Bless his heart, Kirby shut them up while I finally figured out how to cry upside down.

"What the hell?"

I stopped crying.

"For God's sake, Densmore."

Yes, it really was Captain Rye. And he didn't sound very happy with the situation, whatever it was, exactly.

But whatever it was, I could tell he was walking toward Bryce and me.

"Give me that," Rye said, and I heard Jimmy's cameraman put up an argument and a fight. Then I heard an object, presumably that damn camera, land in Karen's fountain.

Proof positive that there is a God in heaven, the spotlight got turned off also.

Jimmy started protesting but Rye ignored him.

"Put away your guns, people," he ordered. "We shoot him, and she goes over. Can't you see that?"

I resumed crying.

"Are you okay, Jessie?" he asked.

"Blackmail," I choked.

"Do what you're thinking, Webb, and you'll follow her over." Rye had moved closer still. "I guarantee it."

"It's Dixon," Bryce said. "I'm Bryce Dixon now."

"Blackmail," I repeated with all my strength. If I were about to die, I was determined Rye would have the whole truth beforehand.

"I'll drop her. I swear I will." Bryce started rocking me back and forth again, which was doing nothing good to my right ankle.

"What did Sweetzer have on you, Webb?" Thank you, God—Rye must have heard me. "Your name? Your family? Your nasty inclination to murder? What?"

"Stan didn't have anything on me, Candy. I swear it!" Bryce kept rocking me. His hands had gone all clammy. Slippery, even.

"Gosh, Bryce." That was Candy. "Then why are you holding Jessie upside down like that?"

Okay, so the world really had gone topsy-turvy. Candy Poppe was now providing the voice of reason.

"How the hell were you paying him?" Rye asked, but I didn't wait for the answer.

When Bryce rocked me forward for the umpteenth time, I took what I hoped was a good opportunity to save my life. I freed my foot, pushed off from the railing, and collided head on with Rye, who must have pounced at the same time I did.

We went down hard, but we were on the roof.

We were on the roof.

More accurately, I was sprawled on top of the prone body of Wilson Rye. There was a lot of running, and yelling, and general commotion going on around us, but I closed my eyes and concentrated on the sound of his heart beating beneath my left ear.

I breathed deep. "Are you okay," I asked quietly.

"Never better. You?"

I let out a gigantic sob. "He threw Snowflake overboard."

That got us moving again. Rye held me tighter around the waist, rolled over and stood up, taking me with him. But being right side up and vertical so suddenly didn't feel so good. I remember looking into his eyes before I passed out. No, let's be accurate—I swooned. Alexis Wynsome couldn't have done it better.

Chapter 29

I opened one eye to see Candy's face a mere inch away from my own. I closed my eye.

"We're not going away," she said. "You need to wake up now, Jessie."

When I realized a cat was laying on my chest and purring, I took her advice.

Yes, it really was Snowflake. I stroked her with both hands and a few tears trickled down my temples toward the pillow as I regained my bearings.

I was lying on my bed. Candy was there, kneeling beside me, and looking far too energetic. Karen was nearby also. She had rolled the chair from my desk over to the bedroom and was reclining on it, her work boot clad feet resting next to my stomach. She was drinking Korbel from the bottle.

"You don't like champagne," I reminded her and reached out. She handed over the bottle.

"You're alive, Jess. Kiddo and I figured that was worth celebrating."

"What the heck happened?" I leaned on an elbow and took a swig, and passed the bottle to Candy. I laid back down. "And this better be good."

"Oh, Jessie!" Candy pulled her knees in closer to me. "It was, like, incredible!"

She took a sip and gave the bottle back to me. Then she started bouncing, but Snowflake scolded her and she stopped. Thank you, Snowflake.

"Why didn't you tell us it was Bryce?" she asked. "And that nice John-guy's a police officer! Did you know that, too?" Candy looked at Karen. "I played two games of pool with him, and I didn't know it."

I decided to sit up a bit. But as Candy slipped an extra pillow under my head, one of the rocks that were under there rolled out and fell on the floor.

Karen leaned over and retrieved it. She held it up and I was relieved to see it was only the light green one.

"It's Howlite," I said, since my neighbors seemed to expect an explanation. I petted Snowflake to avoid their eyes. "Audrey Dibble gave it to me to help me sleep. It's supposed to fix my insomnia chakra."

"Girlfriend!" Karen said. "You keep rocks under your pillow and wonder why you can't sleep? No wonder you're always getting headaches."

I drank more champagne, thankful they hadn't seen the chunk of Rose Quartz I had hiding under there also. According to Audrey, that one promised to revitalize my love-life chakra.

Karen set the crystal on my night stand and got back to the evening's saga. "John and Candy were getting along real well tonight," she said. "Kiddo and her cleavage had the poor guy so distracted he didn't even notice when Bryce left."

"He was coming after me," I said.

"But he told everyone he was sick," Candy said. "None of us knew what was going on until John started acting all funny."

"And then you came to rescue me? What took you guys so long?"

"It wasn't that easy, okay?"

"Jimmy Beak," Karen explained. "He and his crew were getting in everyone's way so it took a few minutes before John saw what was happening. 'Where did Bryce go?' he asked me, and I told him Bryce had left."

Candy jumped. "Oh my gosh, Jessie! John got real agitated then. He shouted some curse words and whipped out his cell phone."

"And then he started yelling into it," Karen said. "'He's not here! Dixon's left the premises! Dixon's left the premises!'" She waved her arms around, presumably imitating John the New Guy.

"He must have been calling Densmore or Rye," I said. "John was supposed to be watching Bryce."

"Well, he sure got everyone's attention," Candy said. "Jimmy Beak and his cameraman ran out, and John was following behind, and he ran right into Gina Stone."

"And the Long Island Iced Teas went flying," Karen elaborated. "What a mess."

"Then we heard the sirens and everyone ran outside to see what was going on," Candy said.

"Everyone?" I asked, the introvert in me cringing at the possibility.

"Sorry, Jess," Karen said. "But it seemed kind of urgent. We saw Densmore run into our building, and then Jimmy and his gang took off. John told the rest of us to stay put, and then he ran off, too."

"He almost got hit crossing Sullivan Street," Candy added.

Karen had the champagne bottle and took another drink before looking at me. "That's about when Kirby noticed you hanging off the roof."

I reached out and she handed me the bottle.

"Oh, Jessie," Candy squealed, "I'm so glad you're okay. Weren't you scared?"

"Well, yeah." I looked at Karen. "But at least I was sure the railing wouldn't give way."

She shrugged. "It held you."

I mouthed a thank you to my friend. If Karen Sembler had built it, that railing would hold an elephant if need be.

"So we all ran over here," Candy was saying. "By then there were more police. It was hard for everyone to get up the stairs all at once like that."

"The elevator wasn't working of course." That was Karen. "I swear, I'm gonna get a license to fix the stupid thing myself."

"That would be nice," I agreed.

"You were still hanging over the railing when we finally got up there," she continued.

"And that's when Rye showed up?"

"Yeah, but not before one of Jimmy's people landed in my fountain." Karen chuckled. "Man, was that gratifying. But anyway, Rye wasn't too happy to find Densmore flat on his back. Kiddo and I still haven't figured that one out."

"He's afraid of heights," I explained. "I think he fainted when he saw Bryce and me at the edge like that."

"Gosh, I hope he's okay," Candy mumbled. She started chewing her knuckle, so Karen leaned over and handed her the bottle.

"But Rye was there?" I tried again.

"And went ballistic when he saw you," Karen said.

"But then you surprised everyone, Jessie." Candy had started bouncing again, so I took the bottle away from her. "You let out this really weird sound and all of the sudden you were sprawled out on top of Captain Rye, and Bryce was screaming that he had a gun."

Karen agreed. "It was kind of crazy for a minute there. Bryce was running around, and John and a few of the other cops were trying to catch him."

"That's when Jimmy Beak picked up the camera from the fountain and threw it as hard as he could," Candy added.

"Which worked really well at knocking John down. Like I said, Jess—mayhem."

When we stopped laughing, Karen twitched a thumb toward Candy. "Kiddo here saved the day. She slipped out one of those high-heeled shoes of hers and tripped Bryce. He landed right on top of Densmore."

I looked at Candy. "Good thinking, Sweetie."

"Gosh, I hope Lieutenant Densmore didn't get hurt."

"It woke him up, anyway," Karen said. "He and Bryce wrestled around some before Densmore got him handcuffed."

Candy started that annoying bouncing thing again. "And that's when everyone noticed you and Captain Rye, Jessie. It was so romantic!"

"Oh?"

"Oh, yeah! You fainted. And Captain Rye caught you and scooped you up into his arms." Candy clasped her hands in glee. "It was just like in one of your books. There was a full moon behind him and everything!"

Karen tried to say something, but Candy was not to be interrupted. "Then he started yelling at the rest of us, 'Listen up people.'" Candy's imitation of Rye's voice was surprisingly accurate. "'Densmore's got Webb, and the rest of you are looking for a cat. Snowflake,' he screamed at us. 'She's pure white, gold eyes. She practically glows in the dark.' he said. 'Webb threw her over the edge.'"

I hugged my cat. She hates it when I do that, but she tolerated me this once.

Candy continued, "But we were all kind of stunned. We kind of stood there in shock or something."

Karen took over. "So Rye got impatient and really started screaming. 'Now would be nice, people!' he said. And the cops, and Jimmy, and the Dibbles, and everyone, all started scrambling down the stairs. 'Bring in SWAT if you have to.' Rye kept hollering. 'But find that cat!'"

"Then he told Karen and me to follow him," Candy said.

"So we did," Karen said. "He carried you down the stairs, and in here, and plopped you on the bed."

"He did not *plop* her on the bed." Candy looked at me. "He gently placed you on the bed, Jessie. It was just like a fairy tale."

I sighed dramatically. If we weren't careful, Candy might start doing some swooning herself.

"That's when Kirby, Gus, and Old Man Harrison came in," Karen said. "Kirby had Snowflake."

"Kirby, Gus and Mr. Harrison?" I asked. "Would someone please hand me that bottle."

Karen obeyed. "The guys found Snowflake on the awning over the front door. That must be where she landed."

I smiled at my very lucky cat and Snowflake yawned.

"I guess none of us noticed her up there earlier," Candy explained. "Since we were so busy trying to get up to the roof and all."

"But Peter Harrison?" I was incredulous. "How in the world did he get involved?"

Evidently Snowflake had been most uncooperative when Kirby and Gus tried to coax her down from the awning, and had crouched up there hissing at the poor guys. Ever-resourceful, they knocked on the closest door, which happened to be Mr. Harrison's. He fetched a ladder and a can of tuna, and helped with the rescue operation—in his pajamas, no less.

"Mr. Harrison's kind of worried about you," Candy told me, and I made a mental note to call on him the next day.

"Anyway," Karen continued. "Kirby handed Snowflake off to Rye and the guys got out of here pretty quick. I think they were embarrassed being in your bedroom."

"Jimmy Beak wasn't though," Candy added helpfully. "He ran in after Kirby left to see how you were doing."

I started whimpering.

"Don't worry, Jess." Karen reached forward and patted my knee. "Remember he had lost his camera by then. And Rye told him if any of this made its way onto the news, he'd hunt him down and kill him personally."

"So, Jimmy left?" I asked.

"Mm-hmm. And then Rye gently placed Snowflake on top of you." Karen smirked at Candy over the 'gently placed,' and Candy nodded approval.

"He told us to take good care of you," Candy said. "And then he told us he had to go and ran off." She flung both arms into the air, performed a little sitting pirouette, and swooned onto the pillow next to me.

I glanced at Karen. "Help me," I begged.

"Hey, don't look at me," she said. "At that point it wouldn't have surprised me if the guy donned a cape and flew out the window."

Candy sprang up and started bouncing again. "Gosh, Jessie, I wonder where Captain Rye is right now!"

I closed my eyes and told her she was giving me a headache.

Epilogue

Even I watched the news the next day. I was anxious to see exactly what Jimmy Beak would end up reporting, and was pleased to note he was informative, accurate, and dare I say it, subdued. Maybe it helped that he had zero footage to accompany his report, and that he actually had some real news to convey.

Indeed, Jimmy did a great job explaining the motive, means, and opportunity behind the murder. Even I learned something. It was Bryce's—make that Keith's— grandfather who had paid Stanley's blackmail fees. I never did catch the full amount, but between Billy Joe Dent and Grandfather Webb, I now had a pretty good accounting of that pesky twenty-seven thousand dollars.

After Jimmy's report, the Channel 15 News anchor interviewed Captain Rye. He explained the outcome of the investigation in more detail and made sure to acknowledge Carter O'Connell's cooperation in remaining in jail until Dixon/Webb could be brought in.

The anchor was closing the interview when Rye interrupted. "I have one other person to thank before we wrap this up," he said. "Jessica Hewitt, better known as the world-famous author Adelé Nightingale, was indispensable in solving this case. Her undying pursuit of justice and truth should be commended."

He looked straight into the camera and grinned, and I was reminded that every bone, muscle, and fiber of my fifty-two-year-old body was in pain from the previous night.

That evening Rolfe Vanderhorn and I finally got around to pondering Alexis Wynsome's predicament. We had left her in the clutches of the vile Derwin Snipe far, far, too long. I had been distracted from the task at hand. And let's face it, Rolfe's cunning could never be considered his strongest asset. The poor guy's rescue plan had gotten nowhere without my assistance. I sat at my desk and stared at The Stone Fountain. Rolfe sat in his garden and stared at his sword.

But then he heard a horse galloping in the distance. It was coming closer! Rolfe leapt to his feet, his sword at the ready. Imagine his elation when a white stallion, carrying Alexis on its back, galloped up the lane and deftly cleared the picket fence into the garden. The lovely—and who would have guessed it—capable Alexis brought the beast to a halt in front of Rolfe and beamed down at her hero. Rolfe promptly tossed his sword aside and helped the lady down.

It seems our triumphant heroine had grown impatient of waiting for help to arrive and rescue her from the dastardly Derwin's dungeon. So she solicited the assistance of her trusty friend Annabelle Goodloe, and together they devised an ingenious plan. Her escape had involved not a little daring, but Snipe and his entourage of vassals were no match for Alexis Wynsome. Indeed, motivated as she was by sweet memories of the rugged and muscular Rolfe, Alexis proved once and for all that she was not a woman to be toyed with. Rolfe rejoiced at her fortitude and forbearance, even before Alexis told him who her father was.

But it was Saturday night, and Adelé Nightingale deserved some time off. I decided to end *Temptation at Twilight* while Alexis still possessed her youthful glow of beauty, and while Rolfe still possessed the considerable store of energy required for the final climactic love scene. I was putting the finishing touches on said scene, trying to think of another word for throbbing, when someone knocked at the door.

"Maybe it's Prince Charming," I said to Snowflake and answered to find Captain Rye leaning against the doorframe.

He looked different in jeans and a white tee shirt. The bunch of yellow roses he was holding also caught my attention.

"We have another problem, Ms. Hewitt."

I crossed my arms and pretended to glare. "Oh?"

"Mm-hmm." Rye nodded solemnly. "Now that Sweetzer's killer has been identified, I've run out of excuses to come see you."

"Oh?"

He grinned and handed me the flowers.

I closed my eyes and soaked in their scent before looking up. "Do you drink champagne, Captain Rye?"

"It's Wilson," he said as I ushered him inside. "And I have a feeling I'm gonna start loving champagne, Ms. Hewitt."

"It's Jessie," I said and headed for the fridge.

The End

The fun has just begun! If you enjoyed *Playing with Poison* and want to read more, check out the other books in Cindy Blackburn's Cue Ball Mysteries series:

Double Shot

Jessie Hewitt thought her pool-hustling days were long gone. But when uber-hunky cop Wilson Rye asks her to go undercover to catch a killer, she jumps at the chance to return to a sleazy poolroom. Jessie is confident she can handle a double homicide, but the doubly-annoying Wilson Rye is another matter altogether. What's he doing flirting with a woman half his age? Will Jessie have what it takes to deal with Tiffany La-Dee-Doo-Da Sass and solve the murders? Take a guess.

Three Odd Balls

A romantic vacation for...five? This wasn't exactly what Jessie and Wilson had in mind when they planned their trip to the tropics. They didn't plan on solving a murder either. But when one of the *Three Odd Balls* tagging along with them seems destined for a jail cell, guess what?

234

Double Shot

Chapter 1

"Candy Poppe has a poodle named Puddles, and I'm suffering from plot plight," I informed Wilson the minute he walked through the door.

He set a bag of groceries on the counter. "Excuse me?"

"Candy, Wilson. My downstairs neighbor? Pretty, perky, petite. Prone to miniskirts and stilettos?"

"I know who Candy is, Jessie. She got a poodle?"

"A puppy from the pound. He's not a purebred."

Wilson blinked twice. "Have you met Puddles?"

"He came up to play today," I said, and we both instinctively glanced at Snowflake, who was perched on her favorite windowsill.

"What did you think of Puddles?" Wilson asked my cat.

She yawned abundantly while I answered, "Puddles pranced around, and Snowflake supervised from where she's sitting right now. All went well until Puddles piddled."

"She disapproved?"

"She was most displeased." I waved at the expanse of wood floors in my condo. "Although wiping it up was pretty painless."

Wilson shook his head. "If I hear one more P-word—"

"You'll pull out your pistol?" I smiled at my profound powers of alliteration, but my beau the cop was unimpressed.

"Maybe we should move on to plot plight," he suggested.

I agreed that was probably a good idea and pulled a bottle of champagne from the fridge.

If you ask me, everything works better with champagne. And trust me, the rather unlikely saga of *An Everlasting Encounter*, my latest literary venture, would definitely be easier to fathom with bit of bubbly. I popped the cork while Wilson got dinner underway.

"Think Cinderella, but with a wicked sister-in-law," I began. I handed him a glass and found my favorite barstool.

"Sarina Blyss has run away from home. She had to leave because her brother Norwood inherited the family estate after their father died. That shouldn't have been a problem, but then Norwood married Agnes. And the altogether evil Agnes quickly turned poor Sarina into a virtual slave."

Wilson tossed a handful of garlic into a sauce pot. "Did you take those meatballs out of the freezer like I asked?"

But, of course. If Wilson Rye wants to fill my freezer with all kinds of homemade Italian delicacies, the least I can do is follow a few simple instructions. I pointed him toward the fridge, and he dumped the thawed meatballs into a hot frying pan.

Snowflake hopped into my lap, and together we watched him do his magic. Spaghetti and meatballs here we come.

"So now it's three years later," I continued.

"Later than what?"

"Three years after Norwood married the bitch. Now, I don't actually call Agnes a bitch in the book, but my readers will get the idea."

"Agnes who?"

"Wilson!" I put down my glass and waved a hand to get his attention. "Agnes Blyss is the altogether evil sister-in-law. Sarina got tired of scrubbing her floors and left home with a small satchel of all her worldly belongings, including her most cherished possession, the golden necklace her mother bestowed upon her the night she died."

"Bestowed upon her?"

I nodded solemnly. "Sarina was a mere child when her mother passed away, and then her father died when she was sixteen. The poor thing is an orphan."

Wilson rolled his eyes, and I suggested he drink some champagne.

"Sarina had an important decision to make the day she left home," I said. "When she got to the crossroads at the end of the lane, she had to choose between walking to Priesters, the charming village she used to visit with her father, or heading in the opposite direction toward the big town of St. Celeste. She knew St. Celeste was twenty miles away, but she had never been there."

"So she chose the charming village, right?"

"No!" I jumped a bit. "That surprised me, too. She decided on St. Celeste. She pulled her necklace out of the satchel and clasped it around her neck for good luck. Then she embarked on her journey to St. Celeste, where she knew not a soul, mind you. But after a couple of hours Sarina grew weary and stopped to rest beside the lavender fields."

"And let me guess, Jessie. That's when she got herself kidnapped by the sinister Lord Snip, or Snap, or Snoop, or whatever." Wilson twirled his wooden spoon in the air for emphasis. "And now she's trapped in this guy's castle, waiting to be rescued by some stupid hunk with a huge—"

"No, Wilson," I interrupted. "That's what happened in *Temptation at Twilight*. But we are now discussing *An Everlasting Encounter*. It's a completely different story." I tossed my head in a haughty manner reminiscent of one of my heroines. "Adelé Nightingale never repeats a story."

"Whatever you say, Adelé." He chuckled over my penname, but I ignored him and moved on.

"Just as Sarina stood up from the lavender field, determined to finish her arduous journey, a handsome stranger driving a white carriage came along and offered her a ride. And of course, the stranger became smitten with Sarina along the way."

"Of course." Wilson shook salt into a pot of boiling water and poured in the spaghetti.

"But unbeknownst to Sarina, the handsome stranger is none other than Trey Barineau, the Duke of Luxley! Can you believe it?"

"Not really."

"The trouble is, Sarina had somehow torn her frock during this whole encounter, and so Trey dropped her off at the dress-maker's shop in St. Celeste. And the proprietress

Winnie Dickerson shooed him away before he could properly introduce himself, or even learn the lovely damsel's name."

"Why didn't the evil baron-guy just kidnap her, Jessie? Isn't that what always happens in your books?"

"Nooo. That is not what always happens in my books. And Trey Barineau is the hero, for Lord's sake. He would never kidnap anyone." I sighed dramatically. "And therein lies the dilemma."

"Huh?"

"Would you please stay with me here? Sarina has found employment with Mrs. Dickerson. Because, despite her delicate hands and fingers, she is quite talented with a needle and thread. And now this lowly seamstress must somehow come back into contact with the Duke of Luxley. Meanwhile, Trey is up in Luxley Manor, simply beside himself with lustful longings for the lovely and lithe Sarina, whose identity he knows not!"

Wilson squinted up at the heavens. Or at least at the skylight.

"So?" I asked. "How will their chance encounter in the lavender field become everlasting?"

"Who's that?"

"Oh, for Lord's sake! Trey and Sarina! Any ideas?" I appealed to my beau for inspiration.

My mother refers to Wilson Rye as my beau, and for lack of a better alternative, so do I. Beau may sound a bit southern and old-fashioned, but I was born and raised in South Carolina, and have lived in Clarence, North Carolina for decades, so I am a southerner. And although I won't claim to be old-fashioned, I am getting old.

Which is why I refuse to call him my boyfriend. I'm fifty-two and he's forty-seven. Boyfriend seems too juvenile. Lover could work, but since the L-word had yet to be spoken between us, that seemed a bit premature.

My beau was staring at me. And from the look on his face, I assumed he had nary an solution to offer Trey or Sarina.

I reached over and turned off the stove. "Okay, what's wrong?" I asked. "You've had more on your mind than dinner ever since you called this afternoon."

He frowned and slowly spooned the meatballs onto a plate lined with paper towels. "I was going to ask you to do me a favor," he mumbled eventually. "But never mind. It's too dangerous."

Too dangerous? Well, now he had to tell me. But how to convince him of that.

I hopped up to set the table and began with the most obvious question. "Does it have something to do with your job?"

"It's kind of complicated," he told the meatballs as he transferred them, one by one, into the sauce pot.

"Why am I not surprised?" I looked up from folding the napkins. "Is this about what happened at the Wade On Inn? Didn't I read something in the paper?"

No answer while he pretended his spaghetti sauce required his urgent attention.

"If you refuse to tell me what's going on, why bring it up at all?" I asked.

"I keep you in the dark for your own safety, Jessie."

"Yeah, right." I dropped the silverware and returned to the stove. "Perhaps things did get a little tricky during the Stanley Sweetzer episode," I said once he would finally look at me. "But that's no excuse for you to be so cagey about your work, Wilson."

"A little tricky? You almost got yourself killed."

I folded my arms and glared. "As I recall, the lead investigator of the Clarence Homicide Squad accused me of killing Candy Poppe's fiancé. Forgive me if I got a little carried away trying to prove my innocence."

"I only accused you that one time."

"Gee thanks."

Wilson took a deep breath. "Okay, here goes. Two murders at the Wade On Inn. Last week. Both victims were regulars at the pool table." He stopped and waited for my reaction.

I pursed my lips and decided to stir the pasta.

"You ever play out there, Jessie?"

"Umm, I might have."

He took the spoon away from me. "That," he said, "is exactly what I was afraid of."

"Come on, Wilson. It was a long time ago."

"What do you know about the game at the Wade On Inn?"

"I know it's the hottest table in town. They shoot nine ball out there, if I'm not mistaken."

He squinted at me, suspicion veritably oozing from his pores. "When were you last there?"

"Oh, for Lord's sake! I haven't set foot inside the Wade On Inn or any place like it for close to thirty years.

"However," I added when he seemed a bit too relieved. "If Adelé Nightingale's books ever go out of style, I do believe I could pop on down there and get enough action to pay my mortgage, no?"

Wilson turned to Snowflake. "That," he said, "is exactly what I was afraid of."

About the Author

Cindy Blackburn has a confession to make–she does not play pool. It's that whole eye-hand coordination thing. What Cindy does do well is school. So when she's not writing silly stories she's teaching serious history. European history is her favorite subject, and the ancient stuff is best of all. The deader the better! A native Vermonter who hates cold weather, Cindy divides her time between the south and the north. During the school year you'll find her in South Carolina, but come summer she'll be on the porch of her lakeside shack in Vermont. Cindy has a fat cat named Betty and a cute husband named John. Betty the muse meows constantly while Cindy tries to type. John provides the technical support. Both are extremely lovable.

When Cindy isn't writing, grading papers, or feeding the cat, she likes to take long walks or paddle her kayak around the lake. Her favorite travel destinations are all in Europe, her favorite TV show is NCIS, her favorite movie is Moonstruck, her favorite color is orange, and her favorite authors (if she must choose) are Joan Hess and Spencer Quinn. Cindy dislikes vacuuming, traffic, and lima beans.

www.cueballmysteries.com

cueballmysteries.com/blog